Kept Darkly

by

Tarrant Smith

Editor: Stephanie Hudak
Cover Design: Scott Smith

 ISBN 978-1461081258 1461081254
www.tarrantsmith.webs.com.

A Toast…

To "the girls" of the Sunshine Social Club who taught me that life should be lived without regrets or apologies, that loving can be both fierce as well as gentle, and that laughter should be raucous and indulged in until the tears fall.

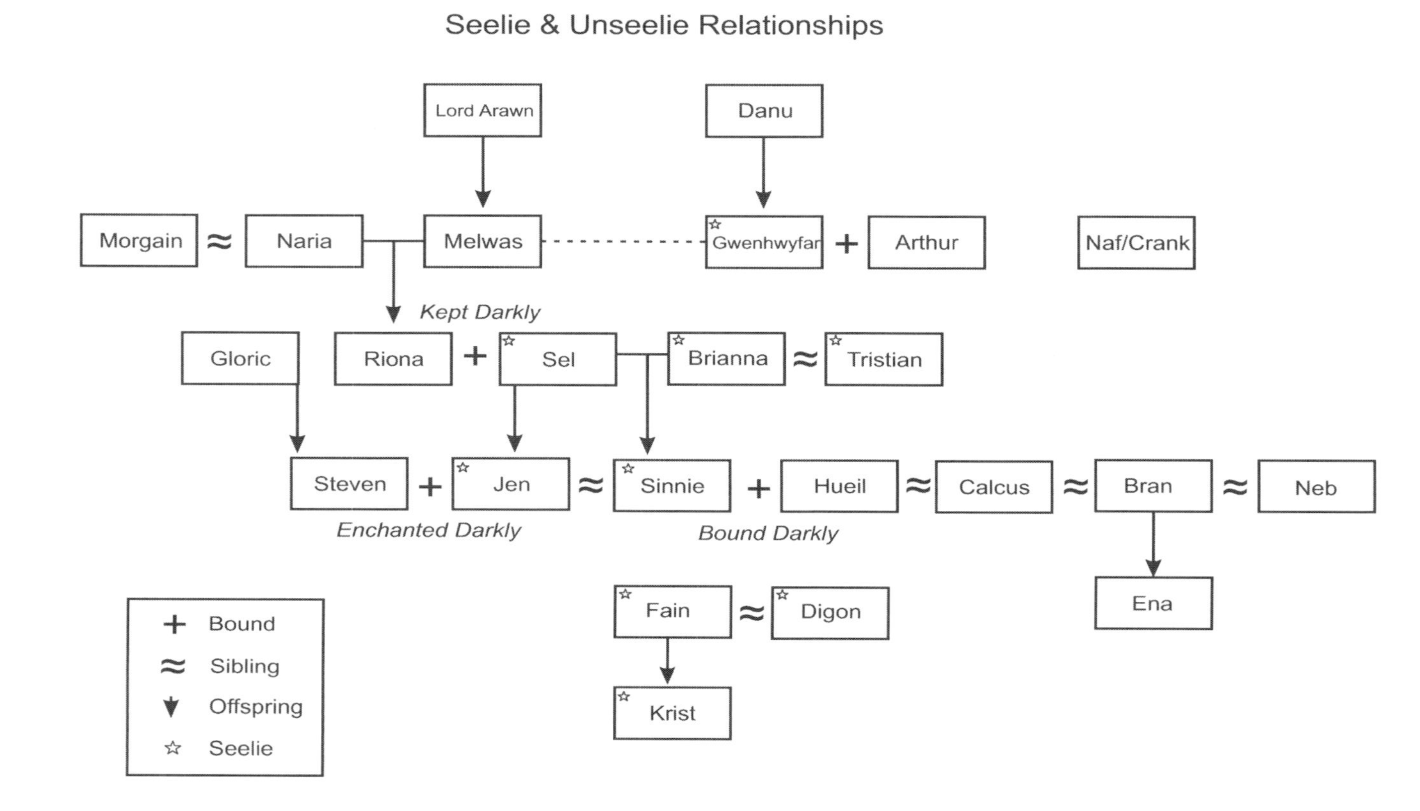
Seelie & Unseelie Relationships
Lord Arawn
Danu
Morgain
Naria
Melwas
Gwenhwyfar
Arthur
Naf/Crank
Kept Darkly
Gloric
Riona
Sel
Brianna
Tristian
Steven
Jen
Sinnie
Hueil
Calcus
Bran
Neb
Enchanted Darkly
Bound Darkly
Fain
Digon
Ena
Krist
Bound
Sibling
Offspring
Seelie

Dear Readers

The Darkly Series draws heavily on Celtic mythology and the laws of magick. As one would expect, it contains many Celtic names and magickal terms. Because a certain amount of familiarity is required to safely traverse the world of the fey, both seelie and unseelie, I have nestled a glossary in the back of this book for the pronunciation of names and places along with explanations for reoccurring terms.

Remember Reader, the fey are nearly immortal and have little in common with humans. Flattery can trick them, iron can kill them, but woe to the person who is enchanted by them.

Tarrant Smith

Enchantress born,
Pure blood of intoxication.

Intentions denied,
Cold and brittle my hollow reply.

Battle of wills,
Soft night and duty soon forgot.

I am lost—oh sweet her spell
Darkly kept, my unseelie desire.

Sel, son of Selgi

Prologue

The balance of power had been upset. The question that plagued the Unseelie King was why.

Melwas often thought of himself in third person, a running monologue forever playing in his head. It amused him most days, but the commentary that accompanied last night's events was disturbing at best. His Queen, Gwenhwyfar, had saved his life. But in doing so, she had stolen not only one of his warriors, but his daughter, Riona, as well. Melwas didn't care about Hueil, the warrior, so much as the loss of his daughter as a tool of power which was his right to wield. And he thought of the traitor Calcus not at all.

Melwas fingered the key around his neck, but made no attempt to remove it. He'd only come to talk and he could do that through the small hole in the face of the door. Standing by the cell's door, he leaned his head back against the cool stone wall and hammered on the enchanted metal with his fist to alert the presence within.

"I have come to visit. Come speak with me," he announced. When time passed without a response from the other side, he pounded on the door again. Melwas was finally rewarded with the sound of movement, shuffling and scraping of wood over stone as the man within took a seat near the door.

"What news?"

Melwas chuckled to himself. His prisoner had always been unfailingly polite. "Our Queen has not been behaving herself. You must remind her of our deal."

"She refuses to speak with me."

"You must try harder. It is her life you protect." It was a

small threat Melwas made, and the cell occupant knew it. Melwas had never raised a hand to his Queen, nor would he.

Silence.

"Let us not forget, I still hold all the cards in this game," Melwas prompted.

"I will do my best," came the disembodied reply.

"That is all I ask."

Silence and then the faceless voice asked, "I am surprised by your visit. What has my Gwen done?"

Through the long centuries, a strange friendship had evolved between he and his prisoner. So Melwas, who trusted no one, relayed the basic details of the disastrous Mabon ceremony to him.

"I remember Hueil as a child." the voice said. "He was a troublemaker even then as I recall." The statement was followed by muffled laughter.

The Unseelie King rose and paced back and forth before the cell door. Hueil's abandonment of the unseelie way needled the great King more than he wanted to admit.

Melwas ignored the unwanted commentary in his head and abruptly stopped his pacing. "Gwenhwyfar has shackled my daughter to her captain. I cannot strike at him without bringing us to open war," he grumbled. "Our Queen is too fond of him."

"I am sorry for your troubles, Melwas. Gwen was always headstrong."

Melwas leaned his hand against the icy metal door. Something had changed. His Queen was taking risks she dared not before. "I think she has seen something new in this game we play."

"A new player, perhaps?"

"I do not know," Melwas grumbled utterly frustrated.

"I am sure you will understand soon. Until then, I fear we

must play on... " the voice suggested.

Melwas glared at the door. His fair-haired Queen had belonged first to the unseelie fey that now slyly mocked him, safe from harm behind the locked door. Gwenhwyfar's continued acceptance of his reign rested on the health of this prisoner. If one died, so did the other. The balance of power between the three of them had stood unchallenged for three thousand years. What was different?

"Are you ill?" Melwas asked, his mind searching for answers.

"Nay, but thank you for inquiring."

"And you say she refuses to speak with you?"

"I profess truly."

Melwas's fist slammed against the door, the soft laughter within only feeding his anger. Melwas had to admit he had been blindsided at Mabon. Whatever Gwenhwyfar was up to, he couldn't allow her to gain control of their game. He needed answers. He needed a plan.

The Unseelie King stalked away from the offending door and out onto the ledge pathway. Out of habit, he fingered the stag-head key once more. Even if she knew where to find Arthur, the Absent King, the Seelie Queen would need more than a key to open the cell door. This alone reassured Melwas. As long as he kept Arthur securely imprisoned, the Unseelie throne was his to keep—as was the reluctant but abiding Gwenhwyfar.

Melwas re-entered the cave and came to stand once more in front of the sealed door. "She still searches for you," Melwas told the fey behind the door.

They knew each other too well, for he had told the old King too much through the years. They were now both enemies and friends locked in a battle from which they could no longer disengage. He had long ago stopped lying to his prisoner—lies of Gwenhwyfar's love for her new King. He didn't share the bond with her that the binding vows forged, nor would he ever. In the beginning, the happy courtship, children born, and idealized court-life of a Melwas rule had been a fantasy woven to torture his prisoner, but Melwas hadn't been aware of the telepathic link between the Seelie Queen and her mate, Arthur. The old King had known of the lies. Oddly, Arthur had never chastised him for the fantasy.

"She will not stop," the voice behind the door prophesied.

"So we will play on then," Melwas suggested.

"Aye. I think it best."

Chapter 1

The black wolf rose from his crouch, his hackles growing. Placing her small hand on his head, Riona stilled him. It was good that Neb obeyed; a loyal unseelie would come in handy, she reminded herself.

"I am Sel, son of Selgi. The Seelie Queen has sent me to you. Calcus is dead by my hand in defense of the Queen. I offer myself to you, and the protection of my house as custom requires. It is the Queen's wish you abide this agreement."

Riona thrust her chin forward to cover her surprise at the captain's speech. "And my father's wishes?" It irked her that the Seelie Captain truly expected her to heel to his announcement. Even here at Tearmann, the Seelie Queen's sanctuary, they had heard the rumors of what had occurred at the Mabon Ceremony. She had known Sel would come, but she had not thought he would arrive so soon.

The Queen's Captain answered her plainly, "He plans to use you as a pawn. In my care you will retain the Queen's protection."

She stalled for time. "Give me a moment to see my friend off. I will meet you in the gathering hall," she informed him regally, giving him a small dip of her chin for good measure. Riona held his gaze unblinkingly as the silence deepened between them. She knew the next to speak would be the loser in this small battle of wills. This knowledge did nothing to calm the sound of her heart hammering in her ears as she waited on his reply.

"The sooner we leave the better. I will wait as you requested." The blond haired captain stiffly bowed at the waist, then turned and walked back the way he had come.

Riona refrained from smiling at his retreating back. It was only a small victory, and she was not yet out of his reach. Beside her, Neb rose from his crouch. She held up her hand until Sel had entered the gates of the castle. Only then did she release the breath she had been holding. Knowing time was against her, she retook her wolf form and ran—ran as if her life depended on it.

She raced through the valley with Neb keeping stride at her heels. After they had traveled a fair distance, she glanced behind her to see Neb's tongue lolling out. He was enjoying himself. Typical, she thought, mentally sighing with annoyance.

When Neb moved up to run next to her, she nipped at him. She had been happy at Tearmann, damn it. But her time at Tearmann was at an end, she now must to look to her future. Riona leaped over a log and continued through the dense brush without pausing.

Neb returned to his position at her heels, content for now to let her take the lead on this merry chase. And a chase it would be once the captain discovered she had fled. Contemplating his reaction gave her another burst of speed. He would expect her to shift from these mountains to somewhere safe; the court perhaps to plead her case to the Seelie Queen.

When Riona caught the sweet scent of water, she changed direction and followed it. Once she spotted the rushing water, Riona plunged into the stream and traveled against the current for half a mile before veering off towards one of the mountains Neb's plaintive whine indicated. Because he was growing tired, Riona let him take the lead. Sensing her willingness, the black wolf confidently loped forward. He seemed to know where he was going, so she was content to follow.

When the grass gave way to loose and jagged rock, they slowed to a jog. Riona picked her way carefully, not wanting to cut a pad on the sharp stones. She couldn't risk an injury, she told herself. It would slow her fight, or worse, it would leave a blood trail for the captain to follow.

The very thought of the Seelie Captain irritated her. Why couldn't he have just stayed away? His appearance had ruined everything. At castle Tearmann she had been able to shed her past life, and in doing so had experienced a freedom she'd never known before. No one had ulterior motives in befriending her. She was just one more unseelie fey under Queen Gwenhwyfar's protection. No one knew she was the bastard daughter of the Unseelie King. Only Digon, the castle's caretaker, had known her circumstances and Riona had kept him at arms-length. She had learned from painful experience that anyone who knew her identity would eventually try to use it to their advantage. Even the Seelie Queen it seemed wasn't immune to the temptation, she mused.

Neb halted, forcing Riona to skid to a stop, just short of running into his haunches on the steep ledge. Bringing her attention back to the ordeal at hand, she concentrated on her surroundings and where Neb might be leading her. The Arach Mountains of Tir na n-Og were hauntingly beautiful but dangerous. She watched while the black wolf put his nose to the ground then scented the air. She didn't exactly trust Neb, but he had once helped her in the past. And with her blatant refusal to the captain's dubious offer of protection, Riona had lost any further protection from the Seelie Queen. If she wanted to remain out of her father's reach, Neb was the sum total of her dwindling list of allies.

Riona waited for Neb to move forward, again sniffing the air, before she inched forward along the path behind him.

Really, what choice did she have? She had grown too

complacent during her short stay at Tearmann, she lectured herself. It had been utter stupidity on her part to believe a happy existence could be attained, even for a limited time. She should have had a plan in place. But she hadn't anticipated Calcus's death, nor the Queen's unusual decision to transfer Calcus's contract with her house to Sel's. It made no sense. It was an ancient law the Queen used, a provision no one paid any attention to anymore.

Neb moved further up the trail.

Riona had welcomed Neb's company when he had appeared tonight. Out of all the guards Calcus had placed near her, Neb had been the most respectful of her title and station. Which explained why, when he found her loping through the valley in sight of the castle, he had insisted that she, a princess of the Unseelie Court, shouldn't be without an escort. So he had joined her for a short romp around the castle.

Naively, Riona hadn't realized they were being watched. It wasn't until the wind had shifted and her wolf senses had caught *his* scent—woodland and male. She hesitated along the rocky trail as her mind replayed the moment the captain had stepped out from the shadows. His massive golden six-four frame commanded attention. Like a doe sensing danger, she had stood immobilized, transfixed by the sight of him. But from the second the captain opened his mouth, it was clear to her that she was only another errand assigned to him by his Queen. She may not have lived at court, but Riona knew about the captain and his Queen. They said he could love no other. Though she had heard rumors about him, in truth, it was the first time she had ever laid eyes him. Too many years spent hiding from court and her father was her only excuse for not knowing him. Riona's mind shied away from his name. He had said it so proudly; his whole demeanor had been cold and unapproachable. But it was his coolness in the matter that had unexpectedly stung.

Neb gave a short yep in her direction; to her wolf ears it registered as a question. Neb had moved further up the trail and was waiting for her, head cocked.

She sniffed in response and followed, thankfully the difficult terrain would keep her mind from resurrecting the captain's image for a time.

After scrambling up the steep trail, Neb led her through a narrow fissure partially obscured by a large boulder. The narrowing path led to a shelter carved into the mountain face. It was crude, but the cave would give them a chance to rest relatively unobserved.

Neb shimmered, shapeshifting to take his true form: blue-tinted skin, a smattering of warrior tattoos, black leather pants, boots, and nothing more but a silver torc around his neck. He wore no weapons Riona could discern so she shapeshifted as well. She chose to dress herself more appropriately for her surroundings than the russet gown the captain had seen her in; a simple tunic, britches, and good sensible boots. Chilled after shedding her thick wolf-coat, Riona manifested a warm gray cloak as an afterthought. It would do, she decided while wrapping the heavy material around her.

"Why are we fleeing?" Neb asked. "The promise of the Queen's protection sounds pretty good," he added.

He wasn't even breathing hard. Riona realized this respite was for her benefit only. "It is not my wish to be handed off to a man like a prized pig at a fair." It hurt that the Queen had simply given her to the captain as soon as Calcus's previous claim had been broken. In the back of her mind, she had expected more from the Queen who had been more of a mother to her than her own.

"Then what do you want to do, Princess?"

"I.." Riona began, then paused. What was she going to do? Her first impulse had been to flee, but now what? And was she running on principle or from the fey himself? Her mind conjured his image with little prompting. To cover her confusion Riona ran her fingers through her recently cropped hair. The once heavy brunette locks now only grazed her shoulders.

"I see you are still working on the solution. No matter. We can rest till dawn if he hasn't found the trail," Neb informed her.

"You are offering to stay with me?" She tilted her chin upward while readjusting her dull cloak around her as if it were the most elegant of robes. Neb, having long since perfected the art of casual-ease, wasn't as affected by her royal airs as Riona would have liked. He was being very accommodating, she thought worriedly. Would he tell her what he wanted from her or would she not discover his trap until after it was sprung?

Neb took a seat on a rock and began laying a fire. "I was not present at the Mabon ceremony. I have no allegiances, and I am not welcome at court for a full year." He glanced up. "I am not needed anywhere at the moment, Princess."

"What if he finds us?"

"I doubt he will. I know how to stay..." Neb paused to smile charmingly at her, "unnoticed."

Riona took a seat on the stone floor and watched him complete his task. A spark ignited the small pile of twigs and the fire sprang to life. Neb fed the flames, larger sticks and then logs until the shelter was warm and cozy. She let the cloak fall from her shoulders. "How do you know of this place?" she asked, filling the silence.

"Once, long ago, I too had to run and hide." The

practiced grin on his face did not match the pain she heard in his voice.

Changing the subject, she asked, "Does this shelter of yours have any food?"

"Nary a bit," he sighed. "I have not used it for some time."

"Then it was providence that sent you to me tonight. Alone, I would not have found shelter," she told him. But what now, she asked herself. She needed more allies than this one unseelie if she wanted to retain her freedom.

"Quite possibly. There have been some strange happenstance of late."

She didn't think he spoke of the uproar at Mabon, which ended with Calcus's death and Hueil's change of allegiance from Unseelie King to Seelie Queen. "Like what?" she asked. When Neb didn't answer right away, Riona assumed he had dismissed her question. They sat in silence, Neb ignoring her completely while he tended the fire, and she wondering what to do next. The captain's image bloomed fresh in her mind and Riona found herself quietly testing his name under her breath, "Sel."

"You wonder about him?"

Riona blushed. She had not intended for Neb to hear her foolishness. Picking up on her discomfort he laughed at her, which made her blush all the more.

"It is natural for you to speculate about the fey. Do you want to know what I think?"

"You think the Queen's protection is not so bad," she snapped.

He grunted to himself as if agreeing then said, "I think the captain is not so bad, Princess. My brother, Hueil, took his daughter as his mate."

"Sinnie? Is that why he now serves the Queen?"

"Aye, Sinnie. Do you know the seelie girl?"

"I have met her," Riona confessed.

A lone wolf howled in the distance. It was a long, woeful cry.

Neb abruptly stood, their conversation forgotten, and went to stand at the mouth of the cave to scan the horizon and landscape below. From their elevation, he would be able to see for miles with his unseelie eyes.

"If it is your captain's call, I canna see him. He should realize by now that you did not travel to court."

Neb had read her mind. Was she that predictable, or were males that predictable?

With a shrug, Neb resumed his seat and poked at the fire. "His pride is no doubt smarting from your rebuke."

"He thinks to much of himself." What would she do if he found her again? If she were honest, there was something about the captain that unsettled her. Riona took a deep breath and steadied her resolve.

"He is changed."

Neb's comment confused her. Her mind had been cataloging the captain's features: the blond hair that curled around his ears, the gray-green eyes that seemed to see directly into her, the strong chin, the high cheekbones. Her mind wandered lower; the breadth of his shoulders, the muscled arms—a result of long service to warcraft. He was a large bear of a man and the thought of his golden presence sent a delightful shiver through her body. "Who?"

Studying her intently, Neb replied, "Hueil."

"How so?" she asked, picking up the thread of their conversation, but her mind stubbornly remained elsewhere. *"He plans to use you as a pawn. In my care you will retain the Queen's protection."* Sel's voice had been strong and self-possessed, not a hint of warmth in his offer or critique of her father's motives. *In his care*, her mind repeated.

"It does not matter," Neb told her. He then quit the fire and took up a post by the entrance.

"Do you see anything?" she asked distractedly.

"Nay. Your captain seems to have lost the scent. It is the dragons I watch for; they are the real danger in this land."

Careful to keep the worry from her voice, she asked, "Should we move on?"

"I would prefer to wait until dawn." He looked back over his shoulder and smiled impishly. "I will keep watch, Princess. Gain what rest you can. Your…" he paused and grinned more fully, "virtue is safe with me. I have a healthy fear of the Queen's Captain."

Riona reached for the nearest stick and threw it at him, causing him to laugh all the louder. Even with the little amount of time she spent at court, she had heard the crude jokes made about her lack of sexual experience, as well as the imaginative places her father might find her if King Melwas chose to look hard enough. Because of the political implications of her station, Riona had not indulged in taking a lover like the rest of her kind was known to do. She was quite possibly the only unseelie to reach the age of womanhood without having known a lover's touch and it had earned her the unfair title of "Ice Princess" among members of both courts.

"I am sorry. I see the tales are true." Neb's laughter died slowly in her ears, until it was just a soft chuckle between friends.

To her annoyance, her cheeks had flamed anew. Ignoring him, she stared steadily into the fire to avoid witnessing his assessing gaze. It was not new to her. Most males looked at her that way, like she was some present they wanted to be the first to unwrap. As casually as she could, Riona reached for her cloak and pulled it around her body. A moment later she felt Neb's attention slip away as he resumed his watch at the cave's entrance.

When the first roar broke the stillness, Riona jumped in alarm. She knew her eyes had grown wide as she looked to Neb for direction. He nodded his head in agreement to her unspoken thought and hurriedly doused the flames with water. The coals sizzled then died, sending up a plume of smoke that choked her lungs and stung her eyes. She felt him put a warm finger to her lips; they would need to remain silent until the dragons passed.

There was an answering scream to the first roar; the dragon's mate perhaps? Riona knew very little about these creatures, but Neb clearly seemed to understand the danger they were in. He moved her to the back of the shelter.

"I have no weapon with me. If we are detected, we will need to shift quickly," he whispered in the darkness.

Without the aid of fire or the moon's light, Riona couldn't see Neb at all, his warrior's blue tinted skin blended into the inky blackness. He kept a tight grip on her wrist and stood near enough that she could feel the heat of his body in the close quarters. Without the contact, she would have lost track of his presence in the gloom of the cave. Riona took comfort in the sound of his breathing—steady and shallow. He was calmly waiting and she tried to follow his example, willing her racing heart to slow.

Despite her efforts to emulate Neb, Riona jumped when another shrieking roar, much closer than the last, heralded a dragon's approach. Neb pressed her backward until her spine was against cool stone. She was trembling, and she hated it. Danger was not new to her, but these creatures knew no reason.

Her sensitive hearing caught movement at the entrance. Peering through the haze of smoke and darkness, Riona thought she could make out a silhouette, but it was too small to be one of the creatures. Not trusting her eyesight, she gathered power to shift but Neb held her firmly in place.

"You trespass. These lands do not belong to the fey," the voice warned. The dragon's voice sounded like stone grinding against stone, an unpleasant grating of bone upon the ear.

Neb didn't respond or move as the new arrival sniffed, testing the air.

"You have a woman with you." It was not a question.

Neb pushed her firmly backward, flat against the unyielding mountain and then he let go. Blind as she was, Riona could only follow the sound of his light footfalls as he walked forward and away from her. When she judged him to be near the entrance he said, "Your nose imagines much. It is only I. You know me, do you not?"

The new arrival inhale deeply again. "Aye. I know your kind. You stink, unseelie."

"Like you and your kin, I am hunted. I will leave by dawn," Neb responded.

The figure gave a loud harrumph then said, "I have seen the one who hunts you. He is close. This is the last boon you will receive from us."

"Thank you, mighty-one. I will not trespass on your lands again," Neb replied cordially.

Riona realized during Neb's conversation that her eyesight had mistaken the silhouetted head of the creature for a misshapen man. There was a shifting and sliding of rock as the great beast took to the air. Neb waited until the dragon was completely airborne before returning to her.

"We need to leave. Now," he told her, gripping her arm.

"Where are we going?"

"Off this mountain."

Neb's power wrapped around her and they shifted in unison. As their bodies floated away from the cave, Riona's eye sight briefly improved. She glimpsed Sel hastily making his way into the hidden shelter, sword drawn—but he was too late to prevent their escape.

In rapid succession she and Neb materialized and shifted again and again. Neb, being more powerful, took easy command of their travel:; the lush valley they had run across, a ransacked bed-chamber, a mineral spring in a part of Tir-na n-Og she had never been, a deserted cottage, a rowan grove, a lake. Eventually, Riona stopped bothering to identify Neb's choice of locations. He was obviously attempting to camouflage their trail. Over time her sense of place became more confused as Neb's constant shifting continued: trees, a castle, a beach, a cave, a tower. The effort of folding space was beginning to take its toil on her dwindling resources of power. So when they materialized next to a tree Riona grabbed at a limb. "Stop," she ordered. It halted Nebs progress but she accidentally had cut her hand in the attempt.

He didn't answer her or give her a moment to rest, instead he pried her hand free of the limb before shifting them once again. Four more locations came and went before her legs began to sag. Gripping her around the waist, he shifted two more times.

They reappeared in a glen, near the edge of a forest. Gently lowering her down into a sitting position, he informed her, "We can rest for a moment. I think I have confused him."

"I need to rest, Neb. Where are we?" Riona was unable to keep the strain she felt from her voice. Her relative youth and lack of power had put her at a distinct disadvantage, the constant travel had rendered her vulnerable. Drained of strength, she would now be forced to place her trust in him.

"Near the northern border. From here we can travel to a place you can safely rest."

She shivered and hugged her cloak to her. The cut to her hand stung but she ignored it. "How long until dawn?" The moon sat low on the horizon. They had been shifting for a very long time.

Glancing down at her, Neb replied, "A few hours." Taking a step away, he scanned the meadow for possible dangers. "I need to retrieve my sword. Go sit in the shadow of that oak." He pointed to a tree several yards away, taller than all the rest. "I will be right back," he told her. Neb then vanished, leaving her all alone.

Riona was exhausted, but she made herself remain standing on trembling legs. Ignoring the familiar fear, she turned in a circle until she spotted the tree Neb had indicated. As ordered, she went to sit and wait. She was being pursued again, alone and ill prepared to protect herself. Would he bring back someone new who also hunted for her? Or would the captain catch up to her? Fleetingly Riona wondered if she could still return to the safety of Tearmann. Dawn had not yet taken the Queen's sanctuary from its nightly resting-place. But then, *he* would be informed she had returned and he'd come for her, Riona reminded herself. If she truly valued her freedom, she knew she couldn't go back. For that matter, Riona thought, it might not be possible to make the jump there…even if she wanted to. At present, Riona didn't think she had the energy to fold space unaided.

Leaning against the great oak's trunk, she gratefully sank

down onto the forest floor and pulled her hood forward, the gray cloak would help her blend in with the shadows. Riona closed her eyes to listen. All she could do was wait, and hope, hope Neb wasn't about to betray her.

Chapter 2

"Who left you unattended?"

A male voice, her mind told her. She had slept, though she hadn't intended to. Opening her eyes, Riona found an unseelie warrior looking down at her, legs apart, hands resting on his hips. She was so use to betrayal that she felt no anger toward Neb. This must be the one Neb had gone to fetch. Only slightly curious, she asked, "Who are you?"

"Gloric." He smiled broadly and then he bowed to her with a flourish. The sun was just peaking over the horizon. She was able to see him clearly in the soft glow of dawn. His hair was cut short, just reaching his shoulders. A leather vest covered his tattooed chest, black leather pants ending at silver tipped boots, and a great war-ax was strapped to his back.

With the tree protecting her back she stood and gave the new arrival a nod, but she did not offer her name. If she were lucky, she might have the opportunity to shift, then attempt to confuse her trail like Neb had done the night before. If she were extraordinarily lucky, this Gloric as he called himself, wouldn't find her again. Riona turned and purposefully walked into the open meadow. She could hear the unseelie following her. Neb was nowhere in sight.

"Are you a sprite, a wood nymph perhaps?" he teased in a feeble attempt at charming her. "Do not think to escape me, lovely one."

She stopped in her tracks, but not out of fear of Gloric. Across the meadow, at the edge of the tree line stood the captain, the rising sun's rays adding a brilliance to his golden image. Her heart picked up its pace. He did not look happy. And why should he? She turned her back on the captain and focused her attention on Gloric. Her new admirer had not yet spotted the captain's arrival. "What do you want?" she asked, raising one haughty eyebrow.

He smirked. "I caught your scent last night in the cave and was intrigued." As he said this, Gloric's voice changed from the musical qualities of their kind to a harsh discord of grating notes.

Her stomach dropped and her mind screamed "dragon" in warning. She took two hesitant steps back from him and plastered what she hoped was a pleasant smile on her face. "Truly? That is quite remarkable, Gloric."

His disturbingly ugly leer told Riona all she needed to know. Gloric was done bantering. The blood drained from her face and she stumbled backward, all pretense of calm evaporating.

Suddenly the captain materialized beside her, and she yelped. With one large hand he shoved her behind him. Riona fell back. Then she felt, rather than saw, Neb appear beside her. Neb grabbed her arm to steady her, preventing her from landing flat on her royal bottom.

By the time she looked up again, Gloric had begun his transformation. The distortion of shimmering air around him camouflaged some the more gruesome elongation of his unseelie body, but Riona could still see Gloric's legs as they gained unbelievable mass. His arms expanded, torso twisted, and his neck stretched. There was a flash of iridescent green as scales replaced skin. As remarkable as the metamorphosis was to witness, it was not what transfixed the threesome. What froze them all in place was the hideous grinding sounds of bone, of ripping flesh, and the emergence of the guttural dragon roar. The captain, who seemed just as stunned as she and Neb, had been mindful enough to draw his sword, though it was held limply in his hand.

Reacting first, Neb shifted her away from the meadow and the captain before Gloric could finish the lengthy change. She didn't offer any resistance as he jumped them from place to place. She wanted as far away from Gloric the dragon as she could get. If the captain had any sense, he'd run as well.

Her heart suddenly constricted painfully in her chest. She hoped he had run. The thought of him hurt, fighting to protect her when she had fled was...distressing.

When they materialized near a lake, Neb paused.

"That was interesting," When she didn't respond immediately, he gave her a hard look. "I know of a place we can go. We need help."

Neb hadn't betrayed her...yet, she amended to herself. "Where?" she asked while trying not to think about the captain and their abandonment of him. Riona attempted to ease her conscience by telling herself that Sel knew how to defend himself, otherwise he wouldn't have become the Queen's champion.

"The human realm. We will go see Hueil."

What trickery is this, she thought. "His daughter is there. What of Sel?" she asked.

"The captain is still looking for you here in Tir na n-Og. We have a little time before he thinks to look elsewhere. We will take precautions. And you've cut yourself. I can smell it," he finished.

She swallowed and clenched her hand behind the folds of her cloak in an attempt at hiding the cuts to her palm. "What took you so long to return, Neb?" she asked suspiciously.

"I was laying false trails all over Tir na n-Og for you, Princess." He handed her a torn piece of her tunic. She hadn't realized it had ripped. "He will think you are everywhere, and yet, you will be nowhere."

She tucked the scrape of fabric into a pocket inside her cloak. She knew she should not appear ungrateful. Whatever his motives, Neb had been true thus far. She pushed her chin forward and looked him full in the face so that he could see that she meant it. "You have proven yourself to be true. I apologize for thinking the worst. "

He held out his hand to her. "We should go."

He didn't look offended by her doubts and Riona was glad of it. She nodded in response.

The air around Neb wavered as he shimmered. His face morphed into that of Hueil's, but Neb's body and voice remained the same."He has permission to pass the watchers. I do not," Neb told her in way of explanation. She held his hand firmly, trusting only because there was no other way. Riona felt his power wrap around her and then they shifted.

* * *

So this was the human realm, she mused. The smell was what she noticed first as a confusing and muddled array of unfamiliar scents assaulted her nose. And that was not the only difference. Unlike the vibrant colors of home, the colors of this world seemed dull to her fey eyes. Riona could not see the appeal of this realm. This world was a poor substitute for Tir na n-Og.

After a series of shifts, Neb's features returned but he continued to hop them from location to location until blessedly stopping beside a tree situated behind a large white two-story house. Riona peeked from behind her cloak's hood. A fey awaited them, his black sword drawn. Standing to his side, a gray horse nuzzled at his belt. His shirt revealed skin that was golden, not blue. There were no warrior tattoos along his arms and his raven hair only reached his shoulders, but the contours of the face were the same as she'd remembered. It was Hueil, but different as Neb had claimed.

Neb grinned at his brother, his joy evident. He was still in his unseelie form, blue-tinted skin and tattooed, a sword now strapped to this hip.

Shoving at the animal's shoulder to send it away, Hueil asked, "What are you doing here, Neb?"

"Brother, I... we," Neb corrected, "need a place to rest. Just a few hours and we will depart."

"Who's the woman."

"A friend."

Hueil's brow pinched, deliberating his sibling's request. "Shift to the upstairs bedroom on the right. Depart by morning. I cannot bring trouble to this house. You may stay no longer than dawn."

Neb offered his hand, and Hueil moved closer to clasp Neb's forearm in a warrior's grip.

"I will explain to Sinnie," Hueil said with a sigh.

"Thank you, brother. I promise, we will not be a burden."

Riona had remained cloaked and mute during the brothers' exchange. She needed the rest Hueil was willing to afford them and she didn't think his knowing her identity would help secure his aid.

"Why here, Neb? Why seek me out?" Hueil asked; his initial concern seemingly turning to suspicion.

She watched Neb wink mischievously and it brought a hidden smile to Riona's lips.

"I can always count on you. And it is the last place anyone

will look for us," Neb answered.

"What have you done, brother?"

"I am only helping a friend; trying to follow my big brother's example."

When Riona felt Hueil study her cloaked form, she remained as still as a statue and willed him not to send them away.

"Who is she?"

"It is better you do not know. Trust me, brother. We will go by dawn. You won't even know we are here." Neb spoke the lie easily enough.

Hueil shook his head as if he knew it was a bad idea. "Fine. But not a whisper, Neb. You have put me in a spot with Sinnie. She will not like this."

"I am sorry to cause discord between you and your mate. I would not, but we truly need a safe place to rest."

"Go. I have your back, as always," Hueil said dismissing them.

Neb reached for her arm and they shifted again.

They reappeared a short distance later in their assigned sleeping-chamber; a room with one conservative sized bed, three large windows, and a fireplace flanked by two upholstered chairs. A large but threadbare rug covered most of the wooden floor. The accommodations were better than Riona had expected. The one bed could be a problem, but then she had slept on floors in the past. It was not so bad. At least this one had a rug on it.

"Let me see your hand." Neb reached for her arm and she passively let him inspect the wound.

It stung and she gritted her teeth against the unexpected pain as he gently opened her fist. The bark had ripped a chunk out of her palm and some bits of wood still remained. Needing to appear strong in strange surroundings, Riona refused to let Neb know his prodding of her injury hurt.

"I am sorry. I dinna realize I hurt you." He sounded genuinely remorseful.

As soon as he released her hand, Riona dropped it down to her side and ignored the throbbing as it work its way up her arm. "I have had worse."

"Let me fetch some water." He turned from her and left through the room's only door. Beyond was a common passageway and she could see another similarly decorated bedroom directly across the hall.

"I swear Hueil, if you don't take your hand off my wrist…" a female voice threatened.

Riona heard someone… no several someones, coming towards them, traveling up what sounded like a flight of stairs. Now what, she thought slightly panicked. Riona reached for her waning magickal resources and waited until the procession reached the landing.

A redheaded seelie stopped in the doorway, her eyes narrowing. Sinnie. Riona recognized her immediately. Hueil was soon standing behind his mate.

Sinnie stalked forward into the room. She was dressed strangely, in blue pants and a tight knitted garment as suggestive as anything an unseelie would choose to wear. "Where is my father?"

Hueil commented from the doorway, "Sin, leave the girl alone. She is exhausted. See how she sways on her feet."

Sinnie turned her back on Riona to argue with her mate. At the same time, Neb appeared in the doorway with a bowl and a cloth. He ignored the bickering couple. Striding past the pair, he gently took Riona's elbow and guided her to one of the two chairs. She had yet to remove her cloak or hood; too tired to do much more than let Neb attend to her hand.

"He searches for her. She was supposed to be at Tearmann. What is she doing with Neb?" Sinnie snapped, her finger poking at Hueil's chest.

"Neb, Sin wants to know why Riona is with you?" Hueil asked, deflecting his mate's question while looking over Sinnie's head at his little brother.

Riona held her tongue. She wasn't about to admit to her initial reaction of the captain's arrival. Her flight had been ill conceived at best. As Neb knelt down in front of her to tend to her hand, Riona was beginning to think she had only succeeded in delaying the inevitable.

"She doesn't like the look of the captain nor being handed off..." Neb peeked into the shadows of her hood. "How did you put it?" He chuckled to himself before continuing, "...like a prized pig at a fair," he loudly restated the objection for the benefit of the room's occupants. Reaching for her hand, he then began cleaning the small wound, taking great pains to be gentle as he removed the bits of bark.

"My father is a kind, honorable man. You should thank the gods your future lies with him," Sinnie spat.

"Sin, this is not the time. Let her rest." Hueil's tone had changed; there was a touch of warning and finality to his words.

"Fine." Sinnie stomped forward and ripped Riona's hand out of Neb's, causing it to bleed anew. Riona eyes teared as the pain stabbed up her arm.

Laying a palm over the bleeding wound, Sinnie quickly held the cut with a surge of searing energy from her seelie hand. "There. Rest. But before you run again Riona, you and I will talk." She released her grip none too gently.

Riona looked up only to see Sinnie's retreating back and

the wisps of dust dancing in the shaft of sunlight left behind by the exiting seelie.

Hueil wore a sheepish grin and shook his head from side to side in some private observation. He then traded leaning against the doorway for the bedpost at the foot of the bed. "Neb, avoid taking a mate at all cost," he cautioned jokingly. "Riona, I think you can safely come out from under your cloak."

Reluctantly she lowered the hood and took the opportunity to study their host more fully. Neb was right, Hueil had changed. The warrior who had escorted her to Tearmann had been full of anger. This fey was nearly jovial. And although a fey could create any glamour he wished, Riona was fairly certain she was seeing Hueil's true form. Some magick unknown to her had transformed him physically.

"When you have rested, and before you tackle Sinnie by yourself, I suggest you talk with Jen. She may help you see more clearly in this matter," he told her cryptically.

"Thank you for this." Riona indicated the room and respite with a small gesture of her healed but sore hand.

Hueil just smiled more to himself than to them. "Well, I will leave you." He stood and walked to the door. "Oh, Neb..." He looked over his shoulder.

"Yes, brother." Neb had risen off his knee and had taken a seat in the opposite chair.

"Dinna think of leaving before Sinnie has had her say. You brought this trouble, so I'll be expectin' you to clean it up before you leave."

Neb and Hueil shared a silent conversation, a nod, a look, a sigh. It ended in an unspoken agreement between the two brothers. She would not be fleeing again without confronting Sel's daughter.

Hueil then smiled crookedly and left them alone, closing the door carefully behind him. With his departure, Riona relaxed and her body sagged into the chair's padding.

"You really do look done in. Take the bed, Princess. I will be fine right here. Do you want me to scrounge up some food?"

She smiled weakly at him. He was being so very kind to her. "Thank you, yes."

"I will be right back."

"You said that before and an unseelie-dragon-fey came while you were gone," she teased.

Neb gave her a lopsided grin, similar to his brother's. "Then I should hurry." After performing a grand bow solely for her entertainment, Neb turned and left, closing the door behind him. Listening to his fading footsteps as he made his way downstairs, Riona pushed herself up and stumbled to the bed. Without bothering to loosen her bodice or remove her cloak, she sank into the soft mattress and sighed. As soon as her head touched the down filled pillow, she was asleep.

Chapter 3

Sel stood at the gates of Tearmann and scanned the distance. Where would she have traveled to and how could he have been so stupid to believe an unseelie would choose to be honorable? *"Give me a moment to see my friend off. I will meet you in the gathering hall."* She had stood there and calmly lied to him. He closed his eyes briefly in despair. Riona had taken one look at him and fled. Sel was surprised at her unwillingness to accept him as a suitable substitution for Calcus, but more surprised that her rebuff could touch such an old ache.

With a shake of his head, he put the disturbing thought out of his mind. His only recourse was to give chase.

Sel strode forward and inspected the spot where she had been standing. He was under the Queen's orders to retrieve Riona and cement an agreement between the house of Selgi and hers. This would keep the Unseelie King from reacquiring his daughter. If the King did finally recover Riona, Melwas was likely to create another alliance not in the Seelie Court's best interest. Riona's unwillingness to bow to the Queen's will was not a factor in the equation, just as Sel's wishes weren't a consideration in his monarch's decision.

He knelt and laid his palm over the bent grass. He could feel no residual marker left behind from her folding space. She had not shifted. Would she have stayed in these hazardous mountains? Quite possibly, if her companion were not a true wolf. Sel was now fairly certain the black wolf had been another unseelie, an informant perhaps. By the way the animal had acted, he was willing to protect Riona and even follow her lead.

Sel unstrapped his sword and placed it on the ground

before shapeshifting into the form of a large tawny wolf. He sniffed the air and in turn received an exorbitant amount of information which his wolf nose easily sorted and cataloged. Riona's scent was distinctive, sweet marjoram and nutmeg. Surprisingly, the combination made his mouth water. The other smelled of ash and steel. Definitely a member of the unseelie warrior caste, he thought. Concentrating on the more pleasurable scent of Riona, Sel scanned the area. He worked methodically until he found a fresh trail leading off towards the west. Mouthing the scabbard and sword tightly in his jaws, Sel gave chase.

He traveled as swiftly as he could, the awkward weapon slowing him more than he would have liked. It felt unnatural and awkward in his lupine mouth. Periodically, Sel stopped to sniff the ground and surrounding vegetation to verify he had not lost her trail. The stops also allowed him to rest his aching jaws.

When a stream hindered him as well, Sel howled with frustration. She had been smart to head for water part of his mind acknowledged, but it forced him to spend precious minutes traveling down river along the bank before Sel realized she had chosen to flee in the opposite direction. Rectifying his mistake, he hastened upstream and found her trail once more. It veered away from the river towards the mountains.

What could she be thinking? The sporadic caves and recesses hidden in and along the Arach Mountains held more than concealment and possible shelter. When the moon reached its zenith, the dragons would awaken deep within their mountain lairs to begin hunting. Time was against him and panic spurred him on.

When the first roar erupted over head, Sel slid to a stop and looked skyward. A large male dragon circled high, its dark body temporarily blocking the blanket of stars. It was scanning for movement below as it hunted. An answering call came from behind Sel, somewhere to the south. A lone wolf wouldn't be of interest to the hunting pair, so Sel dashed up the rocky passage. Riona's scent trail was leading him toward the now downwardly spiraling dragon.

The beast latched onto the side of the cliff just above Sel, talons digging deep into rock. A rain of gravel and stone fell along the path in front of him. Sel scrambled and pressed his wolf's body close to the mountain face just as a medium sized boulder bounced over his head. When the dragon tucked its wings, Sel stalked forward. He could hear the beast address the occupants.

Morphing into his true form Sel quietly approached, pausing only to buckle his sword to his hip before climbing the last few feet. Negotiations had been short between the dragon and the occupants. Not a good omen, Sel thought.

The dragon, having given his warning made ready to depart, but it paused and glanced in Sel's direction. Knowing he was vulnerable, Sel clung precariously to the mountainside. The dragon made no move to initiate an attack, quite possibly because it could clearly see the Queen's insignia and rank on his guardsman uniform.

Unsheathing his sword, Sel pulled himself upward to a place of better footing. Because of his closeness to the Seelie Queen, the dragon might not attack him directly, but Sel didn't trust the creature to keep to the treaty between their two races and not attack Riona and the one who traveled with her.

The great beast coiled then pushed from its perch, unearthing more rock and stone, taking much of the ledge with him in an effort to hinder Sel's progress.

Sel shifted as the ledge above him fell away. He then reappeared to scramble up the last few inches, sword at the ready.

He could not see into the dark interior, but he caught the energy surge needed to shift space and time. Relieved Riona had escaped the immediate danger posed by the dragon, Sel ran to the back of the shelter to follow their trail.

The energy trail was easier for him to follow than chasing after them in wolf form. If he had been slower or the dragon more determined, they might have escaped him, but Sel had been a tracker before rising to the post of captain. As long as Riona chose this means of flight, he would not lose her. Eventually, he would catch her, and the one who traveled with her.

If there was a logic to the leaps through space Sel could not discern it. Each location seemed utterly random. More than once the trail doubled back on itself, which might have confused a less experienced tracker. Not once had the pair attempted to move through time, just from location to location. Part of him wondered if this was on purpose. Riona's escort was making their flight look good, but only just.

At one point the magickal signature thinned. And when he realized the texture had changed as well, Sel stopped to assess the situation. He was standing beside a stone wall. There was nothing but open fields and dawn was fast approaching. Suspecting the reason for the waning signature, Sel took the time to morph once more into his wolf form. Riona's energy had waned dramatically and his wolf's nose could only find the faintest of scents. It was a false trail; Sel was certain. Taking his true form again, he backtracked to find where the false trail had first been initiated.

He reappeared at the edge of a meadow ringed by forest; at its edge a large oak towered above all the rest. He saw no signs of movement, but Riona's scent was strong. As he walked the meadow's perimeter, he peered into the shadowy recesses created by the dense tree growth. The sun was breaking over the horizon and he could not pinpoint her energy trail. Perhaps, he had lost them after all. Perplexed, Sel took one last look across the meadow's breadth.

And there she stood. Inexplicably, his heart once again lodged in this throat and uncharacteristically he hesitated to act. Rooted to the ground much like the trees at his back, he watched as she turned towards him. The moment she spied him, her eyes widened in shock or perhaps it was fear. Beyond her, Sel watched as an unseelie boldly followed her from the shadows of the oak tree. She did not alert her companion to his presence, but turned to confront the unseelie. When she took several hesitant steps backward, putting distance between herself and the approaching warrior, warning bells sounded in Sel's head.

He would have time to ponder his actions later, but somehow Sel knew she was in danger. It might have been the unseelie's body language, or the tone of the fey's voice, but before Sel's mind could articulate the exact form of the danger he had drawn his sword and had shifted to her side.

Sel instinctively placed himself in front of her as a shield; his arm forcibly pushing her behind him as the unseelie began to change into, of all things, a dragon. Sel registered the sudden appearance of another form, followed by Riona's subsequent disappearance as the two abandoned him to confront the unseelie alone. "Typical," he muttered, never taking his eyes off the changing unseelie before him.

He hastily retreated into the center of the meadow while keeping his sword tip between himself and the expanding unseelie. Knowing he was outmatched for now and that he was losing Riona's trail, Sel shifted away before the unseelie could complete the complicated transformation.

He materialized back where it had all begun. Sel sheathed his sword. With dawn's arrival, Tearmann had magickally traveled to another location, leaving no evidence behind that it had ever settled there for the night.

He stood completely alone near an alder grove. This had been the spot where he had first laid eyes on her. This was where he had momentarily been struck dumb by his body's heated reaction to her. She was after all her mother's daughter, he thought sarcastically. He should have foreseen that complication, but wasting time berating himself for his weakness wasn't going to find Riona. "Now what?" he whispered, looking around for any inspiration.

Unfortunately, the energy signature of the unseelie/dragon would erase any traces of Riona's trail. He was going to have to tell the Queen he had lost the princess. He was not looking forward to that conversation. His heart sank; he didn't like failing his Queen.

Just as he made ready to leave, he thought of Urias. It might work, he reasoned. With a renewed sense of purpose, Sel left the Arach Mountains behind and traveled to his private apartments in the Seelie Court.

"Urias!" Sel bellowed while still materializing inside his study. It was supposed to have been a simple task. "Go fetch the princess," he muttered to himself. When Urias didn't immediately appear Sel started pacing the length of the room. "Damn it, where the hell is that sprite?" He paused to look through the doorway leading into his great hall, and beyond into the gardens. Not seeing any sign of Urias, Sel resumed his pacing. He knew every second he was wasting mattered.

"Urias," he yelled one more time.

Urias darted into the room, his iridescent wings nothing

but a blur. "Captain?" he chirped. The sprite hovered directly before Sel's nose and gave a crisp salute.

Urias was one of the lesser fey, an elemental, a sprite. In his natural state he was no bigger than a hummingbird or dragonfly. His undulating wings vibrated expectantly as he waited eagerly for Sel's instructions.

"Riona did not like the look of me, and she has run from the Queen's edict. I need to find her, quickly."

The diminutive sprite's look of complete shock only irritated Sel further; he had to clenched his jaw to keep the growl from rumbling in his throat.

Urias sputtered before he suggested, "Shall I go fetch a tracker, Captain?"

"No, I would prefer to keep this quiet."

Urias nodded, completely understanding. Long ago Urias had pledged himself to the service of the Seelie Queen and to Sel personally. And in some cases the sprite's unerring loyalty bordered on fanatical blindness. Sel had no faults as far as Urias was concerned, so Riona's flight was absolutely astonishing to him.

"Show me her last location, Captain. I can find her."

Sel gladly held out his hand and Urias lightly touched down onto his palm. With a thumbs-up signal from Urias, Sel shifted them.

He brought Urias to her last know location, the edge of the meadow. The dragon was long gone and all was still. This was a last ditch effort for Sel. If Urias's extraordinary abilities couldn't find Riona's magickal trail that now lay buried somewhere under a layer of more powerful magick then he would have to confess his failure to the Queen.

Sel waited impatiently while Urias darted about the

abandoned meadow in a bewildering search pattern. On top of having to track down Riona, Sel now had a bigger problem on his hands. He would have to send several of his guardsmen to find that unseelie/dragon. "Leave it to an unseelie to pass himself off as one of those bloody beasts," he muttered. The treaty between the fey courts and the dragons was brittle at best most days. And with the Unseelie King and Sel's Queen at odds again, all they needed was a trouble-making unseelie masquerading as a dragon. Undoubtedly the rogue was stirring up trouble in the west. With his troubles mounting, Sel had to stop himself from grinding his teeth together; it would only make the throbbing in his head worse.

Interrupting Sel's spiraling thoughts, Urias's sent up a high pitched chirp. By the sound of it, the sprite had good news for him. Coming closer, Sel found Urias pointing to a shallow footprint. Bending down Sel put his hand on the ground, but could read nothing from the faint print. He couldn't feel any trace of a disturbance beyond that of the unseelie's metamorphosis.

"Urias, can you amplify it for me?"

The sprite descended to the ground, landing on Riona's supposed trail. He bridged the space between the ground and Sel's outstretched finger with his body, his tiny hand a conduit of knowledge. Yes, there it was. She had stood here. He could feel the light touch of magick left by her shifting.

"I have it."

Urias grinned broadly, showing all his pointy teeth before jumping once more onto Sel's hand. They shifted together. Now that he had regained the trail, Sel bounced from one location to the next in quick succession. He paused by a lake. The energy felt strong here. They were in the north at a gateway, a leaping off point that connected to other gateways and through them any number of worlds. The exits from Tir na n-Og weren't watched, but the destination gates were. "The bloody idiots!"

Urias sprang off his hand. "Captain!" he whistled.

Sel followed Urias's pointing finger. There on the ground was a scrap of cloth stained with blood. Sel bent over and snatched it up. He inhaled her scent and the metallic signature of blood. Was she hurt? The idea was unnerving to him. From the moment the Queen had transferred the binding agreement from Calcus's house to his own, Sel had been given the responsibility of the princess's well being. It was his duty, and Sel took his duty very seriously. He'd need to hurry.

Sel thrust out his hand for Urias and shifted with the coppery smell of blood still in his nose. For good or for ill, he would not lose her trail now. Her injury meant he had a blood trail to follow, but it also filled him with dread. Was she injured because of her companion? Had she been taken against her will? Or did she flee because she wanted to?

Sel was stunned when he passed through the familiar destination gateway; Riona had traveled into the human realm. Without the masking influence of the dragon, Sel could now clearly identify the unseelie with her. He was the same as the one in the cave; the same unseelie that had been with her outside the walls of Tearmann. They had gotten past the watchers somehow. This bothered Sel as much as it relieved him. Whoever Riona's companion was, he knew how to skirt the gate's deadly defenses. Who the hell was this meddler leading Riona all over Tir na n-Og and now into Jen's realm? An unexpected anger began to eat at him. When he caught him, Sel had every intention of tearing the fool to pieces.

After following Riona through several more random jumps. Sel was left to wonder just how long her companion was willing to run. Fear and rage exploded inside him when Sel materialized beside a pecan tree directly behind Jen's and Steven's new lodgings. "Bloody hell!" Sel hesitated only long enough to draw his sword before moving on.

The next jump brought him inside Jen's house, to an upstairs bedchamber. Urias flew from his hand to hover over the bed, chirping madly. Riona's scent of marjoram and nutmeg filled his nose. Sel was so attuned to her energy and scent signature that for a moment he was quite frankly overwhelmed.

"Be quiet, Urias," Sel hissed. She was alone in the room and seemingly asleep on the bed, a cloak had been partially pulled over her in an effort to keep her warm. The constant travel may not have tired the unseelie warrior, but Sel knew she wouldn't have fared as well. Age brought power to members of their race. Riona was young. Perhaps younger than Sinnie. Sel was also certain the princess had not inherited her father's warrior stamina. Only a select few had made that bargain with the gods.

He slid his sword back into the sheath strapped to his hip. Silently Sel approached the bed; his heart hammering in his chest. Aye, she slept. He had found her. Relief surged through his limbs. Knowing she was safe should have calmed him, but his heart continued to pound and Sel was at a loss to adequately explain his strong reaction to her—at least to his satisfaction, he thought. Yes, her mother's influence clearly showed in her features. But there were some differences. Her mother was famous for her ebony tresses, but Riona's hair was brown, almost chocolate. Riona's skin was equally as pale and luminescent as her mother's, unmarred except for a few faint freckles along her nose. But there was something more to Riona, something he had glimpsed at their first meeting. He could not give a name to it and that frustrated him.

Lingering to study her, Sel could see that she dreamed; the dark lashes fluttered against her pale cheeks. Despite knowing better, he gently entered her mind and laid a sleep compulsion on her so she would not rise from her dreaming until he could deal with her. The fact that he found this momentary vulnerability of hers so damn enticing alarmed him. He didn't need this kind of temptation in his life. But, if he were honest with himself, he wanted nothing more than to touch her.

As if drawn forward by a greater power, his hand inched up to steal a caress along her check. When he felt the temperature of the air around him rise sharply, Sel stopped just short of his goal. When she stirred and turned her face toward his hand, Sel snatched it back and watched as she settled again.

After watching her sleep for a moment more, he found himself wondering if she'd look at him with something other than fear when he allowed her to wake? Brianna, Sinnie's mother, had traded fear for hate, not willing to pause for a more amenable emotion somewhere in between. Would Riona do the same? He gingerly lifted the edge of the cloak and pulled it further up, letting it drop down so that it covered her shoulder. The temperature around him rose again when his fingers accidentally grazed her sleeve. Sel abruptly withdrew his hand as if he had been shocked.

"Captain."

Urias stood on her pillow watching him, tapping his foot, hands on his slim hips. Sel let his hand fall back to his side, the disturbing sound of tumbling dice echoing in his head. He ignored it and concentrated on Urias. "What?"

"What about the nasty unseelie? He's here. I smell him."

Sel's forgotten anger returned three-fold. "Where?" he snarled at the sprite.

Urias gave him a toothy grin before darting from the room. Sel followed the winged harbinger, descending the stars two and three steps at a time.

Chapter 4

Sel jumped over the few remaining steps to land at the base of the staircase next to a large unpacked cardboard box. He was in the central hallway of the antebellum house Jen and Steven had been hastily moved into per his instructions. The main hall accessed four large rooms, downstairs as well as above. Sel could clearly hear Hueil's laughter in one of the front rooms.

Urias sped toward the sound like an arrow shot from a bow with Sel following in his wake. Bursting through the open doorway, Sel rammed past his newest son-in-law and slammed the unseelie up against the wall, his balled fist landing with as much force as he could wield against the blue-devil's jaw. Later, much later, Sel would recall that Hueil had tried to slow his murderous charge.

Ignoring the arm that snaked around his neck, Sel pummeled on the face of the bastard now in his grip. He wanted to beat the grin off the blue face and he intended to do just that.

Steven grabbed for his arm and missed. It took both Steven and Hueil working in tandem before he was dragged backward off the bloody bastard. Sel nearly howled with frustration as he fought to free himself.

"Sel!" Hueil yelled from behind, the effort of restraining him apparent.

"Hold up, Sel. Let Neb explain." Steven slowly maneuvered himself between Sel and his target.

Sel growled low in his throat, but then abruptly stopped fighting as Steven's face came into focus. After a moment, Hueil weakened his hold.

"Are you going to listen?" Hueil grunted.

Sel didn't take his eyes off the unseelie called Neb. The idiot was still smirking even while rubbing at his abused jaw. "Aye, but be damned quick about it," Sel barked back.

Hueil slowly released him and went to right a chair that had been knocked over. "Crap," Hueil said, noticing the shards of a lamp lying on the floor.

"Sel's taking the blame for that," Steven said.

Hueil agreed. "Second one today."

Sel's two sons-in-law chuckled over the private joke.

As if Sel's beating hadn't hurt, Neb casually resumed his seat. "Took you long enough, Captain. I thought you were a better tracker than that."

Sel's next command rattled the windows in their frames. "Explain."

Neb shook his head from side to side. "You spooked her with your little speech, Captain. It left me with little choice but to keep her out of trouble for you."

"You call leading her into the mountain caves of the dragons safe?" he roared. He was having to fight not to lose complete control of his temper again, and Neb's flippant attitude towards Riona's safety wasn't helping. "And lest we forget, in your dubious care she was left alone for an insane unseelie to find. You call this keeping her out of trouble?" Sel spat, stalking towards Neb, his fists balling once more.

Hueil stepped forward, partially blocking his path. "Listen, Sel," he counseled. Talking over his shoulder to his brother, Hueil said, "Neb, get to the point. The captain here would just as soon kill you, by the look of him." Hueil raised an eyebrow, giving Sel a knowing sympathetic look.

With his fun having been cut short by his brother, Neb sighed and leaned forward in his seat, all pretense of amusement wiped clean from his face. "You and I both know the King will use her for his own gain if he gets his hands on his daughter. I am tired of seeing her used by others," he confessed uncomfortably. Pausing, he removed a spot of blood from the corner of his lip and leaned back. "She needed time to adjust to the idea of you. Not that I think you're a good catch, mind you," Neb said sullenly. "We all know I would be more amusing for her, but at least she will be protected from Melwas for the length of the contract between your two houses."

"Neb, finish. The captain's patience is wearing thin," Hueil warned.

"I knew you would follow. I made it easy for you..." he paused, "except for the dragon incident. That was a surprise." Both eyebrows lifted in merriment, a smirk playing at the edges of his mouth.

Sel took one more step toward Neb. He would kill him, he decided coldly.

Hueil put his hand on Sel's shoulder, an attempt to forestall him. "Wait for it." Then he called over his shoulder, "Neb."

Fearing his brother's impatience more than Sel's anger, Neb went on to begrudgingly explain, "I knew the constant traveling would drain her, making her as weak as a new born. And then, I delivered her here for her own good. I knew you would eventually come, if only to see Sinnie."

Sel was astounded by the unseelie's gall. Neb acted like he had done him a bloody favor. "She was injured," Sel accused.

"I am sorry for that...truly I am, but Hueil's mate mended the small wound," Neb said, waving his hand dismissively.

Everything about Neb seemed to suggest to Sel that he thought this a merry game of fox and hound. Meddling, bored unseelie, they were all alike, Sel thought uncharitably. But he now understood that Riona had chosen to run from him. She feared him, just like Brianna had. Ignoring the sinking feeling in his gut, he stated the obvious, "She cannot recover here." It was true. Magick was the force that sustained their kind and this world lacked the resources to foster magick in enough quantities to replace what Riona had lost during her flight from him.

"No, but it will give you time I think. Time you will undoubtedly need," Neb chuckled.

"Time for what?" he grumbled back.

"To court her," Hueil explained, without a hint of sarcasm or jest.

"Why would I want to do that?" Sel bellowed inches from Hueil's face.

Steven shook his head in disbelief as he ran a hand through his dark hair. "Shit, Sel...what you don't know about women."

Sel turned, having almost forgotten Steven was still in the room. His son-in-law had retreated, remaining quiet to let the fey fight among themselves. It had been smart of him, Sel thought. Answering Steven as patiently as he could, given the circumstances, Sel said, "Steven, there is no need to court her. It is a contract, nothing more. I do not have time to woo her. Nor do I want to." The finality of his statement earned him twin looks of disbelief from Hueil and Neb. "This is for the princess's safety only," he told the brothers. Shortly, he would explain that fact to her, and this whole nonsense would come to an end.

Neb snorted and Hueil sighed while plunking down into a brown leather chair identical to his brother's.

"Good luck with that." Steven patted Sel's shoulder and left the room still shaking his head.

"Have you seen her up close?" Neb asked.

"Aye. She sleeps." Sel's mind dutifully resurrected her image and his chest constricted. Hueil and Neb glanced at each other, sharing some private thought between them. "What of it?" Sel barked.

Neb looked pointedly at Sel. "Only that she is… special, one of a kind. Much like her mother."

Suspicious of anything Neb had to offer, Sel asked, "What do you know of it?"

"Who is her mother?" Hueil asked Neb, his curiosity piqued.

Steven walked in carrying a broom and trash can. "Whose mother?"

"Riona's," Hueil informed Steven. He was still waiting for Neb to answer his question.

Steven shrugged then proceeded to ignore the lot of them. Jen's mate busied himself with cleaning up the broken lamp. He swept up the shattered pottery and placed the shade off to the side next to a stack of pictures leaning against one wall.

Sel had scanned the room during the exchange between Hueil and Steven. Hueil had indeed gotten his daughter and mate moved into the large house, though the furnishings were sparse. No trinkets adorned the side tables or fireplace mantle. Two cardboard boxes sat unopened in one corner. The quality of the seating was reasonable, though nothing that could be crafted as well as back home. To Sel's knowledge, Jen and Steven had only the barest of possessions. All the pieces in this room were new. While pleased that the move had been accomplished in such a short time, Sel would have to remember to ask Hueil where he had acquired the extra furniture; if nothing else he would need to make sure it wasn't stolen from some merchant in the dead of night.

Bringing himself back to the conversation Sel informed the room at large, "It doesn't matter. I have no interest in the girl." It wasn't any of their concern what he thought of Riona.

"You have not a wee bit of interest in Naria's daughter? Bollocks!" Neb declared.

Sel gritted his teeth and the pain in his head escalated.

Hueil warned, "Neb, now is not the time to be lyin' to the captain."

"Aye, brother, she's Naria's." Neb's grin returned, broader than before.

Hueil paled at the news and breathed, "When?"

"Shortly after you were banished. The King had to be certain twas his," Neb explained.

"So she is not?" Hueil asked.

"No," Sel and Neb confirmed in unison. Sel glared at Neb even though it did him no good. The bloody fool continued to grin like a cat with a bowl of cream.

Hueil slumped forward. "Thank the gods. Sinnie would kill me." He glanced up at Sel.

Neb laughed at his brother's relief. Standing, he punched Hueil good-naturedly in the shoulder. "Aye, I think she would."

Wearily, Sel sank down onto the sofa, and rested his head on the leather cushions behind him; his head was killing him. He closed his eyes for a moment and felt the breeze caused by Urias's wings as the sprite settled on the armrest next to him.

"Captain. Are you not going to punish the unseelie?"

Sel spared the sprite a glance. His wings drooped with disappointment. "Not at present, Urias." He watched the sprite's wings dip further. "But maybe later, if it pleases me," he offered. That greatly cheered the sprite, and Sel smiled for the first time that day.

Turning his back to the room, Neb moved to look out one of the large side windows.

"Do you wish me to guard your new mate, Captain?" Urias suggested, emphasizing the word 'mate' for the room's benefit.

Sel gave a sharp nod in the affirmative. He didn't trust himself to speak as the word 'mate' bounced off the inside of his skull. Or was that the sound of tumbling dice rolling around in his mind again.

Urias would think guarding a sleeping Riona a worthy assignment, Sel mused as he watched the sprite dart from the room. She was, after all, the mate of the Queen's Captain, bound legally by law if not in spirit, and that made Riona almost as precious as the Queen herself in Urias's mind. Sel looked over to see Hueil watching him intently. To deflect the question forming on Hueil's lips, Sel asked, "Where is Jen and Sinnie?"

While exiting the room after cleaning up the mess Sel had caused, Steven said in passing, "Jen and my mom went to buy a wedding dress. Sinnie went as well."

"It is just us," Hueil assured Sel.

Bored with the view out the window, Neb went to stand near the fireplace.

"When are they due back?" Sel asked. He and Jen hadn't parted on good terms in their last meeting. He hoped he could rectify it somehow and that one day his daughter would find a way to forgive him. Even if he couldn't forgive himself.

"No telling. Women and shopping, there are too many variables to consider," Steven called from the other room.

Sel fought a smile. He liked his halfling son-in-law. Jen and Steven were a good match. Though only the gods knew how he, a seelie, had ended up with two unseelie bred sons-in-law.

Sinnie may have changed Hueil's blue tinted skin when she exchanged vows with him, but Sel suspected Hueil was still very much an unseelie on the inside. No one changed that much.

Breaking into his thoughts, Hueil said, "Jen will soften, Sel."

"Leave it," Sel warned. He then stood and nailed Neb with a contemptuous glare. "You are in Madison, Georgia, and a guest in my daughter's home. Look human, and stay away from Riona or Hueil will have one less brother." Hueil and Neb were acting like his predicament was some great joke of the Queen's. As Sel stalked from the room he growled at Hueil, "Keep your bother on a short leash."

Leaving their laughter behind, Sel headed back upstairs to the bedroom to keep watch with Urias. He wasn't sure what he was going to do with Riona. At some point, he'd have to take her back to court, kicking and screaming if she turned out to be unreasonable. It was a prospect Sel didn't find appealing.

She did not stir as he entered. Closing the door behind him, Sel fought the urge to approach the bed to look on her again. Instead he tried to make himself comfortable in one of the two chairs in the room.

Urias had stationed himself along the bed's headboard and was sharpening his modest weapon to pass the time. It was no larger than a toothpick, but Urias kept it oiled with a special poison that was decidedly unpleasant at best. Catching Sel's eye, Urias gave him a thumbs-up sign, which meant any number of things to the sprite. Sel nodded back, but said nothing. He had no idea where Urias had learned it, but the sprite used the gesture as often as he could manage.

He glanced at Riona's unmoving form. If what Neb said was true, then she would not have the strength to shift if he woke her. He told himself it didn't matter if she found him unacceptable. Theirs was a contract of convenience and she should be grateful. It was a strong argument, but it didn't fully erase the disappointment he felt at her initial reaction to him, nor did it squash the hope that perhaps one day she would look on him favorably. However, neither emotion would interfere with him doing his duty in an honorable way, he decided.

Slipping into her mind again, Sel lifted the sleep command he had selfishly used to detain her. Not wanting to further violate her privacy, he didn't linger to explore her memories. Admittedly, he shied away from delving too deeply. He didn't want to hear for himself what she truly thought of him. Her actions had made it clear enough; he didn't need to confirm what he already knew.

Despite his efforts and the rearranging of the chairs so he could prop his legs in one while sitting in the other, after two hours of waiting Sel began to squirm in the confines of the frugally padded seat. He had also begun to worry. Under normal conditions a fey Riona's age would only need a few hours sleep per human day. He had no idea how long she had been like this. He should have asked. But as soon as he stood, intent on gently shaking her awake, she stirred.

Sel stopped dead in his tracks.

She woke slowly, rubbing at her eyes before moving to sit upright. He was only a few feet from the end of the bed and she had yet to notice him. Urias silently sheathed his weapon behind her.

As Sel had expected, the moment she saw him she jumped in alarm and her eyes grew wide. He said nothing, just raised on eyebrow.

An air of royal entitlement quickly replaced her initial

fright as she schooled her expression. It was a look he had often witnessed on the face of his Queen when dealings with those she was wary of. Riona was quite the little actress, he decided. He would need to remember that.

One haughty eyebrow rose to match his. "Now what?" she asked.

He gritted his teeth and reined in his temper before answering. "Short of me spanking you?" If she was going to act like a spoiled and pampered child, running from a duty place on them both, then he'd treat her like a child. The beautifully arched eyebrow fell, but her chin pushed forward in defiance, daring him.

Silence stretched between them.

Breaking the stand off, Sel said, "What I should do is take you back home. You cannot recover your strength here."

"Where is here?"

"You are in the human realm. Did you not know that?"

"No. I have never crossed beyond the gateways," she confessed.

That was welcome news to him. While waiting for her to awaken, he had decided to treat her with strict cordiality and nothing more. He answered her question as succinctly as possible. "This is my daughter's house. She and her mate are under the Queen's protection."

Pushing the cloak off of her legs, she gracefully swung them over the side of the bed. "Why would Sinnie need protection? Because of my father?" she asked.

"No, though Sinnie and Hueil are here as well." Sel found it irritating to have to explain his affairs to her. "Jen is a halfling, and my daughter. Steven is her mate," he told her.

"Really?" She turned toward him in surprise and ran her

fingers through her hair, letting it fall softly about her face and shoulders.

"Aye. Hueil and Sinnie guard them." He found himself following her hand movements as she repeated the gesture. She was watching him as well, his past failure having caught her interest for some reason.

"From what?" she asked.

How could she not know? His brow creased. Was she playing with him? "Hunters," he answered sharply.

A shadow passed over her features. "Oh."

Wanting to ease the distress he read on her face, he said more gently, "It is not your concern."

She just nodded and remained mute.

Sel had the odd feeling that he was handling their conversation badly and that frustrated him. Taking command of the situation, he pressed forward with his earlier plan. "Are we done with this game? I have no intentions beyond offering you the protection of my name and house. You will be free to conduct your affairs as you see fit as long as you do not bring disgrace to the house of Selgi, or danger to my family," he added.

"You only offer protection?" she whispered, cocking her head slightly in confusion.

His brow creased again. Why did he feel like he was walking into a trap? "Aye."

She ducked her head, took a deep breath, and stood. Turning to him she lifted her chin. "So be it then."

He had the distinct sensation something had been decided between them. Carefully he replied, "Good. It is settled."

Once again, she nodded her agreement but did not speak further.

"I will inform the Queen of your acceptance," he told

her.

"If it pleases you."

"My desires have nothing to do with it," he snapped at her. Then moderating his tone, he asked, "Are you ready?"

"Ready for what?"

"To leave." He knew she wasn't a simpleton, but conversing with her was exceedingly difficult he thought. "The Queen is waiting."

"I do not need to go with you to prove that my acceptance of the Queen's will is true. I have promised to stay here."

"You have made no such promise…"

"I have. And I will stay until morning. Come fetch me then."

What the hell was she blathering on about? "Riona, I have no intention of letting you out of my sight. You have lied to me once already." He itched to close the distance between them and shake her, but he refrained. "I do not trust you to keep your word."

"I promised your daughter. I will not go until she and I have talked," she explained, no outward signs that his gruffness and general frustration with their conversation was the least bit distressing to her.

He didn't know which daughter she spoke of, but if she were lying again, he needed to know. Sel's mind automatically assessed the situation, pros and cons. Jen and Sinnie would be back by nightfall. At least he hoped they would. Steven hadn't made any preparations for going to work. Today must be a day their cafe was closed, he decided. Riona silently stood before him, waiting for an answer. "Fine. You are free to roam the house, but do not leave it. Urias keep an eye on her," he ordered before striding to the door.

"Aye, Captain." Urias chirped.

Sel heard her gasp behind him. Riona hadn't been aware of the sprite's presence, a silent witness to their conversation. Opening the door, Sel headed downstairs. As he went, he struggled to set aside the niggling suspicion that he had gotten the short end of the deal between them.

Chapter 5

Recovering from her fright at the lesser fey's presence, Riona gratefully sat back down onto the edge of the bed. The captain was just another protector now forced upon her. The only difference this time was it had been orchestrated by the Queen to benefit the Seelie Court's aims, and not some disenfranchised member of the Unseelie Court wanting to overthrow her father. She should be used to this by now, Riona told herself, but the depth of her disappointment shocked her.

Ignoring the ache in her heart, she concentrated on her most pressing dilemma—the sad state of her health. She had never been this weak before. The nap should have restored her, but if what the captain said was indeed true, she would remain at a disadvantage until returning home.

Urias carefully bowed, hovering before her at eye level. "Milady, I am Urias. How may I be of service?" the sprite asked.

Riona had had only limited experience with elementals, a few curious pixies when she was very young. She knew them to be secretive creatures, typically keeping to their own kind. Urias's attachment to the captain intrigued Riona and it gave her something to think about other than his coldness. "Why do you serve him?"

Urias alighted on the bedside table beside a plate of fruit. "He did me a favor once," Urias chirped.

She picked up an apple, took a bite, and realized just how hungry she was. The fruit tasted bland, but she ate it anyway. "Must have been quite a favor." She smiled down at him and he beamed back, his wings fluttering excitedly. He took to the air once more, moving to within inches of her nose, his wings fanning cool air across her cheeks. His tiny features had become very serious.

"Princess, he is an honorable man, the best of men," Urias began, then he looked somewhat guilty and looked behind him before confessing, "But, he lets duty to Queen and Court cloud his sight."

Riona bit into the apple again, chewing on it and Urias's personal observation of the captain.

"You will help him in this?" he chirped hopefully.

Knowing the sprite expected a reply, Riona chose her words carefully. "I hardly know him, Urias. What do you expect me to do?"

"Be you. That is all."

The man hardly spoke to her. She didn't think the captain was going to suddenly want to share her company. At the wayward thought of them spending more time together, her foolish heart skipped a beat or two. Idiot, she berated herself. His little speech delivered just moments ago had been business-like and distant. He only saw himself as her new bodyguard, nothing more. He didn't care for her, nor did he give any indication of wanting to care. "Urias, you are mistaken. I can not make a waterfall flow up when it is destined to flow down."

Uneasy with the personal nature of their conversation and intent on exploring her new environment, Riona stood and was hit by a wave of dizziness. Reaching out, she steadied herself by grabbing the nearest bed post. She was even weaker than she had thought. Not good. Definitely not good.

"I will go fetch the captain."

"No!" Riona shouted. Urias stopped and hovered in the doorway. "No, I am fine," she assured him, her tone measured. When her head cleared Riona straightened, squared her shoulders and walked to the door. "I wish to go downstairs."

Urias looked doubtful at her pronouncement, but he accompanied her without argument.

She only made it three-quarters of the way down the stairs before another wave of dizziness hit her. Deciding the best course of action was to sit where she stood, she stopped. Otherwise, she might very well have tumbled down the remaining steps.

As casually as she could, Riona abruptly sat. Noticing her gracelessness, Urias started to say something but she hushed him and pretended that this had been her destination all along. She was no fool; the last thing she was going to do was admit to her weakened state. When Urias whistled his concern, she held up her hand to silence him. Voices were coming from an adjoining room and she wanted to hear.

Respecting her request for silence, Urias flew to the bottom of the banister and sat on the finial to wait. She got the impression he was not pleased with her.

"He cannot stay here, Hueil. He has no allegiance to the seelie or to her safety."

"I have said it before, he will not betray me. I will talk with him. He will keep his word to me."

Riona could tell they were speaking about Neb, but she was not sure of the identity of the "her" Sel was referring to. While she wondered if he was talking about his halfling daughter or herself, the devil walked up and grinned through the banister railings at her. She put her finger to her lips to warn Neb to remain quiet, missing some of what Sel had been saying to Hueil in the process.

"Did you ask her about the unseelie?" Hueil asked.

After a moment Sel confessed, "No. Not yet."

"Could be Gloric. Neb told me he abandoned the others to live with the dragons," Hueil voice floated up the stairs. Riona lifted an eyebrow at Neb, who winked at her in response.

"Another reason I need to get back," Sel replied.

Silence.

"Cheer up Captain, this is not such a bad assignment," Hueil chuckled.

"Where the hell did your brother go?" Sel asked, then he poked his head out into the hall and spotted them. "Care to join us?" His tone sounded depressingly disappointed at finding her eavesdropping. Hueil followed Sel out into the hallway.

Before Riona could muster an answer, Neb came around to the foot of the stairs and gallantly offered his hand. Flattered by Neb's courtly manner, she accepted his assistance and stood. The sour look on Sel's face only served to amuse Neb and his brother. Riona took a deep breath and then descended a few steps before the weakness in her legs forced to halt once more. Neb's grip on her hand tightened as the dizziness caused her to sway.

"Sel, it's Jen on the phone."

A man Riona had yet to meet came striding down the hall with a small devise held to his ear. He was smaller in stature than the others, but pleasant to look at. Glancing up at her only in passing, he motioned Sel to follow him. He showed little interest in who she might be or why she was here.

When Sel followed the new arrival toward the back of the house Hueil commented, "Neb look what you did to the girl."

"She just needs rest," Neb assured him, but he didn't sound certain. Both brothers wore matching looks of concern.

Riona nodded to allay their fears, but she felt absolutely awful. "I just need to rest, like you said. A little time to adjust, that is all I need," she lied. The brothers didn't seem convinced, so she added a smile for good measure.

Sel marched back down the hallway and without warning shoved Neb out of his way. "Not here," he announced and in one swift motion he scooped her up into his arms and shifted.

It had happened so fast that Riona hadn't the time to offer any resistance. They materialized at the heartstone of Tearmann. He had brought her back. Riona was mortified.

While carrying her toward the castle's great hall, he informed her, "We will only stay until you are recovered."

She wiggled in his grip, but he did not slow. "Put me down!" she ordered.

"No."

His body was uncomfortably warm and he held her as if she weighed nothing at all. One thing was clear to Riona, she didn't like being this close to him. For one, it made her heart beat erratically. She glared up at his handsome face and clenched jaw. "I can walk."

"I doubt it."

When she began to struggle in earnest, his grip tightened. Halting in the shadow of the archway that led to the great gathering hall he sighed as if the burdens of this world were more than he could bear. When he finally looked down at her, his features softened.

"Be still, or I will put you over my shoulder and make a show of parading you through the hall."

The threat worked. She stopped struggling which earned her a rare smile. She blushed in response, and her idiotic stomach did a little flip when his smile widened.

"Good. Sinnie said you could be reasonable."

When she didn't offer a reply, he moved forward, swiftly crossing the hall to duck into a passageway that led to a part of the castle Riona had never been allowed to explore.

"Where are we going?" she asked, resigned for now to the humiliation he seemed determined to heap on her.

"To my quarters."

"But I have rooms of my own."

"You will share my rooms. I will have Digon move your things." As if reading her alarmed thoughts he finished, "I can keep a closer eye on you in this part of the castle. Urias will arrive shortly to shadow you when I can not be there."

Her heart sank. "How long do you intend to keep me under surveillance?" He hadn't slowed his pace as he moved them further into the castle's maze. With all the turns, she had stopped trying to commit their path to memory.

"Until I can trust you." He looked down at her briefly and then announced that they had arrived at their destination. Gently, he lowered her legs to the ground and unlocked the door.

Her whole body was aware of his hand on the small of her back. The heat of it seemed to burn through her clothing.

Pushing the ornate wooden door wide, he stepped back for her to enter.

She eyed him suspiciously and then glanced into the room. It was enormous and plush, furnished with dark woods and deep shades of green.

"We don't have all day, Princess."

She yelped when he suddenly scooped her up again to carry her into the room. Not breaking stride, he then carried her into another room where he dumped her without warning onto an elevated and expansive bed. She sputtered in dismay, but otherwise could not find the appropriate words to express her utter outrage at being handle thus.

"Digon will be here in a minute to offer sustenance. You

will appear pleased at the union of our two houses. I also expect you to extinguish any and all hopes he may have entertained in the past. Think of it as a way of getting back into my good graces."

It was becoming all too clear that Sel thought she was very much like her mother. Though disappointed at his unfair assessment of her character, Riona nodded her agreement. She had dealt with the misconception before. Only time could change his opinion of her.

"May I have a glass of wine, with honey?" she asked. Riona sat up and waited as the captain turned and walked into the other room to pour wine into a glass before dutifully returning to her.

He handed her the half-full glass.

"Thank you," she automatically responded. Sipping her drink slowly, Riona tried to ignore him. It wasn't easy with him watching her every gesture. He remained until she had drunk half of the glass's contents. It was unnerving to have his green eyes focused solely on her. Whether it was the wine or the medicinal properties of the honey, Riona started to feel some of her strength returning.

"I can help you feel better... sooner. It is a soldier's trick," he told her in a near whisper.

"What?" she asked, reluctantly meeting his gaze.

"I can give you a bit of my strength," he said more strongly, "or I can continue to carry you from room to room. You decide."

He didn't have to sound so irritated, she thought. Of course if she hadn't run, she wouldn't be in this predicament. "Get on with it then," she said with more bravado than she felt.

"Swing your legs over the side of the bed."

She did as he instructed and took one more sip of wine in

preparation, unconsciously letting out a sigh as the alcohol warmed her insides. The only thing she had eaten that day was the apple and the honeyed-wine he had given her was strong. She could feel her cheeks redden.

He took the glass from her hand and set it down on a table before returning to face her. When his muscular thigh brushed her leg, she stiffened but otherwise offered no resistance. She could once again feel the heat imitating from his body and the close proximity also allowed his scent to reach her. Riona closed her eyes to hide her reaction, but when she felt him carefully slide the strap of her bodice and tunic over the edge of her shoulders her eyes flew open.

He was concentrating hard on what he was doing, his lips had thinned and his jaw had tightened. He didn't look the least bit interested in her possible charms, quite the contrary. She tried to control her rapid breathing when he clinically laid one large hand on the exposed skin of her upper chest, the other he placed in the middle of her back.

"Don't move," he breathed into her hair.

She sat frozen in place, her heart racing under his increasingly hot hands. Glancing up through her lashes she found him staring down at her. When their eyes met and held, lightening flashed across the green of his irises. Threads of power danced between them, vibrating in the charged current. Riona lost track of time, his touch lasting both an eternity and a mere fraction of a second. He was transferring a portion of his power into her, and as her body greedily absorbed what it needed, she realized he had created a bridge between them.

Then abruptly the connection was broken and he backed away from her, turned, and walked out of the room without another word.

Stunned at her reaction to him and his sudden dismissal of her, she jumped from the bed and hurried to the table. Clasping the wine glass in her hands, Riona gulped down the red liquid in hopes of steadying her nerves but she only succeeded in violently choking when the liquid burned the back of her throat. Catching her breath, she wiped the last drop from her lips and waited. No relief manifested. Her blood hummed happily in her veins. She could still feel his touch on her body, a branding that was slow to fade. She then heard a knock followed by male voices. Digon no doubt, she thought.

Catching her reflection in a mirror on the opposite wall, she cringed. No, this would not do. Her tunic was ripped, and blood and dirt were on her pants and bodice. She wasn't vain, but her disheveled appearance put her at a disadvantage and Riona instinctively knew she would need every advantage if she were going to remain in his company. She was stronger now, thanks to his power transfer. It was time to deliver a little retribution and even the playing field, she decided.

Riona shimmered, a distortion of air and heat briefly surrounded her before dissipating. Much better, she thought, smiling at her rectified reflection. She ran her fingers through her cropped hair to remove some of the worst tangles. Yes, the nearly black-green silk gown flattered her pale complexion. It was cut modestly, not too low, but low enough to glimpse the swell of her breasts. It was fitted at the waist, long sleeved, and it flowed nicely over her hips to hang just above the ground. The thick rug beneath her feet kept her soles from feeling the stone below. But in the hall, she would need slippers or her feet would freeze. Like the rest of her attire, she used magick to don a comfortable pair of slippers. She smiled again at the effect. Excellent, this should put him on the defensive. Or at the very least, it should give him pause.

"Are you done?"

She jumped and whirled to find him watching her. He had changed as well, trading his captain's uniform for a white silk shirt, mocha leather pants and matching boots. His sword still hung at his hip. Their eyes met and held and her startled heart picked up its pace. He had caught her admiring her own reflection, and by the stoney glint in his eye, Riona could be certain he now judged her to be vain as well manipulative. Refusing to feel guilty, she went on the offensive. He was after all, just another bodyguard. "I would like some food. The wine is going to my head. Was that Digon?"

"Aye. I told him we would join the others in the hall for the mid-day meal."

"Excellent." She glided past him with all the royal airs of a princess of Tir na n-Og. Let him think whatever he will. She had nothing to be ashamed of, she reminded herself. Riona almost made it to the door before he caught up to her.

"Let me get the door for you, Princess." He swung it wide and gave her a dramatic bow.

He was mocking her now. Let him laugh. He wasn't the first to find amusement at her expense. Moving past him and into the corridor, Riona told herself she didn't care. When they reached the great hall, he would realize what a bastard he had been to her. In this place, she had people who truly liked her. They would have worried and asked after her once they had discovered her missing.

"They called me Molly," she informed him when he caught up to her again. Everyone at Tearmann was forced to assume a false name upon arriving at the Queen's sanctuary. She had picked Molly because it was an unassuming name. As the happy-go-lucky Molly, she had been able to laugh and dance, smile and flirt, without any political reproductions. It had been absolutely wonderful. And tonight, she could do it again. Riona smiled to herself and ignored as best she could the golden seelie striding next to her.

"Tonight you will be Riona, Unseelie Princess, and my mate. You are done with hiding," he informed her. He securely draped her arm over his, intent on escorting her into the gathering hall and into the company of all those she had been forced to mislead.

Chapter 6

Riona sorted through her options in the time it took for them to reach the hall. She could pretend he didn't exist, remaining as cold and distant as she would have with any past bodyguard. She could flirt outrageously with every male in the hall just to spite him. The thought was appealing, but that wasn't who she was—that was her mother. No, if she were honest with herself, it wasn't the disclosure of the contracted agreement with the Seelie Captain that worried her. It was the repercussions that she knew would follow from the revelation of her true identity which made her want to retaliate.

Riona glanced up at his immovable expression and her stomach twisted. He seemed set on exposing her secret. So be it then. Riona lifted her head a fraction of an inch while mustering her courage. She would approach the ordeal like all the ones before it, dealing with whatever came as honestly and graciously as she could.

"Molly!"

Riona couldn't help but grin as Tara dashed across the breadth of the hall to embrace her. Tara was a seelie, and they had become relatively close during her short time here. Riona happily hugged her back.

"Where have you been? I see the captain has found you and restored you to us." She smiled shyly at the captain, batting her eyelashes at him before turning her attention back to Riona. "It was so dreadfully boring without you."

"I missed you too, Tara, but I am only here briefly. I'm terribly hungry, I think I could even eat more than Crank today," she said, changing the subject away from her pending departure.

Tara giggled and tugged her out of the captain's reach toward the food-laden table. At one end of the long banquet table Babs happily waved at her. Riona waved back at the usually shy seelie. The aroma of roasted meat made Riona's stomach growl and she let Tara pull her onward, nearly skipping across the hall. Sel followed at a more dignified pace.

"Good to have you back," Digon stood, greeting her with a genuine smile. Crank also stood and nodded his dark head in her direction, his plum and orange colored kilt clashing badly with his blue tinted skin. He was unseelie and the longest known resident at Tearmann.

Riona smiled at both,while claiming a plate. She then set about filling it. As Molly she had been quite popular, and so she was greeted by most who were in attendance. She returned their good wishes somewhat distractedly for her attention was drawn to the conversation behind her. Her ear seemed singularly attuned to Sel's resonating voice as he gave Digon instructions.

"Yes, I will move her things as soon as everyone has had their fill," Digon said somewhat sourly.

Breaking into Riona's thoughts, Tara whispered, "Are you staying with the captain?" Tara had a nose for gossip and had picked up on Digon's and the captain's exchange like a hound trailing a hare.

"For now," Riona said, unable to stop the blush to her cheeks.

Tara's eyebrow lifted, disappearing under the bangs of her platinum hair. "Are you sure? You know he and the Queen." She nudged Riona's shoulder meaningfully.

"It is none of your concern," Riona hissed back. She didn't want to hear gossip about Sel and the Queen.

"Well pardon me," Tara huffed beside her. "Aren't we

full of airs today."

Riona inwardly cringed. She hadn't meant to be so sharp, but any thought of the captain and the Queen seemed to cause her temper to flare. Tara said nothing further, but remained close as Riona turned to find a seat. She normally sat flanked between Tara and Babs. Babs was was already seated further down the table. But when Riona turned she found Sel waiting, a hand resting on the back of a chair beside his own. By the patient look the captain wore, she knew that he fully expected her to obey the subtle command. Tara grinned, probably finding the handsome captain's gesture romantic. Riona glared at him, only to be rewarded with his cocky smirk. Beside her, Tara giggled.

Left with little choice, Riona crossed to the proffered chair and regally lowered herself.

"A princess should have airs, Tara. Is that not so, Riona?" Sel asked smoothly before assisting her in scooting the chair closer to the table.

Perplexed, Tara cocked her head. Then as Riona had expected, the blood drained from Tara's face as the full effect of Sel's comment registered.

"Molly? Molly is the princess Riona?" she shouted. All eyes turned in her direction as the various conversations in the hall came to an end.

Riona was mortified. The food in front of her no longer looked appealing.

"Aye, Tara. Riona is the Unseelie Princess...and my mate," he added.

There were a few polite congratulations directed at the captain. Riona glanced up to find Tara glaring at her. Taking the opportunity to quit her company, Tara moved to the other end of the banquet table. A few skittish souls casually rose from the table and left, taking what remained of their meals to their rooms.

Riona sighed, but otherwise gave no clue to her distress. No one offered a sympathetic smile, covert glance, or friendly flirtation. No one dared speak to her at all. Sel's announcement had declared her off limits. In a room full of anxious exiles, Riona was forced to eat in utter solitude. No one would dare risk the captain's anger. He was the Queen's man, and on his recommendation alone they might find themselves expelled from what was surely their last safe haven. Without Tearmann as a refuge, her father would eventually hunt them down.

Sel conversed with Digon across the table unaware or uncaring of the tension he had caused. They spent the meal discussing the menial workings of the castle. Both ignored her entirely. Riona forced herself to chew and swallow in a sedate manner until most the food on her plate was gone. She could hear Terrance nervously laugh, talking too loudly and too fast. She witnessed Tara whisper conspiratorially with Babs. All but Crank seemed to have lost their appetite. But then, Riona didn't think Crank was quite right in the head. Indeed, it was torturous dining for all, save for the captain and Crank who ate heartily. As soon as she could, Riona pushed away from the table and stood to leave.

Without comment Sel set his plate aside and stood to offer his arm. Again all eyes were on her. She resisted the urge to berate him publicly for humiliating her and for scaring everyone in the room. Instead, she gave the captain a dazzling smile and allowed him to escort her from the hall. She hoped the gesture was enough to set the residence of Tearmann at ease once more.

Once they were beyond the hall, he said, "Nice performance, Princess." He then chuckled to himself, some private thought selfishly withheld.

She glared up at him. "I had no choice. Your declaration

frightened everyone in attendance. They live and die by the Queen's good will."

"I did not threaten anyone."

"Of course you did," she snapped. "One wrong word or look could have ended their time here." The captain's jaw clenched at her rebuke.

"Then we should keep our stay as brief as possible," he barked back.

When they reached his quarters, he pushed the door wide for her to enter and this time she boldly walked in. The curtains had been drawn and a fire had been cultivated while they in the great hall. It gave the large room a soft glow, an almost cozy feeling. Riona took a seat near the fire's warmth and waited for his next decree.

Urias had arrived. Darting to her side, he gave her a quick bow before going to speak with the captain, hovering just in the doorway.

"Yes, go inform Fain, but otherwise do not seek out the Queen. I will need you with me."

Urias saluted and then sped from the room.

Engulfed in her own current misery, Riona hadn't bothered to eavesdrop. "What prison will you deliver me to next?" Her question was punctuated by the timely sound of the door's lock sliding into place.

Crossing the room, Sel angrily unfastened the sword at his waist and dropped it on a settee. "There is no prison awaiting you," he growled at her.

She watched him pour himself a drink. Not the honeyed wine, but something stronger. Without the strength to out-run him or the allies to aid her, Riona understood that she had no choices left. After all the years of hiding from her father, it seemed the Queen and her captain had captured the prize. She was well and truly caught. She must resigned herself to their contract.

"They are all prisons. Some plush like this." With a wave of her hand Riona indicated the room; lined in books neatly arranged, the intricate tapestries hanging along the walls devoid of shelving, and the finely crafted furniture. "And some absent of all comforts. I have experienced them all, and am prepared for either."

His hand had halted halfway to his lips during her declaration. Lowering the glass to rest on the tabletop once more, he said, "Riona, I am not a punishment. The Queen wants to keep you safe, and I dare say… happy. She is fond of you." His fierce expression had softened, exchanging the tense jaw for a look of pained patience.

Riona raised an eyebrow in response, but she could not believe the contract between them sprang from the Queen's compassion. "So she says, but it is only a kinder prison. My happiness was not a concern, otherwise she would have left me here—as simple, unassuming Molly." With little more to say to him, Riona rose and left him to his drink.

After cowardly retreating to the bedchamber, she gently closed the door behind her. It was an old sorrow she felt, one for a life forever denied to her. Years ago she had made a habit of only crying in the privacy of her own cell, away from those that would use such an open declaration of weakness against her.

Riona waited, but he did not follow. No knock, no requests for her company followed her melancholy retreat. Miserable, she sat on the oversized trunk by the foot of the bed and allowed herself to quietly cry.

Stupidly, she had taken Blodeuwedd's promise to heart

that day in the Queen's antechamber. The goddess had said she had chosen a mate for her, a true pairing blessed by the gods. It had touched Riona that the goddess had taken pity on her plight in life, being forever wanted for political gain but never loved or wanted for herself alone. Just as Riona was about to question the goddess further, Sinnie had burst into the antechamber and Blodeuwedd had retreated to her owl form.

Riona's vision blurred and she wiped at the self-pitying tears. Against her better judgment, Riona had harbored the whispered hope offered by the goddess. In truth, it was an unrealistic daydream; to escape the circumstances of her birth, to find someone to love without fear of betrayal. A sweet daydream yes, but with the enforcement of an ancient and forgotten law the Seelie Queen had ended Riona's foolish dreaming.

Of all the fey, why had the Queen chosen her cold captain? Sel seemed to enjoy humiliating her, having already passed judgment on her character long before meeting her. Riona chaffed at the injustice of it all.

But then perhaps she had done the same, her troublesome conscience suggested.

Riona took a shuttering breath and looked about the room. She had assumed he was a warrior not a scholar, but this room, like the other, was over stuffed with literature, bound in all shapes and sizes. He was quite the learned man. Odd really, she mused.

Riona dried her cheeks with her hands and took another deep breath. She was better than this, she thought. At the very worst, the Seelie Captain would keep her father's long reach at bay. At best, Blodeuwedd would send Riona's true mate to find her after this contract was at an end. In the meantime, she would just have to persevere. With a glimmer of hope for a brighter future wrestled from her current circumstances, Riona started to explore the room. If the captain was her immediate future, then she would at least try to know the man behind the title.

Chapter 7

Sel stopped just outside the closed bedchamber door. What could he say to her? The last thing he wanted was to be tied to an unseelie. They were all manipulative, difficult, pleasure-seeking troublemakers whose loyalties tended to alter with the merest change of wind, Sel thought unkindly.

Although he had chafed at the Queen's decision, he had offered no real protest when Gwenhwyfar issued her judgment. Having served his Queen too long and too loyally to argue, Sel had begrudgingly set out to fulfill Gwenhwyfar's wishes without any care of what it might mean to Riona—duty and the honor of his Queen ruling his thoughts. With such a cold pronouncement of the decreed changes to her circumstances, no wonder Riona had fled from him. The image of her proudly standing barefoot before him with the harsh beauty of the Arach Mountains behind her and the black wolf by her side floated back to him. In truth, the Unseelie Princess was more than he had anticipated, and that complicated matters.

He hadn't wanted to come to Tearmann, much less stay until dawn, but Jen had been insistent. His halfling daughter was taking on the burdens of a seer. And although they had parted badly, Jen had felt compelled to warn him that Riona's strength was dangerously depleted. Jen had also pleaded with him to come here instead of taking Riona to his home in the Seelie Court. Sel didn't understand the difference, but he had given his word he would follow her advice. Having served a seer Queen, Sel was accustomed to receiving counter-intuitive instructions. In the morning, he and Riona would return to his daughter's house so he could speak with Jen in person.

Sel lowered his hand from the door handle and returned to the fire, his drink now forgotten. Every nerve in his body had been completely aware of her close proximity at the banquet table. And now, he keenly felt her withdrawal. Restless, Sel knew he needed something to distract himself from his troubled thoughts; a book, perhaps. Aye, a book would help fill the time and keep his mind busy until Urias returned.

Sel scanned the tomes along the shelves. He didn't want to think about the first moment that he had laid eyes on her, or remember the feel of her skin under his hand as he transferred a portion of his strength into her. Sel especially didn't want to recall the heart-stopping smile she had directed at him upon quitting the banquet table, or the grief in her voice when she spoke of her supposed loss of freedom. He had clearly heard the resignation, and it had angered him as much as it had stung.

Sel bypassed the more scholarly works lining the shelves, knowing that they wouldn't hold his attention, and moved on toward his latest reading obsession. He found a relatively recent book, a western by Louis L'Amour. Novels were his guilty pleasure, and he kept the bulk of his collection here at Tearmann. Lately he had found the genre of the American western strangely appealing. If he hadn't been who and what he was, a cowboy's life would have suited him just fine, Sel chucked to himself. He plucked a book from the shelf and scanned the back.

To feed his library, he had begun to frequent a Madison book vendor after hours, always leaving the monetary fee behind. It wouldn't have been honorable, in his opinion, to take a book without leaving compensation for the merchant. With the paperback in his hand, Sel glanced again at the closed door. Should he force the issue, or let her be? Was this a game she played with him, or was she an innocent as the Queen had suggested? Sighing he set the book down next to his sword and went to lightly rap on the bedchamber door but a deliberate banging on another door stayed his hand. Relief coupled with a hint of disappointment shadowed him as he stepped away from the barrier between he and Riona for yet a second time.

Moving to answer the visitor's knock, Sel unbolted the door and found Digon and Crank had arrived. Crank was balancing a single and modest chest on his shoulder. Sel was surprised at the lack of possessions for the princess.

He waved them in. "Just leave it by the door, Crank." With a sense of renewed purpose Sel went and rapped on the bedchamber door. "Riona, Digon and Crank are here. Show yourself," he ordered.

After a moment, the door opened and she breezed past him with her chin up, a gracious smile for Digon and Crank in place. Having noticed the redness of her eyes, her forced performance irked him.

"Thank you, Digon. Crank." Riona addressed the pair as if they were the oldest of friends.

Crank voice rumbled in his chest, "Princess. Is he treating you well?"

"Yes, of course, Crank. Why would he not?" Riona laughed nervously and then looked past the unseelie to Sel and cocked her head in a silent question.

Crank offered his arm to her and she dutifully, though somewhat hesitantly, accepted his escort. He led her toward the fireplace before answering her question. "Because he is a horse's arse," he exclaimed over his shoulder.

Sel hid his smile. Crank was known for his erratic behavior and crude language, his rudeness being the rule not the exception. The uncharacteristic gallantry was obviously confusing

Riona, who had only known the disguise and not the man. Sel watched as Crank delivered Riona to a seat, like a queen to her throne. "Digon, have a drink, and pour me one." Sel glanced over at the blue skinned warrior and said, "I see we will be letting our masks slip today. Crank, do you really want to do this?

The old curmudgeon grandly bowed before Riona, causing his kilt to be hiked dangerously high from behind. After receiving a acknowledging nod from Riona, Crank nosily dragged another chair over within reach of the fire's warmth and made himself comfortable beside her. "Aye, I trust the girl."

"High praise, indeed," Digon assured Riona while delivering a full glass of liquid amber to Crank.

"Is that so?" Riona smiled at Digon but warily eyed Crank's closeness, wrinkling her nose discreetly.

Crank leaned forward and whispered loudly, "I am a bit of a legend, girl. When I speak, Sel sits up and listens." The unseelie pinned Sel with a steely look and then to prove his point he gave a thrust of his chin to tell the captain to get on with it. "Don't make me order you, lad."

"You are retired," Digon reminded Crank. He moved Sel's sword out of the way and took a seat. He then picked up the discarded book and inspected it.

"Aye, thank the gods." Crank's ever-present lopsided grin then faltered. "Though, I miss her."

"Who?" Riona asked, Crank's cryptic statement having gained her interest.

"The Queen," Sel supplied. "Crank held the post of captain before me."

"But he's unseelie," Riona said, once again looking to Sel to explain.

"You noticed." Crank grinned charmingly and chuckled;

across the cozy seating arrangement, Digon laughed along with him.

Although his attention was mainly on Crank and Digon, Sel could feel Riona's eyes on him. She was studying him. Perhaps she was trying to find the man behind the rank. Sel didn't know whether, after all these years, such an individual even existed.

As their laughter died, Riona took the opportunity to ask the obvious question. "Do you care to explain?" she asked, turning to Crank.

"Let young Sel explain. Let us hear his version of the sorry story," Crank said, saluting Sel with his full glass before downing its contents in one swift motion. He then belched his approval of the captain's good whiskey.

With a sigh, Sel carried his own glass and a nearly full decanter with him into the fire's glow. He refilled Crank's glass and then topped off Digon's before finding a seat of his own.

"Would you like some wine, Riona?" Sel asked, realizing she was the only one without a pour.

"No, I am fine," she said with a touch of impatience in her voice meant to hurry them along.

He nodded and all three males seemed to sober despite the numbing affects of the alcohol.

Sel looked to Crank. "How much do you want me to tell?" Sel asked studying the retired commander. Crank hid his age well from his fellow fey. He had chosen to look only slightly older than Sel, a fey in his prime. The few wrinkles which existed on Crank's naturally blue-tinted skin only gave him the appearance of a human that was perhaps in his forties.

"She's your mate, isn't she? Tell the whole fuckin' thing, man."

Sel didn't know why Crank wanted to reveal his identity

to Riona, but he did as the old warrior bid him. Turning his attention back to her, Sel revealed the secret he had been sworn to keep by the Queen and his old commander. "Crank served both the Absent King and the Queen."

Sel paused when Crank abruptly stood to find what comfort he could staring into the fire's flames. Sel knew revisiting the distant past was not easy for Crank. With the retired captain's back now turned to the room, Sel continued his explanation to Riona.

"Crank served an Unseelie King, but back in those days the lines between the courts were not so well drawn. Arthur and the Queen are true mates, bound by the vows, and so it was logical for Crank to protect both. For if one dies, so does the other."

Riona nodded her understanding but did not interrupt.

For Riona's sake Sel wanted to ease into the truth about Melwas so he carefully said, "Your father rose quickly though the ranks of his unseelie caste; being the son of a god gave him access to power above and beyond that of normal fey. It is hard not to be tempted by such power—to see yourself as destined to rule. Melwas fell into this trap. Eventually he coveted Arthur's throne as well as his Queen."

Crank turned his back to the fire and eyed Sel contemptuously. "You tell a shitty story, lad. Paintin' a pretty picture for her sake. Where's the fightin' and the killin'?"

"Fine, you clear it up." Sel leaned back and waited, relieved the burden had been lifted from him.

"Aye, I will," Crank snapped.

Riona dutifully turned her attention to the grouchy unseelie.

"The long and short of it, girly, is your father's a bloody

bastard, corrupt to his very core. But then, you'd know that, wouldn'tcha. He tricked and murdered his way to the top of his caste. He ingratiated himself with me and Arthur. None spoke ill of him—none that he allowed to live. So, I dinna think it amiss when I accompanied Gwen into the Arach Mountains to negotiate with the bloody dragons. I left the strongest to guard my King. I left him in charge, you see. I let the serpent in. I'm the reason the bastard sits on the fuckin' throne," he bellowed.

"Crank!" Sel warned. His tone giving Crank a mild reminder of where they were and who his audience was.

Crank looked only slightly abashed. "Aye, you're right, lad. She be not him, nor should she bear his sins," he admitted before continuing to disclose his own history.

"So there I was, off with fair Gwen, dealing with the politics of the Dragon Court, leavin' Melwas free to poison the mind of Arthur. Near as I can figure, he convinced Arthur our Gwen was in danger and led him off, for that was the only way Arthur would follow such a serpent. When Gwen and I returned, he blackmailed the Queen into accepting his rule."

"How?" Riona asked.

Crank smiled sadly. "He dinna kill my King, you see. He imprisoned him. Gwen was left with little choice in the matter."

"The Queen searched…" Riona prompted.

"Aye, girl. We have searched all the realms, losing many a loyal fey in the endeavor, but we were never able to find more than a whisper, not much better than rumors of his whereabouts—all different, all of which dinna prove true."

Riona's head swung towards Sel. "Is the Absent King still alive after so long?"

Crank answered her question first. "Aye, as long as she lives, he lives, and vice versa. Bloody fuckin' bastard." Crank spat on the floor. "May his father take him and rid us of his evil doin's, for we would be the better for it!"

Digon raised his empty glass in agreement as did Sel. Unapologetic for his curse, Crank turned to watch the fire again.

Sel thought it was to her credit that Riona held her tongue, choosing silence over the defense of her father. Sel hadn't intended to speak of his mission in front of Riona, but he wanted to give the old warrior hope. And truthfully, he would prefer to travel with Crank on this next mission. "The Queen still searches. And we have recently found what we have been seeking. Will you come with me to finish this?" Sel asked Crank.

"You know I canna leave these walls." Crank's shoulder muscles tensed, his hands tightly gripping the stonework of the fireplace.

Riona looked to Sel and then Digon for an explanation.

Damn it, Sel thought. They had already said more than he had ever intended. "Crank exiled himself here. Tearmann belongs to him. The castle was his home before it was the Queen's sanctuary," he informed her. Riona's eyes had grown wide. Sel ignored it and addressed Crank. "I could use your experience."

"Nay, Sel. If I leave, she dies. I will not cause the death of her, or him."

Riona looked confused by Crank's obscure declaration, as did Digon. Silence was Sel's only response. This was an old assertion of Crank's which Sel had only recently started to accept. Losing his beloved King and friend had nearly killed Crank. He had served the Queen briefly afterward, but the guilt of not being there to defend Arthur had been too much for the unseelie. Some said he had gone mad, but Sel knew better. After long and disappointing years of searching for the Absent King, Crank had grown desperate and finally disillusioned. In his quest to find his

King, Crank had even gone as far as to force his way into the realm of the gods. Upon his return, Crank had appointed Sel to the post of captain before retreating to Tearmann.

In her sorrow, the Queen had enchanted his castle as a way of protecting her champion from Melwas. Sel's old commander was quite possibly the only fey the Unseelie King truly feared. Tearmann now shifted through time and space during the daylight hours, stopping only to rest in the evening. Melwas had lost many a tracker in his search for it.

"Sel, may I have that drink now?" Riona asked. It was the first time she had used his name and it struck him that he liked the sound of it on her lips.

"Aye. I think we could all use one." He smiled and went to pour her a glass of honeyed wine.

"Sel?" Digon held up the book. "Can I borrow this?"

Sel grinned to himself while pouring Riona's drink. He had gotten Digon hooked on westerns with a Cormac McCarthy novel.

Setting the bottle to the side, he said, "No. Not until I finish it. Pick another." He then pointed toward the wall of paperbacks. "Half way up, on the left," he added and watched as Digon stood to make himself at home in his private book collection.

Sel delivered the drink to Riona, casually caressing her hand with his index finger as he transferred the wineglass to her. Again her eyes grew wide, but she did not pull away. Turning from her, Sel caught Crank smirking.

"Digon, make it quick. I think the captain wishes to be alone with the girl."

"No," Riona squeaked and then blushed when all eyes turned to her. "I mean, we enjoy your company. No need to leave so soon."

Crank tsked, but he acquiesced to her mild flattery with a good-natured shake of his dark head. "Sel, how about I beat you at another game of chess?"

Digon returned with a book that he was already thumbing through.

"One day, I might surprise you," Sel said.

"Not likely, lad."

"That's 'captain' to you, you deluded old man," Sel teased. Crank laughed loudly and followed Sel to the gaming table. The chess pieces still rested in their abandoned positions, this particular game having already lasted nearly a fortnight.

Chapter 8

As the afternoon drifted comfortably into evening, Sel and Crank exchanged a few pawns; Sel was one knight to the better. Digon remained engrossed in his book, and Riona occupied her time by covertly studying the three of them while fingering through a play by Bernard Shaw. Not wanting to upset the residents of the castle anymore than was necessary and eager to prolong the helpful distraction of Crank's and Digon's company, Sel suggested that they all dine in his quarters. Everyone agreed, and Riona seemed especially relieved. Digon excused himself from their company to make the arrangements. Leaving the room, his eyes lingered too long on Riona for Sel's taste.

"Check," Crank announced, his lopsided grin growing wide.

Sel tore his gaze away from Digon's retreating back to study the board. Bloody hell. He had overlooked Crank's rook. Sel's king was now cornered. "Give me a minute," he mumbled while weighing his options.

"Take your time, lad." Crank's chair scraped over the stone floor as he moved to stand. "Once you find that you've lost again, you can reset the board." Laughing to himself, he moved to pour himself another drink.

Sel looked up from his study of the board to find Riona watching him. She graced him with a tentative smile before resuming her reading.

Crank carried the wine bottle over to her and refilled her glass. "Princess, the lad is a bit slow. You may have to help him along," he whispered too loudly in the quiet room.

"Excuse me?" she squeaked.

Sel gave up trying to extricate himself from Crank's latest move. "Ignore him, Riona. He imagines much."

Crank just chuckled to himself again while letting the fire warm his backside. Before the old commander could craft a reply or make more mischief, Digon returned from the kitchens followed by three women of the castle who were laden with trays of food. Urias flew in behind the procession before the door swung shut.

"Ah, good, good. It's about bloody time!" Crank announced and moved to follow the parade of dishes to their destination.

The castle's caretaker led the nervous women to a modest size table where they unloaded their burden before scurrying away without once glancing in his direction. Riona's assessment of his earlier behavior seemed to have been correct. Why he had felt the need to so openly lay claim to her, he didn't know—even Digon's and Cranks familiarity with her had struck a cord of jealousy that took him by surprise. He had been acutely aware of all the males, fey or not, in the assembled hall warmly greeting her and had reacted without thinking. Even now Sel found himself completely aware of her every movement. Riona closed her book and laid it down gently in her lap.

Quitting the gaming table, Sel closed the distance between them and offered his hand to lead her the short distance to the dining table. He told himself it was just a precaution, in the event that she might still feel the affects of her earlier weakness. She hesitated, eying him warily before laying her hand in his. When she gracefully stood, he laid her arm over his and brought her to the table, installing her in a chair next to him.

Crank had already claimed his chair and was busy loading

a plate, a smirk glued in place. Digon in contrast looked rather sour, but said nothing. Good thing, Sel thought as he tucked-in to the table beside Riona. Urias dipped a carved portion of pear into a container of honey and flew off to eat his prize in private.

"Where has the castle settled for the night?" Riona asked Digon.

"We are in the Southeast, along the Shannon."

Placing a portion of lamb onto her plate, she asked Digon, "Is it safe for me to take a stroll later?"

Digon glanced anxiously across the table at Sel. "Princess, I think you should ask the captain."

Because of his recent dressing down of Digon, Sel was on the verge of denying her request out of hand. The irritating fact that Digon had stupidly allowed Riona to wander alone outside the castle walls was still fresh in Sel's mind, but then she turned her brown eyes expectantly to him and he found himself replying, "Aye, I will accompany you myself."

"Thank you." She smiled weakly and lowered her eyes once again to her meal.

"Think nothing of it. A walk would be enjoyable," he told her.

With his mouth still packed full, Crank added, "Make sure you hold the girl's hand, lad. They like that sort of thing."

Annoyed at Crank's advice, Sel glared at the unseelie while Riona blushed beside him, refusing to meet anyone's eye. Not unexpectedly a love struck Digon remained mute for the remainder of the meal.

Sel sighed and ate quickly, a soldier's habit. In contrast Riona ate very little, preferring instead to rearrange the contents of her plate. The conversation lagged painfully. Crank was too busy filling his stomach to say much, and Digon was lost in his own miserable love-struck thoughts. So much for a relaxing supper, Sel thought. As soon as Riona moved to leave the table, Sel was ready to assist. He held her chair for her and then offered his arm once more. "Ready for that stroll now?" he prompted.

She gave him shallow nod of acceptance.

"Clean up before you let yourselves out," Sel called over his shoulder. The only response Sel received was a snort from Crank.

After Sel escorted Riona out the door, he guided her through a little known passageway that ended at a hidden door. Unbolting the well-oiled lock, he brought her into what had become his favorite place in Tearmann—the walled night garden. It was a small courtyard, but lush with blooms and heady fragrances.

"Oh, how beautiful," she whispered. She then tilted her face up to him and smiled in pleasure.

Her delight in the night garden greatly pleased him. "When I discovered this courtyard, most of the vegetation was wild and over grown. According to Crank, the courtyard was once dedicated to the cultivation of roses, but because of Tearmann's constant travel and changing weather conditions, the roses suffered. I had Digon replace the sun blooming vegetation with things like this night blooming moonflower vine, night phlox, and nicotiana. So now, the garden can not be fully appreciated until nightfall." Sel pointed to the delicate fairy lilies and the fragrant jasmine clinging to the walls. "The Alaskan Midnight and Nautical Nights are recent lily additions I took from the human realm." As he finished pointing out the newest plants, Sel looked down to find her staring up at him. "What?"

"You are nothing like I expected."

Sel gently pulled her forward so that she walked beside

him along the crescent shaped path. He instinctively knew that it would be easier to maintain his benevolent intentions if he weren't in danger of being mesmerized by her warm chocolate eyes. "What did you expect?"

Riona did not answer, instead she retreated into silence.

Sel could guess her thoughts. He had spent the better part of a night chasing after her, and then he had upset the residents of Tearmann with his heavy handed announcement of the contract between their houses. Sel paused beside a Sweetbay magnolia, its vanilla scent lay heavy in the air. "I feel as if I should apologize for my behavior earlier. You were right to scold me. This contract between us is only for your safety. I should not have overstepped my mandate and threaten those who pose no threat to you."

Her chin inched upward and the air between them cooled considerably. "Apology accepted." Riona removed her hand from his arm and glided forward along the path with her back and shoulders held painfully straight. Her fingers tickled the Franciscan nightshade as she moved past, releasing its perfume.

He wasn't a complete fool. Something in what he had just said had upset her, though he didn't know what. Before she could put too much distance between them he caught up to her and fell into step. "I have said something to upset you," he observed, deciding a direct approach might be best.

"Why would you say that, Captain?" she asked while gently caressing a moonflower petal.

So, she was back to calling him captain. "I would prefer you use my name, rather than my title."

Riona halted her mock inspection of the blooms and turned sharply towards him. "Why would you say that, Sel?"

He smiled at her. Regardless how she said his name, he liked it. "Are you warming to me Riona, or do you still fear me?"

"I was never afraid of you."

The evening breeze had strengthened; a storm was coming.

"You are a poor liar," he informed her.

Sel pushed a stray hair away from her red lips and her eyes widened slightly. As though his hand had a mind of its own, his fingers trailed along her cheek and then her neck, finally coming to rest on her bared shoulder. "I can see your heart hammering in your chest. Is it my touch that scares you?"

Once again he watched her chin jut forward and up. Sel was beginning to understand the mannerism for what it was, a gathering of her courage in the face of danger. And she was in danger, here with him, under the spell of this nighttime haven. He sorely wanted to kiss the parted lips that seemed to beckon to him.

"You confuse me," she whispered. To punctuate her statement the air between them crackled with the coming rain.

He was once more becoming lost in the pools of dark brown gazing up at him. "That is not my intention, Riona," he hoarsely whispered back. The blasted dice tumbling in his head were clouding his judgment. On its own accord his hand inched up to the base of her skull and into her unruly brunette curls. When her chin rose a fraction in that charmingly defiant manner, Sel lowered his head and kissed her. When their lips touched, every muscle in his body tensed. She tasted heavenly, warm and sweet. With infinite patience he teased her lips apart and deepened their slow kiss while his other hand snaked around her waist, sliding along silk to bring her body into contact with his. Only with her body fitted against his, hearts beating in unison, did the sound of the dice come to rest in his mind.

Her taut body relaxed against his and she uttered a sweet

sigh. The delicious combination nearly undid him. Sel knew he must release her or else he would not be able to stop.

Regretfully, he stepped back and watched as her dazed expression cleared. There was a definite blush to her cheeks. May the gods give him strength, he prayed in silence.

With the absence of her body's soft heat against his, Sel's mind cleared. What the hell had he done? Sel deliberately took another step back to put more space between them before dutifully offering his arm. His voice thick with regret, he said, "I think I should take you back inside."

Warily she lifted her hand and he tucked it into the crook of his elbow before striding briskly forward. His lapse in judgment could not be undone. This was going to get complicated, he told himself. He was experiencing desires he had purged himself of long ago, or so he had thought.

Riona said nothing as they left the garden behind. Sel could only assume that she was as confused as he at this turn of events. Some protector he was turning out to be. He was well equipped to fight off all who wanted to take advantage of her, except for himself it seemed.

He was efficiently weaving their way through the castle when Riona broke into his thoughts.

"Where are we going after dawn?"

"Back to the human realm. I need to speak with Jen, then we need to make an appearance at court, but only briefly. The Queen will have a mission waiting for me." They had reached his quarters again. He opened the door and stood aside so that she might enter first. She did not.

"The task you wanted Crank to accompany you on?"

He lied. "I do not know."

One eyebrow arched upward and her lips thinned.

"Do you want to converse in the hallway? The fire is much more inviting, I think," he suggested while keeping a tight rein on his emotions.

She stepped through the doorway, brushing closely by him. Sel caught a whiff of vanilla lightly mingled in her scent. Temptation itself, he thought gritting his teeth. Sel was beginning to recognize the subtle pull her presence caused him. His kiss had strengthened those threads and as a result he found himself following in her wake like a dog on a lead. She resumed her seat near the fire, book in hand but unopened. "Why did you kiss me?"

He started to tell her that it had been a mistake, but he stopped himself. They had only recently reached a tenuous understanding and he did not want to harm the progress they had made. Sel hastily rephrased his response, "I could not help myself. It must have been the garden's influence," he explained while crossing the room to pour them another drink.

She cocked her head, watching him. "I am not like my mother."

"I never said you were."

"No, but you assumed. Believe me, I can tell. Most fey think it is the case."

His jealousy returned and the ugly strength of it fanned an anger Sel did not recognize. Straining to maintain a congenial tone, he said, "I am not like the others." What other fey, his mind railed.

"No you are not. Until you kissed me, you only looked at me coldly, distastefully," She then stood, the chin again inching upward. "So which is it going to be?"

Sel was at a loss. Why was she pressing him on this? "Riona, I am sorry if I confused you. I..."

"I understand. Good evening, Sel. I will be ready to

depart in the morning." Riona gave him a slight nod, and then in an elegant flourish she retired to the bedchamber. Urias's wingtips just made it through the closing bedchamber door before Riona shut and locked it.

"Bloody hell," Sel muttered before gulping down the contents of this glass.

Chapter 9

Riona spent the remainder of the night trying to understand the seelie just beyond the bedchamber door. He was irritatingly distant, cold and guarded most of the time, but then she had witnessed his easy friendship with Crank and Digon. The pair obviously knew the captain well and she envied them that; so far he had done naught but confuse her. She paced the room, too agitated to sit for more than a few minutes.

Drunk on honey, Urias was too busy cleaning the sticky sweetness off his wings and person to offer his opinions. Of that, she was grateful.

At present, she felt surrounded by the captain. She could feel his presence and power just beyond the closed door, the kiss having only intensified his affect on her. Sel had allowed her to glimpse some of his hidden joys, the books lining the shelves and the discovery of his love of beauty. The courtyard garden had truly taken her by surprise. She paused in her pacing to remove a book from its home, A Midsummer Nights Dream by William Shakespeare.

Truthfully, she had never been so lost in a such simple kiss, not that she had been kissed by many. As the memory replayed itself, her heart danced in her chest. Why? Why had he? Why tell her one thing then do another? How was she to respond? She replaced the tome without bothering to thumb through it and leaned against the wall of leather bound books. He had said he was sorry; sorry to have humiliated her in the hall, sorry to have kissed her, sorry to have confused her.

Perhaps the Queen's choice for her wasn't so random. Riona was now tied to a man that could awaken her well-guarded heart, and that scared her as nothing else had ever done. By the gods, it had only been a day and look how unsettled she felt. What would become of her after a century, two centuries? To fall in love with the captain knowing that his affections lay only with his Queen would be torturous. Was this maddening fey Blodeuwedd's choice for her? How could he be?

With her immediate future so uncertain, Riona's first priority should be the continued restoration of her health but sleep eluded her. Because Urias was somewhere in the room and would no doubt report to Sel in the morning if she did not appear to rest, she pretended. For hours she lay unmoving on the bed, continually replaying the day's events in her mind behind closed eyelids. But by the time dawn approached, Riona still had not come to a solution. She had no answers, no decided course of action. And despite knowing he would want to leave Tearmann at dawn, the knocking on the door startled her.

The sprite was suddenly before her, bowing to her in greeting.

"Good morrow, Urias," she said, hastily covering an escaping yawn with her hand.

Urias beamed at her, showing a full mouth of pointy teeth. "Morning, Princess," he squeaked, before darting to the door to await her.

While still running her fingers through her hair, she dutifully rose and crossed to the door. She closed her eyes and yawed wide once more as she pulled on the latch.

Sel stood on the other side of the swinging door as if he had been impatiently waiting for her to rise. "Well rested?" he asked seemingly amused.

She clamped her mouth shut.

"I had Digon bring a light meal. We should leave as soon

as you have eaten," he told her, the warmth of the previous night missing from his voice.

She nodded and followed his instructions. Maybe he thought of her as just another member of his Guard, to be instructed, ordered, commanded. While he looked on, she ate a bite of melon and then a bite of pastry. She had not bothered to change from the night before, so unsettled were her thoughts. He, however, had taken the time to prepare himself for seeing the Queen. He had donned his guardsman uniform, green and gold, the insignia of rank on his chest, the sword strapped to his hip. The gold accents gleamed, as did he.

She glanced down at her wrinkled gown. Popping the rest of the pastry in her mouth she shimmered and rectified her disheveled appearance. She left the color the same, but changed the styling so that it draped off the point of her shoulders. "Should I leave the length?" she asked him, swallowing the last of the raspberry tart.

His eyes wandered over her figure and he swallowed before answering. "Aye. It is adequate."

His lack of enthusiasm for the silk gown irritated her. After all, she had wanted to flex her feminine power last night, hence the seductive nature of the gown's fabric and cut. She swallowed her sharp retort and said a little too sweetly, "Then I am ready."

He held his arm out to her and she demurely accepted his escort. They traveled through the castle in uneasy silence. Sel didn't pause in the hall to speak to Digon, but whisked her onward to the heartstone of Tearmann. Crank was waiting with her meager possessions, his usual smirk firmly in place and his kilt slightly askew.

"Princess."

She smiled brightly at him. "Crank."

He transferred her trunk from his shoulder to that of the captain's. "Remember what I told you, girl. He's a wee bit slow, the captain is," he said, as if she might confuse who he meant with someone else. Lifting her hand to his black lips, he grinned over the top of her knuckles and whispered across the skin, "It's been a pleasure, my beautiful Molly."

Riona had to refrain from laughing at Crank's courtly antics. Mostly because the captain was growling his displeasure right beside her. Crank paid Sel no mind, even when the captain took her hand from Crank's grasp, abruptly shifting them out of there. Crank's bellowing laughter followed them long after his image and Tearmann disappeared from view.

A heartbeat later they materialized in the house that belonged to Jen, same bedchamber as the day before. Without warning Sel dropped the trunk at his feet and narrowed his green eyes at her, but he said nothing. Abruptly he turned and stalked out the door. She could hear him travel down the staircase with purpose. Riona followed.

By the time she reached the bottom of the stairs, Sel was no where to be seen, the hallway was vacant. Hearing muffled dialogue, Riona followed the sounds of female voices until she located Sinnie. The other female, Riona could only assume was the often talked about Jen, Sel's other daughter.

Riona was struck by how very alike in appearance and dress the two sister were, save that of hair coloring—one being red the other blonde like her father. In unison the two looked up. Only Sinnie's eyes narrowed. The seelie had not gotten her say before Sel had taken her away. It was a thorn that Riona might have to be extricated before it festered.

"Riona!" the blonde said brightly. She set her cup down

and stepped forward, thrusting her hand out between them. "It's wonderful to meet you. I'm Jen."

"I am honored to meet you as well." Riona returned Jen's enthusiastic greeting with measured reserve. Jen's offered hand was left untouched. At Tearmann, Digon had warned her of the consequences of touching a human. It would be disastrous indeed if she accidentally enchanted the captain's daughter.

Jen lowered her hand and the sisters grinned at one another. The blonde brought her full attention back to Riona and Sinnie leaned back against the counter, folding her arms across her chest. Picking up her cup again, Jen asked, "Can I fix you somethin'? Did you eat already this mornin'? I keep fruit around for Sinnie and Hueil, though mind you, they don't eat much of it."

Jen had an unrushed musical way of speaking that was easy on the ear. She was trying very hard to set her at ease, Riona thought. "I do not need sustenance, but thank you. You are most kind." She had not found yesterday's apple very appealing, but judging by the aroma of roasted meat in the air and the basket of fresh fruit on the counter next to the sinks, Riona was left to assume that she had stumbled upon the kitchen in Jen's home. Though many of the items were foreign to her, it was well organized and it sparkled with recent cleaning, she absently noted.

"I'm not affected by contact with the fey. Relax Riona, it's fine." Jen's easy smile broadened.

"Why not?" Riona asked.

"My sister is bound to her halfling mate by the vows," Sinnie explained proudly.

Riona brow creased with confusion. "But how can a halfling do such a thing? I thought it not possible." Riona watched as Jen sipped at the steaming brown liquid in her cup. A halfling using the fey vows of binding was absurd. Only a few could hope to accomplish a true mating, one blessed by the gods to last for all eternity.

Sinnie rolled her eyes at her sister. "My sister is," she paused, smirking at her near twin, "special."

"Thanks, Sinnie." Jen shoved at Sinnie's shoulder and then leaned against the counter, the two sisters completely at ease in each other's company. "You make me sound slow-witted."

"Now that he's back, you need to tell him about the dreams," Sinnie told her sister.

Jen shook her head and quietly replied, "No. It will pass."

Sinnie glared at her sister, but to no avail. Jen would not yield. Turning her attention back to Riona, Sinnie said, "Nice dress by the way. Off to see the Queen?"

"I believe so," Riona replied. She was an outsider in this close knit group. There was so much she did not know. She wished Sel had explained more about Jen's history. Why were the hunters looking for her? Why was the security around her so tight? What made her "special" as her sister had suggested?

"Really?" Jen snapped angrily. She shoved away from the counter she had been resting against and stalked towards a glass door which opened to the yard beyond. Opening the door, she stepped out just far enough to yell, "Steven, where's Sel?"

Riona could not hear the reply. She glanced at Sinnie, but the red head offered no explanation for Jen's behavior.

"Tell him to get in here!" the halfling ordered. She waited a moment more for a yelled reply from her mate before closing the glass door.

Sinnie cocked her head at her sister. "Important?"

Jen mumbled a curse to herself and nodded in the affirmative. Both sisters looked at Riona, Jen worrying her lower lip.

The door swung open and Sel entered, one eyebrow raised as his gaze met Jen's glare. Hueil, Neb and another seelie guardsman filed in to hear what was to be said, the modest kitchen filling quickly. Hueil moved to stand next to Sinnie along the edge of the two metal sinks. The guardsman positioned himself near Neb in the archway that opened to a sitting area. Sel had stopped his progress in the middle of the kitchen, his full attention on the daughter that had all but ordered him into her presence. Riona kept her thoughts to herself. Surely Sel would reprimand Jen for her impertinence.

"Yes, Jen." Sel's stern features softened.

Jen cut her eyes to Riona then back to her father. "She's not..." the halfling paused in frustration, "It's too soon."

Sel sighed before answering. "It cannot be helped."

The creaking of the glass door's hinges announced Steven's arrival. "Horses are done," he paused, "Is there a problem, Sunshine?"

Jen looked past Sel to her mate "Yes."

"No," Sel said over his daughter declaration. "Jen, the Queen cannot wait," he said forcefully but not unkindly. "Riona, did the unseelie call himself Gloric?"

The change of topic caught Riona off guard. "Yes, how did you know?" By his change of expression, Riona realized that she had confirmed something for Sel. The captain's jaw tightened and he all but growled to himself.

"We have been doing a bit of conjecturing outside," Hueil supplied for her benefit, a wary eye still on the captain who was studying his boots or perhaps the dirt on the white tiles.

Addressing Hueil, Sel said, "Remain here until I send Krist. The three of you track Gloric. We can't have the treaty with the dragons crumbling."

Neb grinned at Hueil from across the kitchen, obviously pleased at the prospect of another adventure.

Riona noted Jen's face had paled considerably, but Sinnie looked unconcerned that her mate would have to track down the unseelie. "Sel…" Riona began. The captain turned his green eyes to her, causing her silly stomach to do a happy little flip. "What is happening?"

"Gloric is a danger and must be contained. Hueil, Neb and Krist will find him. No need for you to worry." Sel's attention swung to the other guardsman in the room. "Bradwen, Sinnie will relieve you at next dawn."

"Aye, Captain," the seelie replied.

Sel held his hand out to Riona and she stepped forward to take it. Gently pulling her closer, he tucked her hand through the crook of his arm. She studied his chest instead of his face, else she blush with the closeness of him. She could detect his gathering of power, as it wrapped around her. He was about to shift them to Tir na n-Og.

"Sel, wait." Jen stepped forward, staying him with her hand at his elbow.

Patiently he asked, "What is it, Jen?"

His daughter huffed with frustration before giving in to some private debate with herself. "Damn it, Sel. I'm still angry with you." She released his arm.

Sel said nothing, just waited for Jen to say her peace before shifting to the Seelie Court and the Queen.

"You should have listened to me." Jen poked at his arm, then worried her bottom lip again before turning to Riona. "Ask for a hound, nothing more. It'll help you find what you seek." Then she looked into her father's face. "She can't leave your side, not for a second. If she does, you'll risk losing her."

If his daughter's warning caused Sel any worry, Riona couldn't detect it. Her grip tightened on his arm. In response, Sel laid his other hand over hers, his thumb absently stroking the back of her hand.

"All will be well, Jen."

Even though Sel's eyes never left his daughter's concerned face, Riona had the feeling he was reassuring her as well.

"It won't." Jen turned from Sel and reached for her cup again. "Because you didn't listen and do what I told you must be done," Jen said petulantly over her shoulder.

"She's been having nightmares, father," Sinnie offered.

"Sinnie!" Jen pivoted to glare at her sister.

Sel absently patted Riona's hand and looked from one daughter to the other. "What are in these dreams?"

"She refuses to tell me," Sinnie explained. Hueil's arm encircled Sinnie's shoulder. It wasn't clear to Riona if Hueil's gesture was meant as a show of support or if he was preempting a fight between the opinionated sisters. "But she wakes up screaming," Sinnie finished.

Though he still stood by the glass door, Steven came to Jen's aid, his tone a warning to the room filled with fey. "That's enough. If she could explain the danger she would, but the images are too vague."

Riona was starting to understand. Like the Seelie Queen, Jen was a seer. No wonder they all deferred to the halfling. Riona felt a sudden kinship toward Jen born out of sympathy for the halfling's plight. From a young age, Riona had learned what it was to carry the burden of hope not of her own making, to suffer under a destiny not of her own choosing. Like being the Unseelie Princess, everyone wanted something from this halfling.

"Jen," Riona gave Sel's daughter a hesitant smile, "we have

just met, but I thank you for your counsel. I promise to do as you say." This gained Riona a light squeeze from Sel's hand, and a weak smile from Sel's youngest daughter.

"Jen, I will take every precaution," Sel promised.

Jen mutely accepted Sel's assurances, but her worried eyes were only for Steven.

Riona didn't mind it when the room and its residents disappeared from view. It seemed Sel would wait no longer for their interview with the Seelie Queen.

Chapter 10

He had brought them to his study. Sel crossed to his writing desk and scribbled a message. While he was busy, Riona took the opportunity to take in her surroundings. It had not changed. She found the dark green and warm wood hues of the study comforting. She had been here once before, delivered by another seelie after being stolen by the Queen from under the nose of her father. She had then been rushed through the captain's grand hall and out into the gardens. There, Hueil had appeared and delivered her to Tearmann. That well orchestrated escape had only just occurred. Mabon had not been so long ago, though it now seemed as if an age had passed. Within the space of just a few days she had been consigned to Calcus by her father, rescued, hidden, and retrieved by a completely different mate—the title of ownership of her person having been transferred by the Queen's edict. The swiftness of the changes in her life was rather sobering.

"Princess." Urias hovered before her. "Your things are this way," he chirped.

With Sel was still intent on his note making, papers being stacked and shuffled through, Riona followed Urias beyond a set of large ornate double doors into what appeared to be a bedchamber. Off to the side of the very large bed sat Riona's unopened trunk "Thank you, Urias. I will see to it after we have visited the Queen."

Urias settled beside a decanter full of amber liquid atop the credenza. A pitcher and wash basin, candles, and of course the ever present stacks of books were dotted about the room, distributed mainly between two smaller side tables. The room's decor was similar in styling to that of the study; in predominately masculine colors of green, blue and browns . The heavy wood of the canopy bed dominated the space and her wild imaginings.

"This will be your room," Sel's deep voice brushed against her ear, his tenor notes dancing through her body.

She turned to find him leaning against the door jam. Feeling the sudden flush to her cheeks, Riona all but stammered, "I would not think of taking your room from you. I will be fine in another."

His brow creased, but as he guessed at the path of her thoughts a boyish grin replaced his temporary confusion. "There is only the one room. Tis yours. I have no need of sleep." He pushed off the door's frame and stalked towards her.

In two paces he was uncomfortably close.

"I do not use this room. Be at ease, Riona." He then spoke past her to Urias whose wings had noticeably drooped. "Urias, go find Krist. Take him to Jen's. Hueil and Neb are going to hunt for Gloric. I want Hueil to command, Krist on point, and I want you to act as messenger to keep Fain updated on their progress."

"Aye, Captain," Urias chirped, saluting half-heartedly before darting out the door.

"I will give you a tour of my private and public rooms as soon as the Queen blesses the union of our houses. At which point, you may come and go as you please. You need not fear, the wards protecting my quarters will protect you as well. Are you ready?" Sel asked.

Riona squared her shoulders, lifted her chin and met his untroubled gaze. "Of course."

He took her by the elbow and they shifted.

Riona and Sel arrived a second later in the Queen's private rooms, or more precisely an outer waiting chamber. Two guardsmen stood post on either side of the bronze doors, the entrance into the Seelie Queen's enter sanctum. In unison, both guardsmen crisply saluted their captain, fist to heart.

Sel responded with an identical motion before asking, "What news?"

The guard on the left answered, "She awaits. Fain and Tristian are in council with our Queen."

"Open the doors then," Sel ordered.

Unlike the automatic swinging doors of the Queen's audience chamber, these heavy bronzed doors required a level of brute force to open. Both guards struggled to move the triskele mounted on the right door a full quarter turn, unlocking the bolts that barred entry. After the thunderous noise of the bolts retreating from the locks reverberated against the white marble walls, the left door was swung open on silent hinges.

Sel stayed Riona with a gentle pull when she took a step toward the open doorway. "We must wait for the Queen to call us into her presence. Without a summons, the magickal wards will not allow us to pass through. Arthur put this extra protection in place."

"Does it still work after so long of a time?"

Sel glanced down at her, "Aye, it does. Though I fear the knowledge to create such a ward has been forgotten."

Fain and Tristian emerged. They were followed by the Queen herself, who stopped just inside the protective ward.

"Captain," the guardsmen said in unison while saluting Sel. Riona's eyes were drawn to the moon shaped scar marking Fain's left cheek. Tristian gave Riona a rakish glance, then remembering where he was, cut his eyes back to his captain.

A muscle in Sel's jaw twitched before he returned their salute. "Fain, I have sent Hueil and Krist after Gloric, and unseelie who could be stirring up trouble with the dragons. Urias will act as messenger." Fain responded with a sharp nod of the head, then he and Tristian left to see to their duties and the Queen's instructions.

Moving into the archway of the door, the Queen smiled at her captain and then at Riona. "You are here. This is good."

Sel released Riona's arm and bowed. Riona thought Gwenhwyfar's gaze lingered longer than necessary and somewhat hungrily on her captain. When Gwenhwyfar's green eyes left her captain, Riona gave a shallow curtsy but nothing more.

"As you instructed, I have fetched the princess," Sel told his Queen.

Riona frowned. *The princess?*

"Come, we have much to discuss." Queen Gwenhwyfar gracefully pivoted and strolled away, disappearing further into her private rooms.

Without turning to look at her, Sel thrust his elbow at Riona, fully expecting to escort her into the Queen's presence.

Riona glared at the side of his handsome face, then she lifted her chin and breezed past the captain under her own power. After all, she was of a higher rank, Riona thought peevishly. Let him trail behind.

Her rebuff only lasted a few seconds. After a few paces, Riona slowed to a halt. As a very young child she had played in this room; scurrying in and around the magnificent crystal council table, brushing up against the legs of the Queen and her advisers. But that was so long ago and this was not how she remembered the Queen's private council room. Riona was struck by the diminished size of, well, everything. The table was not so immense, the space not so open, and it was not as magickal as her girlish memories recalled.

The Queen smiled at her. "I dare say, you remember this

room differently, Riona."

Riona absently nodded, not trusting herself to speak.

The Queen's seer eyes slide away from Riona to once again concentrate on Sel. After a moment of silence the Queen nearly gushed with well wishes. "You two make a striking couple. Yes, I knew it was a good match." Pleased with her handiwork, the Queen clapped her hands together with all the enthusiasm of a young girl.

Riona's eyebrow lifted when Sel remained as mute as she. It seemed he wasn't willing to offer any assurances of the rightness of the Queen's choice. Gwenhwyfar stood directly before him full of happy tidings and Sel was, for all the world, trying not to look sour over the Queen's decision to substitute him for the now deceased Calcus. Riona watched him gallantly offer his arm to the Queen to escort her to the council table. A belly full of soured wine could not have made Riona sicker than watching Sel and the Queen together. He was besotted with her. When the two reached the table they leaned over a map of sorts, blonde heads together, talking low.

"Riona, come," the Queen said in a tone that rang of reprimand to Riona's ears.

Dutifully, Riona joined the twosome.

"And you think he is here?" Sel pointed to a mountain range.

"Yes. But I cannot be sure." The Queen gave Sel a key, which he pressed into a pocket near his heart. "She must travel with you," she told him.

"Surely not."

"Yes." The Queen replied, and they both looked up from the map to study Riona. "You will go visit your grandfather," the Queen instructed. "You will be safe enough with him. It will give

Sel the opportunity he needs to search."

Too shocked to answer, Riona simply nodded. In return Sel narrowed his green eyes while continuing to stare at her. Whether he was annoyed or concerned, Riona could not tell. She had to fight the silly urge to stick her tongue out at him from across the table, certainly a very unprincess-like thing to do. Instead, she dropped her eyes to the map of Annwn, the underworld, a place she had never intended on visiting until the day death came to claim her.

The Queen was showing Sel the location of several gateways, their fingers meeting and touching first one place then another. Thankfully, the roar in Riona's head and the churning of her stomach left her deaf to the near whispered conversation. She only caught snippets of the planning between the two. They were going back to Tearmann first, then on to Annwn after dusk. She heard Crank's name and the phrase "three days". Beyond that, Riona could not recall anything. She was just too miserable in the couple's company.

The movement of Gwenhwyfar abandoning the planning table with Sel at her heels alerted Riona to the end of their royal interview. She crossed to stand beside the captain so the Queen could give her official blessing to their union, the body of which was simply more well wishes peppered with flowery language and the pomp and finery found in most royal rituals. Riona paid little attention to the Queen's speech. When Gwenhwyfar was done speaking, Riona curtsied because it was expected. Sel bowed beside her. Capturing her hand and pinning it to his arm, he then escorted her out of the Queen's presence. Once beyond the bronze doors, Sel's immense power wrapped around her and he transported them back to his study.

"What is wrong with you?" he barked as they

materialized.

She only glared at him. He was in love with the Queen—besotted with her. It wasn't just a harmless rumor Riona could ignore. It was heart-breakingly real and she knew herself well enough to understand she needed to run now, before it was too late, before he could hurt her. She took a deep breath to steady her nerves. There was only one way for her to honorably dissolve the contract between them. "Have you bothered to read the contract your precious Queen has condemned you to?" she snapped. That got his attention. Riona raised her chin a fraction of an inch to ward off the intimidating bark she knew would follow.

"No. What of it?"

Calmly she explained, a reckless and dangerous plan forming in her mind. "I have seen it." In truth, her father had made her read it so she'd understand that despite the agreement with the house of Caw, she would remain her father's property. "Calcus was preoccupied with having legitimate heirs. Specifically a son, a daughter would not be enough. Calcus would not waver on this. My father took exception to Calcus's perverse insistence on this point. I am bound to a mate until I bear a son." Remembering her father's anger sent a shiver down Riona's spine. "To say it angered him, would be an understatement," she told Sel. "So, the moment I was able to present Calcus with a son—the contract ended. Calcus would get his heir, but my father would regain his right to my person and title, so he could peddle me off at his discretion on another alliance as a proven broodmare." She had known such an arranged alliance would be forged for her. Her father had only allowed her to grow to adulthood because he saw the political advantages that could be gained from it. A son, Melwas would have slaughtered on the spot. But her father had understood the value of a daughter. It was a commodity that could be used repeatedly to his advantage, without fearing the loss of his throne. "Those are the terms of the binding contract you have been forced into assuming."

Sel looked startled at her stark declaration. "The Queen only wants you protected, Riona. I will not press the terms of the contract," he assured her.

"Then you dishonor me," she told him. Having just witnessed his glowing adoration for the Seelie Queen, she felt emboldened by her anger. Taking two tentative steps toward him, Riona pressed forward with her plan. "I want freedom granted to me from this alliance, without bringing dishonor to myself. And the only way to get it is to bear a son. With Calcus dead, the contract no longer dictates who the father must be, only proof that I can create an heir."

Riona knew she was crossing a line with him, but like her father, she was determined to find a benefit where none seemed to exist. Political ramifications didn't matter anymore. She was officially the mate of Sel, son of Selgi. Her house was tied to his in a politically blessed arrangement that had only one way out. As long as she was discrete she could finally take a lover, snatching a few years of happiness in the process. And if the gods were willing, she would then return to her life of hiding or Blodeuwedd would honor her promise and send a true mate to her. Either way, she wouldn't have to watch a love-sick Sel adore the Queen night and day.

Riona narrowed her eyes at him. "Is the duty so distasteful to you? Is it because I am unseelie?" His jaw was so tight it looked as if he might break his teeth under the pressure. His eyes burned into her, but she found the courage to move a step closer. She didn't think the captain was the type to hit her.

"Riona." Lightening sparked across the green of his irises.

"I will not be cuckold."

She shimmered and the black green of her gown thinned, leaving her charms visible beneath the sheerest of fabrics. She was able to hide her embarrassment under a layer of anger, their audience with Queen still fresh in her mind. Sel's sudden intake of breath left her shaking nervously, but Riona did not retreat.

"Bloody hell!" he roared. "Why do you press me?"

Her mind was fevered with wild thoughts, images of Sel and the Queen together. "I press only for my freedom. If you cannot perform the task, I will seek out Digon, or pick another guardsman whose coloring is more in keeping with yours." She had no idea why the thought had occurred to her, but the threat was a last desperate attempt at gaining a kind of control over her life and fate.

She had reached him, though it took an eternity. With a shaking hand Riona touched his cheek, softening the rigid set to his jaw. He was on fire, his skin nearly burning her fingertips.

"Are you certain this is what you want?" His voice, low and strained, was almost unrecognizable to her.

"Surely a trivial duty for you," she taunted. If he didn't give in quickly, Riona knew she would lose her nerve. She was not like her mother, and she was beginning to think that seducing a man was more difficult than her mother made it look. She dropped her hand from his immovable face, and then doubt made her drop his gaze as well. Afraid she had made a mistake in pursuing such a ill thought-out plan, she moved to retreat. That's when his large hands cupped her face.

Riona froze, and watched as the last tethers to his control snapped.

"Do not run from me," he breathed more than said. Then, lowering his lips to hers, he kissed her hungrily, brutally. With his tongue, he probed her mouth, tasting then devouring. The air around them vibrated with his power, winds swirling in a invisible whirlwind of terrifying strength.

Sel abruptly paused in his assault on her lips and drew back. Dazed, Riona leaned into the void his absence left. Her mind, still stunned by the intensity of his kiss, was slow to give warning to the danger she was now in. The once tame captain was on the precipice of losing his cherished restraint. For better or worse, she had awakened the fury and wildness that he had kept at bay. Whether planned or not, Sel held her immobile until her vision cleared and a kind of sanity returned. Only then, did Riona truly recognize the tempest she'd unleashed. The storm had arrived, and only a complete surrender to his demands would gain her the freedom she sought.

* * *

Sel could not make his hands release her. His body craved her, and the kiss had not been enough to satisfy the hunger she fanned in him. All promises and gallant intentions were torn from him by the whirlwind at his back pressing him forward into her arms. She stood before him with naught but the sheerest of coverings; her breasts rising and falling in a near pant, her heart racing like a terrified bird in her breast. Her eyes, half closed with desire, mouth red from his kiss and partially open to him, his hands joyously tangled in her silky tresses now anchored the temptress close. He should release her, the last logical thoughts in his mind warned.

"If the Queen has truly purchased a broodmare for me, then I would see my gift well appreciated," he said harshly, angry that she had so effortlessly pushed him to this point. Sel then tilted her head to the side, leaned forward and inhaled her scent along the vulnerably exposed length of her elegant neck. The taunt, which was meant to end this madness only succeeded in adding to his hunger. "Be rid of the gown," he growled low in his throat.

Obediently, she shimmered, giving him glorious access to her luminous skin. With the prize in his hands, Sel found he was afraid to move. He had balanced on a razor's edge for far too long, replacing honor and duty to Queen and Court over his own base needs. The innocent kiss in the garden had set his blood on fire, now Sel was afraid that if he moved to take what she offered, he would turn to ash, like a leaf in a flame.

She moved first, reaching with both hands to capture the sides of his face. Slowly, she guided him down to her lips to kiss him.

In one swift motion Sel lifted her up off the floor, one hand around her waist and the other at the base of her skull. Her long legs wound around him as he tasted her lips again and again. But his body screamed that this was still not enough.

Lunging across the room, he slammed her back against a solid surface. The wall, he thought dimly. Shimmering he rid himself of his clothes, skin finally touched skin. No skill guided his actions, there was only the blinding carnal desire to ram his cock repeatedly into her, to take what was before him, to claim her as his own.

When she gave the sweetest of whimpers in her throat, it nearly undid him. He could not wait any longer, his body demanded hers. With her securely pinned between him and the wall, he reached down and found her slick entrance. He then lifted her hips once more and dropped her onto his throbbing hard cock, swallowing her shocked scream in the process. She was so tight and hot, Sel thought he might die with the pain and pleasure of it.

He pushed repeatedly into her, hard and fast, over, and over, and over again, completely out of his mind with hunger. He pounded into her until his legs burned from the repetition of it. Reaching through the fragile threads dancing about them, He called to her magick and passion so that the first of many orgasms rolled through her.

Her slick muscles tugged at his cock as pure, unadulterated pleasure contracted her womb. Gritting his teeth against the bliss, Sel slowed his rhythm to relish the sensation of her muscles pulsing around him. Fevered with the knowledge that he hadn't yet had nearly enough of her body, he realized this position would no longer serve his purposes. Like a madman Sel scanned the room for a better surface to feast upon.

Finding none, he howled in frustration. Breathing hard with her still impaled and clinging to him, Sel carried her to the bedchamber and the bed. He tumbled them onto it, Riona ending up on top and astride him. An aftershock of pleasure traveled through her and he pressed into her, lifting his hips as he gave in to his own orgasm, filling her with his seed.

The binding vows now taunted him, skipping through his mind like a poem they sat waiting on the end of his tongue. He clamped his mouth shut so he would not utter them, sure his body had confused love with lust. Sel hugged her close to him, still astride but cradled in his arms. She relaxed contently, and kissed the hollow of his neck. He could feel her heart's rapid beating, in timing with his own. Maybe this wasn't going to be such a bad duty to Queen and court after all.

"I did not hurt you, did I?" he asked.

She gave him a muffled reply. "No, the deed is done," she sighed lightly, easily against his ear.

A disquieting feeling began in the pit of his stomach. "What deed?" he whispered back. His sated mind supplied the answer by offering up the vague memory of resistance when first ramming himself into her. Gently he pushed her off and found blood, virgin's blood. "Bloody hell. Why didn't you stop me?" he yelled at her.

Her eyes were wild with panic for a moment, then her composure descended. "I pushed you too far. It was too late to stop. No fault lies with you," she explained while laying her hand on his chest in an effort to soothe him. "It does not matter."

"Damn it, Riona, it does matter. I would not have used you so roughly if I had known." She did not answer except to purse her lips, a little gesture, but one that he was learning announced a pending retreat. The fact that he was her first lover, astounded him as much as it appalled him. She had been willing, but he had been past the point of stopping. That was no way to introduce bed-play, at least no way he ever wanted to introduce the pleasure of bed-play. He gently pulled her to him and slowly, lightly kissed her.

As she warmed to the leisurely manner of his kiss, her hand began its exploration of his torso, each ridge, peak and valley. His cock jumped to attention as the heat between them built, his body's needs having been too long ignored. Sel knew he would recover quickly, but he would go slower this time. There were no thoughts of disengaging. The threat of her straying to Digon or another one of his men had pushed Sel over the edge of reason, and with her mother's courtesan blood in her veins, he could not be certain her earlier threat had been a hollow one. Yet, he craved her—even knowing all her family's history and knowing he would never be able to completely trust her. If she wanted to bed him willingly, then by the gods, he would have her begging his name by nightfall. Sel had no intentions of fighting fair. He possessed the knowledge that could chain her body's needs to him. And being her first lover, only made that task easier.

He left her red and swollen lips to travel down to her luscious breasts, fondling one while suckling on the other. He was rewarded with a pleasurable gasp when he paused to lavish attention on one taut peak. When she started to squirm, he pinned her under him, sliding his hips between her thighs. "Riona, look at me."

Slowly she opened her eyes, the brown irises almost black with desire.

"I am going to wash the blood away. Then we will do this again, the right way."

She smiled shyly at him before he bent his head down to kiss each breast. He then trailed his tongue down to her navel before regrettably leaving the bed.

Sel poured water from a pitcher into a bowl. After setting the pitcher down, he put his hand in the cold spring water and heated it—a simple trick. He then dipped a nearby cloth into the steaming bowl, rung out the excess water and turned to find her watching him. Her eyes were absolutely enormous. He followed her line of vision to his erect and mildly bloodied cock.

"Me first then," he said lightly. He efficiently cleaned himself, re-wet the cloth, and set his mind to the happy task of cleaning the blood from her inner thighs.

She did not flinch at his touch, but passively opened her legs to him. To set her at ease, Sel wiped the blood from her with as much detachment as he could muster. "Riona, you will undoubtedly find that I have a rigid sense of duty. If you wish to conceive, I will aggressively make sure you do. At every opportunity, and in every position I think might accomplish the task. From this day forward, until you conceive, you are not to leave my side. Do you understand?"

"You do not trust me."

"No," he confessed coolly. "You have already lied to me." He finished the task but lingered to clean some of his seed from her pink entrance. "And you have already threatened to look elsewhere." His hunger was growing to a dangerous level again as he inhaled their mingled scent warmed by her skin.

"Do your duty, and do it well... and I will not look elsewhere," she told him quietly.

Sel smiled from between her legs at her bold words. "You will not look elsewhere because I mean to chain your body's desires to me. It will only be my name that you beg for." He leaned down and licked at the pink folds and was rewarded with her squeal. "I can drop you to your knees with a thought, Riona. I am that powerful," he told her. Capturing her gaze, he then sucked on her tender bud until she lifted her hips to press herself closer to his mouth and tongue. Abruptly he released her and she sank into the soft bedding with a shutter.

"Do not attempt to manipulate me," he warned her. As easily as he heated the wash water, he again called to the desire deep within her and the orgasm took her. Sel then confidently knelt down and lapped at the gates of heaven until her passion was spent. Only then did he rise up and push his engorged cock into her once more, inch by delectable inch.

By the gods this was a sweet torture, and Sel repeated it over and over again. Riona was a quick student, learning his body's demands and arching to meet him. Circling her waist, Sel supported her bowed back and took his time gliding in and out of her wetness. Sometimes faster, sometimes slower, but just as she reached the edge, Sel would withdrawal or stop and Riona would whimper under him for the loss of him. At these times he would hold her close, breathing across her earlobe, "What do you want?"

And she would beg, near tears at times. "Sel, please. Oh, please." When she grew desperate for him, Sel would relent and call to another orgasm along their bonds, releasing his control over his own body, pumping and shuttering only after she lay sated beneath him. After a short respite Sel would clean her, heal her sore muscles if needed be, and then the process would begin anew, for there were many hours until dusk and he intended his ownership to be absolute.

But sometimes the best laid plans can go awry. Dusk came and went, night fell and they still had not traveled to Tearmann. Sel had finally allowed her to sleep, but he could not bring himself to wake her. Riona was curled around him, draping her arm over his chest, a leg, a thigh over his hip. He left her alone to rest for an hour beside him then gently slid his cock into her. She cooed in her exhaustion and wiggled closer. Slipping into her mind, he deepened her sleep and she settled once more, tightly wound around him. He was well content to simply lay quietly joined with her.

Still awake in the predawn, Sel reexamined his hand and arm. His skin glowed faintly in the dancing shadows of the firelight, a sure sign she was the one, the only one destined for him. Sighing, Sel shimmered to hide the effect she had wrought on him. It wouldn't do him any good to let her gain the upper hand so soon. No, he held the key to her body, and for now, that was enough. His mind quietly suggested that maybe, one day, her heart would follow if he were lucky. They would need time for their bond to grow, for trust to grow. Only then could he hope to bind the temptress laying beside him with the vows. Until that happy day, he must keep his heart's longings to himself.

She mumbled something in her sleep and Sel smiled down at her, carefully moving a stray hair from her check. He chuckled quietly to himself in the dark. He seemed destined to collect unseelies.

"Sel…"

"Shhh, sleep," he told her, then he kissed the top of her head and she sighed, lost to her dreaming.

Chapter 11

Sel selfishly kept her under the sleep compulsion until well past dawn. This gave him the time he needed to call on the Queen, making new arrangements for Tearmann's destination that evening. Because the castle could not settle in the same valley twice, they picked another location just twenty miles east of the castle's last resting place. It meant he and Riona would have to ride hard for the doorway to Annwn, but it could be managed.

Next, Sel met with Fain and Tristian, calling them away from their training time in the sand pit. In the event of his not returning, Sel appraised them of his current mission along with the plans he had left with Hueil concerning Gloric. They in turn updated him on the unrest and political squabbling in the Unseelie Court. Calcus's doomed generals, Aeron and Brodie, seemed to have cooled the Unseelie King's wrath by offering up the third general, Durstian, for execution. Sel couldn't help chuckling to himself over the unseelie's sense of proportional retribution.

Both of Sel's lieutenants were wise enough not to comment on his forced agreement with Riona's house. Sel knew they thought the Queen was punishing him for some unknown reason. He didn't broach the subject to set them straight, but instead, he let them think what they will. Finally with his duties done, Sel left the Guardsmen's Hall.

His last stop was the kitchens of the Queen's palace where he ordered a platter of sweetmeats, nuts, and fresh fruits to be delivered to his private study. He assured the nervous servant that the ward's sting would be temporarily lessened, if he hurried.

Only when these things were done did Sel return to his quarters and his sleeping Riona. As he passed through the wards protecting his private rooms, he siphoned off much of the power maintaining the energy field. But even before he fully materialized inside his bedchamber, he was hit by her terror.

She was alone in bed, thrashing, sobbing, caught in a dream she could not wake from, his compulsion being too strong for her to break. Panicked, Sel gathered her to him, cradling her against his body and hastily pushed into her mind to lift his will's sleep mandate. He had to breach a wall of fear, but once his mind was connected to hers, Sel understood her terror. Vivid memories bombarded him: murky darkness, fear; a child's hands beating against solid air, trapped; the repeated sting of an invisible lash against her backside, caught; the never ending pain of *his* discipline, despair. Sel was horrified by the images of her father's treatment. The scenes ignited Sel's anger, his furry flowing hot in his veins.

Released from the compulsion, Riona surfaced quickly from the nightmare and curled into a shaking ball next to him with tear streaked cheeks and a racing heart. To soothe her Sel stroked her arm and back while maintaining a calming influence in her mind. *Riona, you are safe.* He should not have left her alone. *Shhh, I'm here. Nothing can hurt you*. He enveloped her in a cocoon of security fashioned from the strength of his presence. *I can protect you.* As the heat of his body seeped into hers, her shaking and heart rate slowed. *I promise. Nothing can hurt you now.* When the shadows in her mind cleared, he felt her tentatively touch his mind through their connection.

Abruptly Riona pushed him away and sat up, clutching the blanket to her breasts. She glared at him and forcibly and rather painfully expelled him from her mind. "You have no right!" she hissed. "Stay out of my head."

"I am sorry." What else could he say? That he had

purposefully kept her asleep so he could go about his duties without having to entertain the nagging worry of what she might do without him there? Or confess it wasn't the first time he had compelled her for his own selfish reasons. "I promise, I will not trespass again." Sensing she needed it, Sel stood to put distance between them. "I will wait for you in the study. We must leave soon for Tearmann."

Sel retreated and left her to compose herself, trading the bedroom for his study and ignoring the confusion on her lovely face. She seemed caught between anger at his intrusion into her privacy and hurt at his cool manner after last night's intimacy. The wisest course of action was to move slowly, but what he would rather have done was toss her on her back and repeat the previous nights lessons. But such a action would only be addressing his own need to hold her safely in his arms.

As he closed the bedchamber door, he had to remind himself that if Riona was indeed his true mate then this battle to win her heart and loyalty wasn't going to be a trivial skirmish easily won by overpowering her defenses. No, the gods had set before him a campaign, a campaign where both sides must ultimately emerge victorious.

Sel settled down at his desk and exhaled slowly. He knew too little about her. She had a history, one that he had not expected, and one he had only been able to glimpse. Her bid for freedom from her father's influence and now her bid for freedom from the contract which bound her to the house of Selgi wasn't just spiteful willfulness as he had assumed.

A servant halted in the hall archway with a sliver tray and cleared his throat to gain his attention.

"Just set it on the ottoman." Sel said, pointing to the round leather footstool he had obtained in what was once called

Persia. "My thanks to the cook," he told the servant right before the boy departed.

Sel looked down at his desk and tried to concentrate on the reports in front of him, but his mind continued to mull over the crux of the problem between. He shuffled through a few notes on his desk and wrote a quick observation for Fain to find but his ear was singularly attuned to any movement beyond the bedchamber door.

He didn't hear her enter as much as he felt her, like a lost part of him gratefully reattached. Sel kept his eyes on his paperwork, even though he no longer had any interest in what information it held. "I had the kitchens send a light meal. We should leave as soon as you are ready," Sel informed her, then rose to strap his sword onto his hip before looking up. She wore the same modest russet dress as when he had first encountered her. It was soft and feminine, impractical for Annwn. Sel had to remind himself to breathe.

"I am not hungry. We can leave at your discretion." Her tone was neither warm nor cool, perfectly obedient and without opinion.

Sel picked up the key from his desk and hung it around his neck before tucking it under his uniform. "As you wish." The Queen's diplomatic greeting for Arawn was already stashed in a pouch at his waist. He offered his arm and shifted them as soon as he captured her hand.

She remained silent as they wove their way from Tearmann's heartstone to the gathering hall where Digon was quick to notice their arrival. The hall was nearly empty, the morning meal already having been cleared away. Sel reluctantly halted their progress to speak with the rapidly approaching caretaker.

"Digon."

"Sel." Digon returned the captain's greeting before turning a pleasant smile to Riona. "I worried when you did not arrive yesterday, Princess."

"We were detained," Sel informed Digon, rudely preempting Riona's response and gaining Digon's full attention again. "I need to speak with Crank. Please go find him and send him to me."

Digon snatched a quick look at Riona before replying. "Crank was in a bad way last night. Can it wait?"

"I do not care if he has drunk the whole of the cellar's stores. Find him and deliver him to my quarters before the hour is out." Sel's uncommonly sharp command sent Digon on his way.

"Feeling out of sorts this morning?" Riona asked.

He moved off, sweeping her along with him. "Crank has information about Annwn that I need. I respect his experience, but not his predisposition for self-destruction."

"He is tormented and should be pitied."

Sel did not give her a reply until they had reached the door to his quarters. "He does not want your pity, Riona." Sel opened the door and stepped back for her to enter first. "I will see the Queen's task successfully completed. And if that means that Crank must suffer my questions while hungover, then so be it."

"Forgive me, I forgot that everything you do is for the Queen," she replied, dropping his gaze. "I will not forget again." She glided past him, the fabric of her dress brushing against his thigh.

She had done it to him again. With a clever quip, she rendered him off balance. Was she talking about his treatment of Crank and Digon, or about his treatment of her? He bolted the door behind him. When he turned to continue their discussion, she preempted him.

"How will we reach our destination?" She stood with the fireplace to her back, chin raised, a royal air wrapped closely about her like a defensive cloak.

He thought her absolutely magnificent, irritating for sure, but magnificent nonetheless. Though younger in age, smaller in frame, and weaker in power, Riona was every bit his equal and would not quake under his glare or surrender her opinion because he might speak sharply in a fit of temper. Sel had to admit, he had always hoped for such a woman, a woman who could match the grace and strength of his Queen. "When the castle settles for the night, one of my men will be outside to meet us. We will have to ride for the gate. Once through, we will cross the waters to Annwn." Sel unstrapped his sword from his hip and leaned it against a chair. "Crank has spent time in Arawn's Keep, and knows the lay of the land better than I."

"Will you press him to come with us?"

Sel hesitated. Crank could be a great asset, but he was unpredictable. "Aye. I will try," he said, knowing it to be a lost cause. "On the Queen's behalf," he added.

"Then I will help see it done," Riona said.

Sel raised one blond eyebrow. "And if the Queen's request can not persuade him, why would your plea accomplish such a feat?" He sat down while studying her, his long legs crossing at the ankle. He noted her nervous swallow, but it was the only visible doubt she showed him.

"I think he will offer to see me safely there and back if I request it of him."

Sel grinned. She was showing her inexperience, he thought. "Shall we wager on it?" Sel knew Crank hadn't stepped outside of Tearmann since his self imposed exile. Sel was certain the old commander would refuse her no matter how prettily she pleaded.

"If it pleases you. What are the terms?" she asked.

He could see her interest was piqued. "I will grant any boon that is in my power to give… if he agrees to come with us on our little adventure." A bold offer, he thought.

"And if he refuses?"

Sel grew serious. "You tell me who hurt you," he said, knowing he trespassed on a painful secret. Riona turned her back to him. "I am sorry, Riona. Let us pick another consequence for losing. After all this is a friendly bet."

She turned to face him, raising her chin. "No. I accept your terms."

He was proud of her for not backing down. Sel rose from his chair and crossed to her. "Then let us seal the bargain with a kiss." Perhaps, he was pressing his luck after this morning's drama but, as if daring him, Riona raised her lips to him. Not letting the opportunity to kiss her go by unanswered, Sel quickly brushed her siren lips with a chaste kiss before disengaging. He then walked away from her fearing he might get swept away once again by her charms.

He glanced over his shoulder. Riona wore a look of confusion and Sel had to bite down on the inside of his cheek to prevent himself from smiling. Fatefully, the door rang with the banging of a fist, thus ending their flirtation.

"I will see to it." Riona moved swiftly to the door, unlocking and opening it for a disgruntled Crank. Her smile wavered when she took in the disordered state of the belligerent commander. By the look and smell of him, and the hastily donned kilt, Digon had located Crank passed out cold in the stables. Riona ignored the smell and threw her arms around the unseelie's neck and her body against him in greeting, as if he were her savior.

Crank held her close in stunned confusion, his hand came to rest naturally on her buttocks.

Sel's vision narrowed dangerously as a wave of jealousy hit him.

"I am so glad you are here," she whimpered in mock relief. "I am so afraid, Crank. They are making me go."

It took Crank a moment to clear his fussy brain, but when he did, he moved his hand up to Riona's waist. Still holding her, he came into the room and shot Sel an accusatory look. "What is she babblin' on about, lad? Why do you summon me thus?"

Riona continued to cling to Crank as if her life depended on it. If she didn't let go soon, Sel was certain he'd kill someone. "Riona, let go of him." The command came out less like words than a low deep growl. His warning only succeeded in causing her to cling tighter to the mad old unseelie.

"You see what he's like?" She craned her neck back to plead her cause to Crank. "He is taking me with him to Annwn. Crank, please don't let him." A tear leaked out of the corner of her eye.

After reading the murderous intentions on Sel's face, Crank tried to gently untangled himself from Riona's grasp. He partially succeeded, but she would not let go of his hand and arm. "Sel, what is this?"

Sel could see Riona's acting had already gained the unseelie's sympathies, and his violent reaction to seeing her in another's embrace had only strengthened her performance. Reminding himself that he had originally wanted Crank to accompany him, Sel tried to calm himself, but it took a few tries before he was able to explain. "I have the key to his prison. I need

Riona to entertain her grandfather while I search. She will be in no danger. She is of his blood."

"Aye. True enough, but only if his wife is not in Annwn while Riona is there."

"She will be absent for the next three days," Sel said.

Surprised by the information, Riona's pretense of fear slipped. "You did not tell me that."

Looking down at Riona, Crank told her, "Sel will not let harm come to you, girl. Of that you can bloody well be sure." Crank absently patted her hand, the crisis to her having been averted in his mind.

"But what of him?" she asked Crank, her eyes growing wide with worry. Sel watched her smoothly change her argument. "He does not know Lord Arawn like you do, nor the lands." When that line of argument didn't seem to touch the heart of the blue warrior, she tried another. "I need you, Crank. I trust you. You must go with us to keep me safe. Sel's heart belongs to the Queen. I have seen it. You know this to be true. If sacrificing me, a mere unseelie, will ensure success for the Queen's quest, then I fear I am doomed to remain in the underworld. You know if he must choose between me or his Queen, he will pick the Queen." Again a tear or two leaked down her cheek.

Crank eyed Sel and then Riona suspiciously. "Do you use her to persuade me?"

"You know I would not. The Queen asks that you go."

"She would," Crank mumbled, finally removing himself from Riona's grasp. The unseelie crossed the room, poured himself a drink and swallowed it in one swift motion before answering Riona. "We travel to Annwn, and nowhere else. I can never appear at court again."

Sel watched Riona vigorously nod her head in the

affirmative, her eyes still watery with false tears. At least Sel hoped all her tears were false.

"Aye. I will see this done then," Crank sighed.

Riona went to throw her arms around him again but the unseelie caught her in mid fling, stopping her.

"No child. Your mate contemplates murder because you keep throwing yourself at me." Finding Sel's torment amusing, he chuckled. "I will not have his death on my conscience." He released his hold and took a step away.

Riona turned from Crank to give Sel an impish smile before returning her attention back to the unseelie.

"We leave as soon as the castle settles," Sel curtly informed Crank.

"Aye. I will be ready." Crank then kissed Riona's knuckles and excused himself.

Glaring at Riona behind Crank's retreating back, Sel followed the bloody blue bastard to the door. Once the unseelie was beyond the doorway, Sel slammed the bolt home with more force than was necessary. He didn't begrudge her winning the bet, so much as the way she had won it. Wanton manipulation was so very much like her mother. He crossed the room and poured himself a drink. What boon would she ask for? Could he ever be sure of her? Could he ever trust her?

"It was my father I dreamed about. As a small child I was too willful for his tastes. He would beat me for the fault and then have a healer mend the marks afterward."

Sel set the glass he had been holding down on the table. Her unsolicited confession held no emotion, as if it had been someone else's life instead of her own. "How often?" he whispered.

"Whenever he happened upon me."

"And Naria, she did not offer to protect her own child." It was a statement. Sel knew Naria would look out for her own best interest, not her child's, but Sel held out hope that the seductress possessed hidden depths of character.

"She hid me away." Riona's chin jutted froward. "But I think it was so she could have his sole attention. She has never liked sharing adoration with others."

The nightmarish memories replayed themselves in Sel's mind. Not raising his voice, Sel declared, "I would kill him for his treatment of you." He didn't care that such an act would start a war between the two courts. No child should suffer such abuse.

Riona crossed the floor to stand beside him. "Nay. It was a long time ago. I would not have you start a war for me. I am not worth it."

Sel studied her, his hand straying to her cheek. There was so much he did not understand about her. "Aye. You are," he told her. Sel then bent down and carefully kissed her lips.

Because he had promised to stay out of her mind, Sel refrained from telegraphing his desires along their link. It went against his nature to remain passive, but she needed to initiate the contact along their bonds, to touch the power she wielded over him. He was the most feared champion of the Queen, but the enchantress before him ruled his existence without even being aware of it. The second she had embraced Crank, Sel had wanted nothing more than to pummel his old friend to death. And if she smiled at Digon one more time, Sel knew he would finally erupt into a jealous snit.

So, because he had glibly promised to stay out of her thoughts he did, even though it made reaching his ultimate goal of gaining her love rather troublesome. Sel, however, did allow himself the joy of teasing her lips apart so that he could taste her more fully.

When she moaned in pleasure, he felt her mind brush his. He moved from her lips to the hollow of her neck and then the tender spot right behind her earlobe. She sighed and leaned into him. He happily encircled her waist to pull her up against his hard body. The threads between them vibrated with her sudden desire for more contact, both physical and mental. Smiling against her soft skin, Sel trailed kisses and teasing nips along her jawbone until he reached her lips again. Offering up a small prayer to the gods to protect his heart, Sel then breathed across her cheek the plea his soul most craved, "Reach for me, Riona. Call to me."

Chapter 12

His body was so hot Riona thought it might burn her, but she leaned into him anyway. Through the haze of desire, Sel had urged her to call to him, but she still held back. He had completely dominated her will with his skillful bed-play the night before. She had lost herself to him and it frightened her. Could she trust him with her heart when his belonged to the Queen?

"Riona, reach for me," he again whispered across her ear, a warm breath and even sweeter melody.

Warnings rang in her mind, but his hand was gently teasing her breast and she sighed with the pleasure of it. Drunk with her body's wanting, she brushed against his mind again and was surprised by his acute need for her. Though it caused him pain, Sel was holding back, giving her the opportunity to demand from him what she craved. She caressed his mind again, gently but with more confidence. He moaned in response to her touch.

"Aye, free me, Riona."

He kissed her deeply again, leaving her weak in the knees, only his arm holding her against his body kept her from melting onto the floor. He then put his lips against her ear and whispered, "Call to me," before he leisurely kissed her neck. "Call to the magick." He nibbled at her jaw, then paused. "Call to my power. It is yours for the asking," he hoarsely breathed against her skin.

It was an erotic thought, and she heard herself sigh. He was offering her all that he was, so that her body might find the pleasure it whimpered for. Her mind warned he loved another and the Queen's image rudely intruded into her thoughts. But her body did not seem to care about what was safe or prudent. He had awakened her physical needs, shaped and schooled her to want him. He was holding her now and her intoxicated mind did not have the will to deny his request, much less have him continue to bear the pain his restraint caused him.

Riona guided his lips to hers and decisively reached through the link he had forged between them, slipping easily into his mind. The wall containing his desire collapsed and she was swept away by the force of his longing. The waves of the first orgasm engulfed her senses, washing through her as the ocean breaks against the shore.

She could not remember how they arrived at the bed, nor when the barriers of clothing had fallen away. With her mind passionately melded with his, Riona was only aware of him and the glorious feel of his body surrounding her, penetrating her, cradling her. His strength flowed freely into her, filling her until her blood hummed with the power of the ancients and of the gods. For the first time in her life Riona knew what it was to be sheltered. At last, here in his arms she found the safety she had sought.

As he slid in and out of her, Riona pushed deeper into his mind, searching. Instead of meeting with resistance, she floated in his joy at her probing. He had no thought save that of her; of keeping her by his side, forever and at all cost.

"Sel," she pleaded, straining for yet another release. Responding, he quickened his pace, pushing forcefully into her while cradling her head between his palms.

"Call to me," he said, his voice straining with the effort. "Take it."

He had relinquished all control to her, and she reveled in the sweetness of it. Riona fanned his fevered mind to the point of madness, propelling them both toward sweet release.

Her mind was firmly entangled with his. If it had not

been, she would have missed the one thing he tried to hold back. At the very moment he breached the final point of his body's control and the second before he shuttered with release, he swamped her with a wave of love which pierced her heart; a god bolt of truth he could not contain. And for good or for ill, Riona answered by surrendering to him completely; her body, her mind, her heart, and may the gods have mercy on her... her very soul. As she rode the crest of her own orgasm she knew he would never betray her. She had found Blodeuwedd's blessing in the form of the Queen's Captain, her captain.

When Riona settled back into her body, he was still joined with her, holding her close by his side. She pulled back from his thoughts, a habit born of self-preservation. She would keep the discovery of his secret to herself, its truth too astonishing for her to believe. They needed time.

"You will be with child very soon. I fear I do my duty too well," he told her while caressing her cheek. "I will hope for a girl." He smiled weakly at her.

"Surely it will take time to accomplish."

"Nay, not so much time. Sinnie's mother, Brianna, conceived straight away."

It was silly, but the mention of Sinnie's mother caused Riona's heart to constrict painfully. "Another contracted agreement?"

"Aye. Though, not a happy one. Brianna dissolved it as soon as Sinnie was born. It was an alliance not of her choosing. She had been convinced by her brother that it would be a good thing."

"I am sorry."

"It was a long time ago, and I have forgiven Tristian for his ambition."

"Oh, that is why he looked at me so disapprovingly."

Sel did not bother to contain his growl at hearing the news. "If he ever gives you any slight, no matter how small, tell me. I will not permit such a thing." He then kissed the top of her head and carefully hugged her to him as if he could protect her solely with the mass of his own body.

"How many hours until we leave?"

"A few. How do you wish to fill them?" the smile in his voice teased.

She could feel him grow hard inside her once more, but he stayed out of her mind as he had promised. Reaching for their connection, Riona lowered his lips to hers. *Do your duty, and do it well. Only then will I let you leave this bed.* She telegraphed the thought into his mind and deepened the kiss.

He chuckled into her mouth and spent the next several hours fulfilling his contracted duty to her with a single-minded joy that humbled her.

* * *

That evening they found Crank waiting for them just beyond the gates of Tearmann. Though cleaner in appearance, his haphazard attire now bore the addition of two swords cross-strapped along his back, a dagger at his waist, and knife secured to his bare calf just above the heavy black boots.

Sel clasped Crank's forearm in a warrior's handshake. "We have miles to ride. Are you sure you want to wear that?"

Crank looked down at his kilt before answering. "Aye. My balls are as hard as stone. Worry about my horse, not me," he laughed. Turning to Riona he greeted her with more formality, "Princess."

Aware of Sel's eyes on her, Riona kept her tone neutral, "Crank."

At the bottom of the hill, a lone fey appeared with two bridled black steeds.

Upon spying the sleek fairy horses, Crank grinned until his cheeks might split "She sent us phookas!" he roared in delight.

The magickal animals were shapeshifters, and though they chose to appear most of the time as long-maned wild horses, they could also take the outward shape of a goat, bull, eagle or an ass if the mood struck them. The phookas were pranksters by nature, and so they shared many of the same traits as the unseelie; moody, malevolent, and unpleasantly unpredictable.

Riona shared a look of doubt with Sel before following the happy old commander down to greet the phookas who would soon convey them to the border lands separating this realm from Annwn.

By the time she and Sel reached the guardsman, Crank was busy stroking the neck of one of the phookas while conversing with it in a language Riona had never heard.

"Liam." Sel acknowledged the guardsman before exchanging a salute. The guardsman handed Sel the reins to the second phooka. His assignment completed, the fey vanished, leaving just the three of them and the two fairy steeds.

Crank slid the bridle from his mount. "Sel, they will take us without these." He dropped the leather to the ground and then turned to the captain. "Trust me."

Riona thought it a bad idea. The fairy mounts were members of the elementals and hardly trustworthy, but she kept her opinion to herself when Sel also removed the bridle from their mount. Sensing her unease, the phooka went so far as to nuzzle her arm in greeting.

Crank swung himself atop his mount and the phooka danced under him, eager to be off. He patted the animal's black withers and then adjusted his position so his buttocks bore most of his weight.

Sel followed his example and after he was astride, he offered his hand to Riona. "You will sit in front of me. Give me your hand."

The soft black nose of the phooka gave her an encouraging nudge, but when she continued to hesitate it bared its blood-stained teeth to demonstrate its annoyance.

At the gruesome sight, Riona brushed against Sel's lower leg in an attempt to put more distance between herself and the phooka's sharp teeth. A squeal escaping her lips when Sel reached down and caught her around the waist to haul her up. One minute her feet were firmly on the ground and the next she found herself wedged between his warm thighs, her back pulled tightly against his chest and one arm firmly around her middle, securing her in place. She wiggled to find a more comfortable position and he stiffen behind her.

"Be still," he grunted into her ear.

Guessing at the source of his discomfort, Riona blushed. But before she could apologize for her thoughtlessness, the phookas broke into a canter, heading west. Startled by the speed at which the phookas traveled, Riona pushed back into the security of Sel's embrace, afraid she might slip from the beast's back.

"I've got you," Sel said against her ear.

"Yes, but who has the phooka?" she squeaked.

Her question did not receive a reply, though Riona thought she could feel his chest shake in suppressed laughter.

With time Riona adjusted to the speed and the steady

rocking motion of the phooka's gait. Sel's strong grip never wavered and, after a time, Riona was able to relax and take in the beauty of the ever-changing landscape of Tir na n-Og as it flowed past. Their magickal mounts kept the same steady pace until they had to skirt the edge of the Arach Mountains. There, the easy rocking canter slowed to a bone jarring trot as the soft meadows and forest floor gave way to terrain that favored goats instead of the solid hooves of horses. Even though it was more difficult for them, true to Crank's assurances, the phookas pushed onward without changing shape.

The moon was high in the night sky by the time they reached the end of the rocky mountain trail. The meadows returned along with the tangy aroma of the sea. Their mounts whinnied their delight and broke into a swift gallop, tripling their speed.

"We will need to jump when we see the stones," Crank yelled over his shoulder. Having less weight to carry, his phooka had pulled into the lead.

"What does he mean, jump? Will they not stop?" Riona hollered at Crank's fleeing back. She could feel the phooka beneath her strain to catch its companion, its legs flying as the smell of the sea grew in its nostrils.

"They race for the water and we cannot be astride them when they reach it," Sel informed her, speaking once again directly into her ear.

They had been riding the phookas for hours and Riona wasn't sure her legs would support a hasty dismount. She tensed, waiting for the stone archways to come into sight; closing her eyes Riona tried to prepare herself for the coming impact.

Sel's arm tightening around her waist was her first warning. Riona's eyes flew open and she witnessed Crank vault off his black phooka, hit and roll. And then all at once she too was airborne, Sel still holding onto her. He grunted when she landed heavily, sprawled on top of him in the wild grass, the sound of retreating hoofs dying in the distance.

"Sorry," she squeaked. He did not offer any resistance when she quickly rolled off. Riona hid her embarrassment by taking the opportunity to brush the dirt from her tunic before attempting to stand.

Sel was already on his feet, hailing Crank. He adjusted the sword at his hip and checked that the Queen's message had not been lost before offering to help her to her feet. A rider she was not, so she gratefully accepted his assistance. He efficiently brushed the dirt from her bottom, then patted it fondly. Her mind was temporarily jolted with wave of desire along their private link.

"This way," Crank called.

Sel motioned to Crank he had heard, the touch of his mind abruptly leaving her along with the heat traveling through her blood. Riona wasn't sure Sel had been aware of tapping into their link. At least there wasn't any outward sign of it.

Without a word, Sel took her hand and pulled her along beside him until they reached the grove of trees. He then pushed her forward until she was walking between the two of them, Crank on point and Sel guarding the rear. The phookas, it seemed, had strayed off course, leaving them just short of a mile from their destination. Crank had recognized the grove, a mixture of silver fir and yew trees. The grove was unique in that they formed a protective ring around the doorway they sought.

After several minutes of walking, the feeling in Riona's legs returned along with the apprehension of entering the underworld. "What is waiting for us on the other side?" she asked

Crank's back. Crank didn't slow his pace and for a minute Riona thought he hadn't heard her question. She would rather know what lay before her, hoping it might distract her from pondering the seelie behind her.

"The landscape will not look so different than these lands. It is lush and green, but do not mistake the benign and familiar appearance of Annwn. There are many dangers, but it is the whispers you must stridently guard against."

"The whispers?"

"Aye. They are the voices of bodiless souls who promise ease and contentment; a home, a hearth, a place of rest. If they sway you, then the doors leading out of Annwn will forever be closed to you. They are strongest at night. They are why we must gain entrance to Lord Arawn's Keep."

"Riona, it will be fine. I will not let any harm come to you," Sel said from behind. She looked over her shoulder and gave him a weak smile.

"Once we pass into Lord Arawn's realm, we canna use magick to leave. There will be no shifting home, nor can we bring anything back," Crank continued. "Except Arthur, who dinna belong there. You mustn't forget what I tell you, girl. Your life may depend on it."

"We will remember, Crank. Now, where are these doorways we seek?" Sel asked the old commander.

"There." Crank stopped and pointed to the three stone archways in the grove's clearing.

"Yes, but which one?" Riona asked.

"The left," Sel and Crank said in unison.

Sel placed his hand on the small of her back and murmured against her hair. "If you have to leave on your own, always take the archway on the left as you approach the three doors. Do you understand?"

She looked up at his serious face. "Yes, but you will be with me."

He just nodded but did not promise her.

"The sun will be rising soon. We should hasten." Crank strode forward and passed under the left arch, disappearing from view.

Sensing her shock and apprehension, Sel took her hand in his larger one and together they crossed the border into Annwn.

Once beyond the door, they were knee-deep in bog water. The fog, as if sensing their arrival, raced toward them from either side. The moon was brighter in Annwn than in Tir na n-Og and so Riona could clearly see Crank as he moved through the brackish water.

"We need to get to shore," Sel indicated the shoreline just ahead where the marsh ended and incredible white sands began. "It is not deep, but if the fog catches us, we could lose our way," he instructed while tugging at her arm.

Unlike Crank, who was surrounded quickly by the fog, Sel and Riona fared better. The wisps of milky white clouds shied away from them, thinning as they trudged forward. At first, Riona thought it was only a trick of the mind, but Sel noticed the odd behavior of the fog as well.

"Your grandfather knows you come," he explained, gripping her hand tighter.

By the time they reached the beach of Annwn, Crank was dry and waiting for them. He handed them bits of wool to plug their ears, then motioned for them to follow. Riona took a moment to shimmer, drying herself as well as ridding herself of the odor and mud left by the pungent marsh water.

Sel shimmered as well then they left the powdery sand

behind, traveling past grass covered dunes and through a flowered meadow that ended at a line of ancient Rowan trees, the tree of life. While passing through the grove, Riona reached to touch one of the huge trunks as a sign of deference, but Crank snatched her hand away before she could caress the tree's bark.

"Do not," he yelled so she could hear him past the stuffing in her ears. He did not attempt to explain.

She dropped her hand and dipped her chin so he could see she had heard him. For the rest of their journey, she kept her eyes open but her hands to herself. She had to remind herself she did not know these lands, or its traps.

They walked for a long time but as gray rays of dawn broke against a night sky, her grandfather's home finally came into sight. It was a lone circular tower surrounded by a moat filled with black water. The tower was plain and shockingly ordinary, its choice of location just as unremarkable. Fields of grain, golden and heavy with seed, the harvest imminent, surrounded it. Riona had imagined her grandfather would have a grander residence with a more dramatic setting, for he was after all one of the ancient gods.

Guessing at the direction of her thoughts, Crank hollered close to her ear. "He has no one to impress. Come. We will need you to gain us entry." Moving forward, Crank cut a path for them to follow through the field using just the bulk of his body.

Riona followed. What choice did she have? "How am I to get us in?" she yelled at Crank's muscled blue back.

"Talk your way in. You'll soon see," Crank replied.

Behind her Sel said nothing and Riona fought the urge to reach for his strength. She could do this, she told herself.

In less time than she would have liked, they reached the moat whose expanse was bridged by rotting wood. A single man stood on the other side, legs apart, arms crossed. Three great white hounds with red tipped ears rested at his feet. His skin, untouched by the passing of time, was the color of warm mahogany and his brow was wreathed by a single band of gold. Arawn the god/king of Annwn had come to greet them. Or challenge them, Riona thought uneasily.

Riona saw Crank remove the packing from one ear, and she followed his example. She could not hear the whispers, the seductive promises of the dead Crank had warned her to guard against. She suspected that her grandfather was somehow keeping them at bay, for now.

"Naf, Arthur's first and truest defender, I expected you long ago. Has death finally brought you to my borders?" The light of recognition sparkled in the god/king's eyes, but it did not translate into a warm greeting for their guide.

"Nay, Lord Arawn. I escort your granddaughter and her mate." Crank, whose real name and title was apparently well known to her grandfather, held his blue hand out for Riona to take. When she did take it, he led her forward to the edge of the moat.

Lord Arawn's crystal blue gaze settled on Riona and he smiled. "My dear, you are welcome in my home, but these two are not. Send them on their way. They can return to escort you home after we have visited."

Knowing Sel and Crank were relying on her, Riona squared her shoulders and raised her chin before locking eyes with her grandfather. She now understood what Crank had meant. She knew this was a test of sorts, and only she could pass it. Instead of bantering, she decided to insult him, a negotiating ploy often successfully employed by her father. "I will not. If you will not freely offer the warmth of your hearth to my mate and guardsman, I will return to Tir na n-Og and tell all who will listen how ill your hospitality is to your kin." Behind her, she heard Sel suck in his breath.

Instead of taking offense, Lord Arawn erupted in laughter, a deep belly roll of amusement. One sleek animal stood in excitement, its tail wagging. It was the size of a wolfhound, its withers reaching his master's waist. Still chuckling at her audacity Lord Arawn replied approvingly, "Done. They may warm themselves, but they may not eat at my table."

"Then I will depart, and tell all who will listen that your stores of grain are low, your fields fallow… that any who seek your hearth will soon starve." Sel placed his hand on the small of her back in a silent warning.

Her grandfather sobered at the threat and pierced her with his crystal blue eyes. "So be it," he replied, this time less amused. He then offered his last challenge. "They may warm themselves and feast at my table, but they may not roam my lands unattended."

Riona was running out of ideas, and she didn't think she could get away with another offending slight to her grandfather's hospitality without angering him. One of the hounds beside her grandfather wagged its tail again, a rhythmic thumping against the ground. Remembering Jen's instructions, she smiled sweetly at her grandfather. She then said, "I will be delighted to stay, only if you grant me the loan of one of your white hounds as a companion for myself and my mate. This will allow them to enjoy the plentiful hunting on your lands during the day, and bring them safely to your hearth before nightfall, in this way they will always be faithfully attended."

Arawn did not answer her, and for a moment she thought she might have failed in her task. Finally with a sigh escaping his lips and a wave of his hand the bridge of rotten planks were restored to wholeness. "Come, I greet you all."

Riona waited for Sel to offer his arm before she moved forward with all the regal air she could muster. She didn't want her grandfather to see just how nervous she was in his presence. Thankfully, Sel covered her shaking hand with his own.

With Sel beside her and Crank behind, the threesome followed Lord Arawn into his stronghold.

Chapter 13

The interior of her grandfather's hall wasn't any grander than the crumbling exterior. Only the basic comforts were provided, and cleanliness was not among them. Though the dust and cobwebs were in abundance, the furnishings were sparse. A few rickety chairs sat in disrepair by the open hearth. Two more where stationed at the end of a roughly hewn table which was flanked by weathered benches. A motley assortment of discarded items were piled in disarray about the hall: weapons, farm tools, cauldrons of various sizes, and some items Riona could not identify.

She hid her surprise and disappointment at the state of her grandfather's home behind a fixed smile. By the time Lard Arawn turned to face them, she was prepared.

"You may take the stuffing from your ears. No whispers will breach these walls." He waited expectantly, his faithful hounds had all settled at his feet next to the flickering flames of the hearth's fire.

With a quick nod from Sel, Riona removed the wool from her other ear. "Grandfather, may I present my mate, Sel, son of Selgi. He is the Queen's Captain." Beside her, Sel bowed to her grandfather.

"Queen Gwenhwyfar sends her greetings." Sel pulled the Queen's message from the pouch at his waist and offered it to Lord Arawn who took it without comment, read it quickly, and then tossed the crumpled greetings into the fire.

"She is most complimentary of you," Lord Arawn told Sel. "We shall see." He then turned and waved them toward the table. "Come, eat and let us know one another." Two hounds rose to follow their master, but one remained, its eyes fixed on Riona.

Riona hesitated, though Crank did not. The unseelie grinned with the mention of food and followed her grandfather to the empty table.

Standing at the head of the table, her grandfather indicated the bench to his left. "Come, Riona, sit beside me."

Noticing her hesitation,Crank cryptically said to her grandfather, "They do not have the sight, as of yet."

"Ah." Arawn nodded in understanding. "Come." He motioned to Riona again with his hand.

With Sel giving a small push to her lower back, Riona moved forward to stand beside the ill constructed, dirty bench. As if tethered by an invisible lead, one lone hound followed and sat his great haunches down at her feet.

"I am not so unfortunate, my dear. Take my hand and I will show you." Lord Arawn held his hand out to her, palm up. "Sel, take her other hand. No need in performing this trick more than once."

Sel laced his fingers with hers. "Done."

"Now, if you would my dear," Her grandfather said, his hand extended towards her, untouched.

Briefly glancing across the table at Crank for reassurance, Riona lifted her hand and placed it in the outstretched hand of the god/king of Annwn. As soon as her hand touched his the tattered appearance of the hall changed. The rough stone walls were now glazed in sheets of gold which sparkled in the candlelight, and instead of the rush covered plank floor she saw a polished and intricately tiled design underfoot. The table before her was polished to a high sheen and laden with copious amounts of food, but what was most astonishing were the abundance of people and servants milling about, all richly dressed and merry. There was lively conversation, musicians, and dancing which she could see but not hear. Turning to her grandfather she asked, "How?"

He smiled broadly at her, pleased that she could now see the richness of his hall. Her grandfather remained simply dressed, though his gold crown was more richly embellished. "My land bridges two worlds. In one, I am entrusted with the souls of the dead. The other is a place of the living. I have neglected the living somewhat," he paused but did not show any embarrassment by this confession. "I live alone, save that of my wife who is," he paused to glance at Sel speculatively, "conveniently absent."

When his blue eyes traveled back to Riona, Lord Arawn's features softened. "Because death has not come to you, one of my lands is hidden from view. But as long as you are in my Keep, I do have the power to allow you to see its wealth. This gift will have to satisfy your curiosity." He bent down and kissed her hand before continuing. "When you step outside these walls, Riona, do not listen to the whispers from the dead. They promise much, more contentment than can be found in the hard task of living. If you are persuaded to linger with them, then you will not be able to return home. And as much as I would enjoy having you in my care, I have a feeling that you, granddaughter, have much to do in your life." He released her hand, but the brilliance of his hall and its residence did not vanish.

Despite her grandfather's gentle manners, Riona's heart pounded a warning in her chest. "I will remember your instructions, grandfather," she replied evenly. Sel lifted her other hand to his lips and grazed her knuckles with a kiss before assisting her onto the cushioned bench.

"Good, Good!" Lord Arawn said approvingly, settling himself in his chair at the head of the banquet table.

Crank tucked-in and greedily loaded an embarrassing

amount of food onto his plate before shoveling it into his mouth. Riona averted her eyes, rather than risk losing her appetite.

"Crank tells me your lands are fat with game," Sel began. He offered Riona a choice portion of venison from his plate. "Perhaps you will honor us with a tour?"

His thoughtful gesture made her smile.

"A fine suggestion, lad," Crank chimed in while waving a carving knife in approval, the pork still dangled from its end where he had stabbed it.

Lord Arawn held back a smirk, his knowing blue eyes traveling from one male-fey to the other before settling on Riona. "My dear, is this your wish as well?"

Riona looked up without glancing at Crank's too full mouth. "Yes, a ride would be lovely. I fear I know little about my own kin."

Lord Arawn studied her for a moment before answering. "Then I will see it done." Leaning back in his chair, he motioned to one of the attendants to approach. "Have my horses readied. We ride after our meal." The servant bowed, mouthed a reply that none heard but Lord Arawn and then hurried off to see the god/king's will done.

Leaning forward Riona anxiously asked, "Pardon my asking, grandfather, are they real horses?"

Lord Arawn laughed loudly, gaining the attention of all in the hall. Every individual stopped to listen with rapt delight to the god/king's good humor. "Yes, my dear." Patting her hand, her grandfather continued to chuckle to himself. "I would not entrust you to anything as unpredictable as a phooka. Though my horses are just as swift, they are well mannered. Never fear."

She blushed and he squeezed her hand. He seemed to want to please her—for now. So far, they were doing well, Riona thought and she began to relax in her grandfather's presence. She had gained them access to her grandfather's Keep, and now they were going to be given a tour of his lands. Tomorrow, Sel and Crank should have enough information to search for Arthur on their own. But Riona wondered how her grandfather had known of the phookas. No one had mentioned them.

* * *

Sel was worried. Except for the initial test to gain entrance, Lord Arawn had not offered any resistance to the Queen's request. Sel knew the contents of her letter. Either the god/king truly wanted to spend time with his granddaughter and thought Arthur too well hidden to be found, or he had already warned Melwas that the Queen was searching again in his realm.

Arawn's first allegiance would be to his ill begotten son. He had, after all, helped Melwas achieve the unseelie throne. Could Riona, as the Queen hoped, gain the god/king's affection as only a girl-child could? Would Lord Arawn let his son fall from power if urged by another of his blood? Sel wasn't certain, despite the fact Riona had, on more than a few occasions, successfully persuaded the unsympathetic into aiding her. But now that they were in Lord Arawn's realm and under his powerful influence, Sel wasn't so sure the Queen's plan didn't border on desperation.

Upon learning the extent to which Gwenhwyfar intended to use Riona, Sel had become torn. The Queen expected him to orchestrate events so that Riona was alone in Lord Arawn's company at every opportunity, essentially putting the princess in danger of incurring the god/king's unpredictable anger. If it had been any other woman, Sel would have done so simply because he trusted his Queen. But Riona wasn't just any woman. She was his contracted mate, and may the gods help him, she was also his true mate. All he need do was say the binding vows and coerce her into doing the same to tie them eternally together; one fate forever entwined upon Arianhrod's silver wheel. How could the Queen ask this of him?

Lord Arawn excused himself for a moment and Riona leaned close and whispered, "You are troubled. Have I done something wrong?"

Sel rubbed her arm reassuringly. "Nay. I am fine." He took the precaution of guarding his thoughts, should she decide to probe his mind. "I do not like having you in danger," he confessed in a whisper. He was pleased she seemed so attuned to his moods. Surely it was a sign their bond was strengthening. "I would have preferred you remain in Tir na n-Og where my guardsmen could watch over you, or at Jen's where Hueil and Sinnie could protect you."

"I am not so frail," she snapped under her breath.

"I do not mean to offend," he started, but refrained from finishing his explanation when he caught sight of Melwas trailing behind Lord Arawn as he returned to his guests.

Crank's and Sel's bench scrapped the floor in unison as they stood, each reaching for their swords. The hound that had attached itself to Riona scrambled out of the way of the moving furniture and then taking sides, bared its teeth at the Unseelie King.

"Hold," Lord Arawn bellowed before anyone's sword could slide free from their scabbards.

Sel stayed his hand, not that he had much choice. Arawn's god powers had frozen his sword arm in place. With the other, Sel pulled Riona behind him in order to better protect her. Melwas took no notice. The Unseelie King's glare was aimed at

Crank alone.

"Let me kill him father," he requested as easily as if ordering a dish from the kitchens.

While still behind Sel's protective arm, Riona said, "No! Please…"

"Shut up girl," Melwas snapped, never turning his head in her direction.

Sel's hand strained for his sword. When his limb would not obey, he growled back, "Hold your bloody tongue, or I will carve it from you."

Without taking his eyes off Crank, Melwas responded with a crude hand gesture.

Crank wasn't wasting his energy on threats. Instead he continued to struggle against the will of Lord Arawn in drawing his twin blades. Sel could see he was making a small amount of progress.

"Enough," Lord Arawn roared. Turning his stormy glare onto his son, he said, "No. You cannot lay a hand on him or any of my guests. The prophecy stands. You made your choice. Live with it or take your place in my court." The god/king then motioned to a servant who nervously approached his master. "Escort my son to the stables. He is leaving." When Melwas hesitated, Lord Arawn reminded him, "You have a court of your own. Go see to it."

Melwas paused to fix each of his father's guests with a hateful stare before reluctantly bowing to his father's wishes. "Yes, Father." But before he turned to leave, he said to his daughter, "Time is on my side, girl. Have no fear, we will be reunited soon." Then he strode from the hall, followed by an anxious servant and several of the darker souls who found Melwas's malevolent nature attractive. One by one they separated from the shadowy corners and recesses to drift out of the hall after the Unseelie King.

With Melwas' departure, Arawn released his hold on Sel and Crank. Sel slid his arm around Riona's middle to keep her close, to give her time to settle her fearful thoughts. Just as his body had shielded hers, Sel's protective instinct had flooded their bonds with the strength of his presence.

Crank forcefully slid his two swords back into their sheaths before lowering his hands. "Bloody fucker," he snarled. If the unseelie thought his words unwise, he didn't show it. "Arawn, for a reasonable god like yourself, I canna figure how that bloody fucker could spring from your bloody pecker. He should be the son of the Morrigan, the twisted bastard."

"Crank, remember where you are," Sel warned. Despite standing close enough to feel the heat of her body, Riona had withdrawn from all of them. Like the souls of the Keep, she was a phantom. Sel rubbed her chilled arm. It worried him how pale she looked.

"Yes, Naf, remember to whom you speak," Lord Arawn warned. His clear blue eyes had become the eerie gray of a brewing thunderstorm.

Righting the bench he had knocked over, Crank mumbled, "I'm just sayin'..."

"Riona, come with me dear. I think a ride is in order." Lord Arawn held his hand out to his granddaughter, his eyes once again a clear blue.

Sel didn't urge her forward. He would rather have taken her in his arms and held her until the dark shadows her father caused could be chased from her mind. That, however, was not a part of the Queen's plan so Sel didn't hold her back when she floated away from him into her grandfather's reach.

Lord Arawn's arm encircled her shoulder protectively before he escorted her from the hall. Sel silently trailed a few feet behind, while Crank mumbled curses under his breath behind him.

"I can hear you, Naf," Lord Arawn called over his shoulder at Crank.

The unseelie clamped his mouth shut, leaving only the companionable clicking of the hound's nails upon the tiled floor to be heard.

Chapter 14

Lord Arawn let Riona, who had not spent much time on horseback, set a leisurely pace for their ride. As often as the path allowed, Sel rode next to her. Crank trailed behind and the hounds darted in and out of their company while hunting along the brush edging the path. None spoke due to the stuffing in their ears, yet some communication occurred. There were periods of frantic gesturing as they happened upon the vast assortment of game Annwn was famous for containing. Sel would have counted the day as a pleasurable one, except for Melwas's appearance and the fact the sun never fully rose into the sky. Instead it seemed determined to remain just above the trees as it skimmed across the horizon. Though excellent conditions for hunting game, the gray light of Annwn would likely depress the spirit, Sel mused.

After riding for several hours and leading them over a large tract of his lands, Lord Arawn turned their party back towards his Keep. He had shown them much, but the god/king had not gone near the cliffs Sel and Crank would need to search. Noticing this, Sel tried to calculate the time it might take to cover the distance. They would start tomorrow, as soon as the sun began its journey across the horizon. Perhaps, he could conjure an excuse to bring Riona with them. Sel still couldn't stifle the conflict that leaving his mate behind in the god's care created for him, even if she was his kin, even if the Queen thought Riona would be safe.

Once their procession reached the backside of the Keep where the stables lay, Sel dismounted and hurried to help Riona down from the sedate bay mare she had been riding. Admittedly he held her a little longer than was necessary, his hands resting on her waist, but she did not pull away. It wasn't until Lord Arawn came to collect her that Sel reluctantly released his hold.

While in the courtyard, Lord Arawn removed the wadding from Riona's ears, dropping the bits of wool onto the cobblestones at their feet. "My dear, let me show you to your rooms."

She gave him a little smile. "Yes, it would be nice to freshen up."

Her biddable reply and accommodating attitude seemed to please her grandfather. It irked Sel for reasons he couldn't name. Tucking her hand into the crook of his arm, Lord Arawn led her into the Keep. Once again, hardly acknowledged, he and Crank trailed behind in the company of Arawn's watchful hounds.

Sel held his tongue until Lord Arawn left him and Riona alone in their assigned accommodations. One hound remained outside the closed door, satisfied to block the threshold's span with his bulk. The bedchamber wasn't large, but it was dazzling to the eye. Precious jewels were embedded within painted murals which served to only further embellish the walls of gold. The exotic depictions were enhanced by wisps of incense curling next to a pillowed pallet. Sandalwood and frankincense drifted on a light breeze, floating lazily out through the brightly colored silks which hung gracefully over the open widows. Sel didn't bother to bolt the door. He suspected that anything he might say in Annwn would be reported back to its king.

She stood near one of the open windows, her back to him. Riona had not asked for his help or shown any outward weakness after the confrontation with her father, but Sel could see the tilt of her chin, the stiffness of her shoulders. He had seen the paleness in her cheeks, though he doubted anyone else had noticed. The day had not been an easy one for her.

"Riona," he began. When she didn't turn her gaze to him he came up behind her and slipped his arms around her waist and whispered into her ear, "Tell me what you need."

"To be someone else," she breathed.

Whether she realized it or not, she leaned her back against his chest. Her body sought comfort, even if her mind refused to reach for him. "If you were not who you are, who would you be?" he asked, taking the opportunity to inhale her scent.

She sighed and her shoulders relaxed. Leaning the back of her head against his shoulder, she said mournfully, "It is only a matter of time. You cannot protect me from him."

Sel smiled into her hair before greedily inhaling her scent once more. "Aye, I can," he told her in all confidence.

She shook her head, her face still turned from him. "The contract will end one day. Perhaps if you and the Queen are pleased enough with me, she will continue to offer her protection. That will have to be enough." There was no self-pity in her reply. She walked out of his embrace and busied herself with washing her hands, arms and face in a basin of water.

Confused by her defeatist attitude, he watched her without comment. Did she not feel the connection between them? Whether he or she wished it or not, they were a true pairing, true mates destined by the gods to share one fate. If he weren't actively hiding the glow of his skin, it would be obvious to anyone who saw him that she was his true mate. And contract or no, he would never let Melwas rule her life again. Once the vows were exchanged, they could not be undone.

"There is no reason to fear returning to your father. I will not let that happen. Once we return home, Riona, I will say the vows."

She angrily whirled to face him. "You cannot."

"Why?"

She sputtered in anger before saying, "You love the Queen."

"Aye, I do."

Riona threw her hands up in frustration. "Keeping my father from regaining his rightful control over me is no reason to tie me to you. And what if I refuse? Will you force me, like the Queen forced you into this contract? I am sick of being a pawn between your Queen and my father!" Her eyes flashed in anger. "I will not bind myself to you," she shouted at him.

Sel's had clamped his jaw tight during her tirade, afraid he would say something in anger he could not take back. Was she insane? "I will not have this argument with you."

"Why?" she yelled.

"Because it is silly, and beneath both of us."

"You… you eedjit!" she screamed at him.

That's when he had to duck. Sel had missed her palming the object, but he got a close look at the bristled brush as it passed inches from his head. Next he dodged what he thought was a goblet. Another careened by his shoulder to smash against the wall behind him when he stepped out of its path.

"Riona, enough!" he shouted, but she ignored him while reaching for larger and larger objects to hurl. When she went for the previously used bowl of water, Sel charged across the room and grabbed for her. The bowl slipped from her grasp and fell to the floor where it hit and cracked, the water splashing over both of them.

"Let go of me," she hissed through gritted teeth.

Sel held her as carefully as he could while she struggled to free herself. Coming to the conclusion that she could not break his hold, Riona's sudden tantrum ended and she became very still in his arms. May the gods give him strength, his blood was on fire. The incense could not cover the intoxicating scent of her skin when he was holding her so closely to him. "Riona. Are you done? I like my head on my shoulders," he chuckled over her head. "Is it safe to let go?"

"Release me," she replied in a calm and queenly manner.

Feeling the fight had gone out of her, he slowly released her. Looking down, he hoped to catch her eye but she would not look at him. So instead, Sel watched the swell of her breasts as they rose and fell with her rapid breathing. "Your grandfather will know we quarreled. Kiss me and forgive me."

"You do not know why you were in the wrong."

"Aye, I do not know why. But I know I am at fault. That's the best I can do." She looked up. Reading the annoyance on her face, he smiled foolishly at her. "Besides, Crank warned you that I needed to be helped along… a bit," he added.

Sighing dramatically, she admitted, "A daunting task."

He lifted her chin and when she did not pull away, he brushed his lips against hers. "I could not abide taking instruction from anyone else." Indulging himself, Sel took the opportunity to kiss her more deeply. As the kiss dragged on, her body softened and Sel had to ignore the pain her more willing demeanor caused him. Their privacy was limited and so he would need to stop soon, or risk a possible interruption by the Lord of the Keep. Reluctantly Sel pulled back. "I fear your grandfather's far reaching influence will keep me from my duty to you," he teased.

She replied with a hint of sarcasm in her voice at his simple jest, "Ah, yes. Lest we forget, your duty."

Reasonably sure she wasn't going to pelt him with anything else, Sel stepped back and shimmered, changing his attire to something less formal than his seelie guard uniform. "You should change into a gown for tonight."

"Do you have a preference in color, style?" she asked waspishly.

By her tone, he could tell she was angry again. The swiftness of her changing emotions was downright frightening. "No." Not knowing what he had said to renew their fight, Sel chose to compliment her. "You are fetching in everything I have seen you in." She looked mildly shocked and a bit confused at his simple confession. Sel was pleased his compliment had worked and he filed it away as a viable strategy to use in the future.

"Go. I need a moment to myself."

Though dismissive, her tone wasn't unpleasant so Sel bowed to her. "As you wish." With a kind of peace restored between them he turned to leave, but his dignified exit was marred by his tripping over the prone body still blocking the door. The massive white hound had made no effort to move out of his way. " Bloody beast," he grumbled, catching balance.

* * *

Despite her anger, she giggled at Sel's ungraceful departure. Riona called the hound to her with a wave of her hand and then crossed to close the door on Sel's handsome face. The man brought out the absolute worst in her. How could he stand there and offer to recite the vows, but not confess that he loved her? Bloody idiot, she thought. As she scanned the destruction her temper had wrought, she had the good grace to feel abashed at breaking her grandfather's things. She only wished her aim had been better, or Sel slower, so that the porcelain and glass hadn't shattered in vain.

Now what? She had used her father's upsetting appearance to no avail. Sel would protect her from her father; she knew this. He would because he loved her. She had felt it, but he seemed determined to keep this truth to himself.

"Duty," she spat the word from her lips. Duty was the shield he hid behind. Duty to the Queen was the excuse to retrieve her, duty to the contract was the excuse to bed her, duty to the gods was the excuse to bind her and keep her. She had to find a way for him to confess his need for her, beyond that of simple duty. But how? The threat her father posed to her, and them, was not sufficient it seemed. Jealousy had moved Sel along once, but who was she to flirt with here. Crank? She couldn't picture it.

Riona prepared for the evening meal, knowing Sel was just beyond the door waiting for her. She shimmered, donning a gown much like the ones she had seen on the ghostly residents of the Keep. The floor length blue silk was the same hue as her grandfather's eyes. She added a simple draped belt at the waist. The voluminously long bell sleeves were impractical but in keeping with the fashion she had witnessed in the hall earlier. It would do, she decided. "It would be nice to have a trinket or two for the neckline," she told the hound.

The beast looked up, but did not comment.

"Well, it is the best I can do, under the circumstances," she said continuing her one-sided conversation. Giving the room another glance, she went and retrieved the bristled brush from the far wall and gave her hair a bit of attention before returning the item to its original resting place on the side table. There, in the cracked bowl's vacated home lay a jeweled necklace with matching ear bobs. The blue of the sapphires matched her gown perfectly. It seemed Sel had been correct, her grandfather had indeed been watching and listening. "Thank you, grandfather," she said, knowing he would hear her.

She donned his generous gift and motioned for her grandfather's hound to follow her to the door. It stood, wagging its massive tail approvingly before accompanying her.

Opening the door, Riona found Sel leaning against the wall. She had somehow known he would be there and realized she found his constant presence as comforting as she found it irritating.

If her attire was to his liking, he didn't profess it. No compliment dripped from his tongue, which surprisingly disappointed her. Instead, Sel graced her with a shallow bow and thrust his arm at her so he could escort her down to her grandfather's hall. Her captain it seemed was a man of few words, and more times than not, the wrong ones she decided.

Stowing away her irrational disappointment, Riona moved to lay her hand on his arm. But before she could, the hound wedged himself between them and no amount of shoving on Sel's part could get the beast to relinquish his position by her side.

"Sorry, Sel. It seems you have been replaced for now." Riona smiled sweetly up at him.

Sel didn't look pleased, but after a moment he silently waved her forward, and fell into step behind her. "Bloody beast," he muttered to himself.

Riona patted the hound's white head and smiled to herself. Perhaps the key to unlocking Sel's heart lay in her carefully played withdrawal. She had seen her mother deny her father, but only just. Sometimes desire burns brighter when missed for a time. But could she stay true to such a plan? Honestly, Riona didn't know. And to think, only few days ago she had run from him as if her life had depended on it. He pursued her then, perhaps a chase was exactly what was needed now.

"My dear," her grandfather called from the foot of the staircase. "You look lovely."

The hound bound down the last few steps and padded over to the hearth to make itself comfortable.

"Thank you, grandfather. These are lovely." She laid her hand on the necklace at her throat.

"You shouldn't have," Sel said from behind her.

"Oh, I think you will indulge me, Captain." Lord Arawn held out his hand for Riona to take. Unlike that morning, he had dressed himself richly. He wore fabrics of gold and red in a fashion that complimented his broad shoulders and trim waist. Even the jewels in his crown had been changed to rubies to match his evening attire.

"You are most kind, grandfather," Riona informed him. Smiling brightly, she let him lead her to the banquet table. The hall was already full of silent revelers, dancing and singing. It was disconcerting to see someone laugh, but not have the joy of hearing it.

"Think nothing of it." He kissed her knuckles before calling over his shoulder, "Captain, do you not think your mate beautiful tonight." He winked at Riona.

"Aye, I do," Sel dutifully replied.

"Next time you should tell her," Arawn instructed the captain. When their little procession reached the table, her grandfather relinquished her hand and moved to speak with a servant.

Sel came up beside her and placed his hand on her lower back in a show of ownership. She ignored it, and him. Scanning the hall, Riona could not find Crank. "Where is Crank?" she asked her grandfather.

"Sit, my dear. I have never known Naf to miss a meal," Arawn told her. "He will be along shortly, after he has finished riffling through my things. He searches for a map, I think."

Though her grandfather's casual statement alarmed her, neither Sel nor her grandfather seemed surprised by Crank's actions. "I am sorry he abuses your hospitality, grandfather,"

Lord Arawn took his seat at the head of the banquet table. "It was expected. Was it not Captain?"

"He is predictably rude," Sel admitted.

"And brash," Lord Arawn supplied. "Come, sit. Do not worry yourselves. He is on his way now," he told them.

Riona looked to Sel, who gave her a simple nod of assurance, before she took a seat to the right of her grandfather. "You know everything that goes on in your Keep?" she asked.

"Aye, my dear. I am afraid I do." He patted her hand but did not elaborate further.

Riona kept her mouth shut, and hoped the god sitting beside her could not read her thoughts as well. She was grateful when Crank/Naf arrived.

"Lord Arawn, I have taken the liberty of studying some of your maps so Sel and I are more familiar with the lay of the land. Never fancied the idea being lost."

"Ah," Lord Arawn replied with a hint of curiosity or amusement at Crank's professed reason. "And what are you two hunting for?" he pleasantly asked.

"Game of course." Crank grinned back, completely at ease with lying.

"Ah, I see." Lord Arawn turned to Riona. "Do you plan to ride out tomorrow, my dear?"

"Come, you will enjoy it," Sel insisted.

His statement had all the charm of an order to her—an order Riona had every intention of ignoring. She smiled sweetly at Sel, then turned to her grandfather. "Nay, I have come to spend time with you. If you will not mind my presence, that is, grandfather. I do not wish to be a burden or stay you from your affairs." She could feel Sel stiffen beside her. He wasn't happy with her refusal, and that greatly pleased her.

"What a delightful child you are. I would be honored to have you by my side." Lord Arawn's eyes sparkled with amusement. "Now, with tomorrow's plans laid, come, enjoy the bounty of my house." He motioned toward the scrumptious dishes that suddenly appeared before them.

Crank didn't hesitate in availing himself of Lord Arawn's hospitality, nor did Riona this time. Only Sel was slow to partake of the table's abundance.

The conversation was brisk, and the food endless. Riona could declare she was truly and contently stuffed by the time she finally pushed back from her grandfather's table. The only strangeness to the dining had been the entertainment, which for their safety had been performed completely without sound. The acrobats and jugglers she could appreciate, but Riona had longed to hear the harpist and the singing. She sighed, but otherwise tried not to show her disappointment.

Her grandfather leaned forward and whispered, "Believe me, my dear. It is better this way."

She turned to him. "Do not think me ungrateful. I have seen much in the way of spectacle."

"You are a good child, and it warms my heart that you are here." Lord Arawn smiled again at her.

She grinned back, her fear of him having left her completely. "I am sorry to have waited so long in coming to visit," she honestly told him.

"Do not concern yourself with such things," he replied.

Her grandfather then pointed to a new batch of performers taking the impromptu stage, and so Riona turned her attention away from him.

Lord Arawn's voice whispered, "But this is not the time to speak of regrets." He was so close to her ear Riona could feel the warmth of his breath against her skin and smell the sweet spices that flavored the pork they had dined on. "There will be time later to talk of more serious things. Yes?"

Riona cut her eyes towards him to answer, but discovered that he was several feet away, leaning back into the cushions of his chair while watching the new performers. He could not have been so close. Startled, Riona forgot what she had intended to say.

"Lord Arawn," Crank interrupted. "When I do grace you with my eternal presence," Crank paused to belch loudly. "If you could put in a good word for me with that wench over there." The unseelie pointed to a buxom female soul, pretty but casual in her state of dress. Her gown, having slipped off one shoulder, was now displaying a healthy portion of her overly large breast.

Arawn chuckled. "Naf, if you are lucky enough to enter my lands again, I will do my best. But, she is a handful," he warned. "Or so I am told," he amended after glancing at Riona.

"More than a handful, by the look of her," Crank said, laughing at his own jest. "A man would need six hands, me thinks." Crank and Arawn shared an appreciative grin, one male to another. Riona pretended the conversation between her grandfather and Crank didn't embarrass her. She was use to such things in the Unseelie Court, but she had not thought to find such concerns in the underworld.

Scraping his chair loudly on the tiled floor, Sel stood.

"Lord Arawn."

Reluctantly turning from his and Crank's conversation, Lord Arawn's attention turned toward Sel. "Captain."

Placing his hand on Riona's shoulder, Sel announced, "My apologies for cutting the evening short, but Riona as you know, must take her rest."

Riona glared up at Sel's tight jaw. "You make me sound like a child."

"You are, compared to the rest of us," Sel told her, his eyes never leaving her grandfather.

After a tense moment, her grandfather said, "My dear, Sel is right. I forget your limits, and I would have you well taken take of while in my lands." Lord Arawn then rose from his chair. After a weary sigh Crank also reluctantly stood.

Left with little choice, Riona pushed back and rose from her seat. "Grandfather, I look forward to the morning," she said brightly. Right on cue, Sel captured her elbow.

"As do I, my dear," her grandfather replied cordially.

She gave her grandfather a respectful nod then turned to the fey who felt more like her keeper than her mate. She said tightly, "I can find my way alone. Stay and enjoy the company. I am sure you and Lord Arawn have much to discuss." She didn't have to see Crank to know he found her forced politeness amusing.

"I will see you safely to our rooms," Sel smoothy replied.

"It is not necessary." Riona laid her hand on the white hound's head beside her. "I have an escort," she told him.

"Then you shall have two. All the better," Sel almost growled back.

She could have pushed the captain further, but Sel's grip on her elbow was becoming painful and she detested making a scene in front of anyone, much less her god-grandfather. "As you wish," she said, keeping a tight lid on her temper. Riona was sure her jaw would crack with the effort of maintaining her pleasant smile.

When they were halfway to the steps, Crank called after them, "Take your time, lad."

If it wasn't for Sel's controlling grip on her elbow, Riona would have whipped off one of her slippers and thrown it at the irritating unseelie.

Chapter 15

"You have delivered me to our rooms. Now go away Sel," she said more kindly than she felt. Riona had her back to him when she heard the metal bolt slide home, locking them in. All the broken items had been restored to wholeness and the room set to rights by unseen hands.

"Riona, tell your grandfather you changed your mind and wish to ride with us tomorrow."

Again his request sounded like an order. Her first inclination was to flatly refuse him but when she turned to confront him the worried expression on his face made her reconsider. "Sel, I do not think I am in any danger from my grandfather. If anything, you and Crank are."

"You must not anger him. He has power that neither you nor I can fathom." Sel crossed the distance between them.

"I have no intention of doing any such thing. I have not forgotten the power he wields."

"I still would prefer for you to come with us in the morning." His finger traced downward along the neckline of her gown until his hand came to rest at the swell of her breast.

Through the fine fabric of his clothes, she could feel the heat radiating off his body and had to fight to keep herself from leaning into the safety that his embrace would offer. Riona took a deliberate step back from him and he dropped his hand back down to his side. "We will talk of this in the morning. As you have told my grandfather, I must take my rest. Go back downstairs. The hound guards the door."

Confusion clouded the green of his eyes. "You do not wish me to stay?"

"Not with my grandfather's eyes on us, no." Not liking her reply, Riona watched as he unconsciously gritted his teeth.

"Riona, I can provide us with a ward for privacy."

"Perhaps tomorrow, Sel. For now, let me rest. There is much I have had to adjust to recently," Riona weakly argued, all the time knowing that if he was intent on bedding her she would not have the resolve to stop him. Already her body was anticipating his touch. Hoping he would take the hint and leave, Riona moved toward the unconventional bed and stepped out of her slippers. Instead of taking offense at her polite refusal and quitting the room, he seemed a statue, frozen and mute, perfectly happy to simply watch her.

She removed her grandfather's necklace next, and then the jewels at her ears. Riona turned towards him, one eyebrow lifted. "Will you take this back down to my grandfather? Tell him that I would not wish for such exquisite stones to be misplaced here in the room. They are much safer with him." Riona held the jewels out to him, sapphires dripping from her fingers like raindrops. Her request got him moving and he crossed the floor to take them from her.

Capturing her hand in his, Sel kissed her knuckles before relieving her of Arawn's gift. When he kissed her empty palm, her stomach did a happy little flip. Riona swallowed uncomfortably, her mind warring with her body's desires.

"Call me if you find sleep slow in coming," he whispered thickly. His green eyes found hers and held. The fevered light blazing within promised so much that it nearly collapsed her resolve.

All Riona could do was mutely nod. She dare not encourage him further. It had only taken one smoldering look from her captain for her body to go up in flames.

Finally, relinquishing her hand, he said, "As you wish." He then slowly turned and left her. This time stepping over the resting hound barring the doorway.

* * *

Sel returned to Arawn's hall, to find Crank and the god/king entertaining each other with tales of past exploits. Crank was single-mindedly drinking his way through their host's cellar, but Arawn didn't seem to care as he listened to Crank's graphic description of a pair of twins he had had occasion to bed. As Sel listened to Crank's booming voice, he was acutely aware that this was the last place he wanted to be. His mind and heart had not left Riona's company, and the unnecessary physical separation she wanted pained him.

Both Lord Arawn and Crank burst out laughing, breaking into Sel's sullen thoughts.

Catching his eye, Crank called, "Sel, come. Let us makes plans for our hunt on the morrow." He waved a scrolled piece of parchment at him in encouragement.

Sel moved away from the base of the stairs toward an animated Crank. Lord Arawn said nothing in protest, though Sel suspected the god/king knew of their ruse.

"What game do you crave? Shall it be stag or boar?" Sel asked Crank with little enthusiasm, the specters parting before him like smoke in a strong wind as he crossed the hall.

Arawn raised an eyebrow, but again the god/king said nothing to dispute the Queen's cover story.

Crank grinned lopsidedly at Sel and unfurled the parchment, revealing a map of Annwn. An exact duplicate of the same map resided with the Queen. Sel had not thought to ask how she had come to possess it. Perhaps Crank had taken its twin the last time he was in Lord Arawn's realm.

Moving closer to the recently cleared banquet table, Sel studied the artist's rendering of Arawn's kingdom. For all intents and purposes, Annwn was an island, surrounded by water that lapped upon silvery beaches except in the south where swamps led into pungent marshlands none would want to traverse. The mountains he and Crank sought were centrally located, and Sel judged the distance to be a two hour's hard ride north of Arawn's Keep. After that, Crank and he would be constricted to traveling on foot the remainder of the way. Once they located the cave they sought and found Arthur, Sel would have to ride back for Riona. Crank and Arthur would travel east, straight for the beach and gateway back to Tir na n-Og. The Queen was certain of Arthur's location this time, and now that they possessed the key to Arthur's prison. The rescue of the Absent King did not worry Sel—getting out of Annwn with Riona did though.

While pointing to a meadow in sight of the mountain they aimed to search, Crank suggested, "I saw a fat herd of deer just north of here. Why don't we start there and see what fortune can be had."

"So be it," Sel replied flatly. "I would prefer Riona to hunt with us, but she has refused me."

Crank snickered but did not comment on what he obviously thought was a lovers' quarrel.

"There seems to be some discord between the two of you," Lord Arawn observed from his seat.

Sel, leaning over the table, glanced up from his inspection of the map. Lord Arawn was studying him as intently as Sel had been examining the terrain of the god/king's lands. "Aye, but nothing of consequence. We are newly contracted."

Lord Arawn did not argue, nor did he press his inquiry. "Well, if all is settled, I will leave you til the morrow. I trust my hounds will keep you out of trouble," he said, looking pointedly at Crank.

With his hand laid over his heart Crank assured him, "Lord Arawn, mischief is the furthest thing from my mind." It would have been believable except the unseelie was never quite able to wipe the smirk from his lips. "There is not a wench to be had in this ghostly Keep of yours, so I will simply have to make due with your cellar's stores. As long as the wine flows, I dinna plan to leave this hall til daybreak."

Lord Arawn pushed his chair back and stood. "Impressive plan, Naf. I wish you well." The god/king smiled then dismissed Crank's unseelie antics and turned his full attention back to Sel. "Sel…"

Sel pushed off the table's top so he stood facing their host. "Lord Arawn."

"Riona will be safe in my care."

However doting Lord Arawn appeared to be today, none of it would matter once Arthur was removed from Annwn. "It is not your care that worries me," Sel lied. Melwas would fall, and Sel could not bring himself to trust Riona's safety to anyone, even to a god's budding affection.

Arawn's blue eyes turned dark gray. "Let us speak plainly then."

Sel nodded. "I would prefer it."

"Riona is the key, not the brass you wear around your neck. This fact has eluded you, Sel. Your Queen has manipulated events, dared even to step across time to tilt this game in her favor. I do not want to see Riona a casualty of her or Melwas's fight."

"Nor do I," Sel said, his jaw tightened. He did not fully understand what Lord Arawn meant by Riona being the key, but Sel would give his life to protect his mate.

"Good, then we are agreed."

Lord Arawn knew they were here for Arthur; Sel had suspected as much. He felt better not having to maintain the ruse. Sel nodded. "Aye, agreed. Riona is an innocent in all this."

"Sel, you should know by now… there is no such animal as innocence. You are your Queen's hound, here to do her fetching. Thanks to Blodeuwedd's infernal meddling, Riona's fate is now tied to yours. "

"Not entirely," Sel confessed. He had not bound her to him with the vows. He couldn't stop the words from tumbling through his mind, but he could refrain from saying them out loud if it meant keeping Riona safe.

"Perhaps," Arawn speculated, "in the meantime, Riona will stay with me while you search."

"She should come with us," Sel pressed.

"It will be too dangerous tomorrow. She is better off here."

"Dangerous how?" Crank asked.

Arawn ignored Crank's question, his stormy eyes never leaving Sel's face.

"Do you take your son's side in this?" Sel asked.

Arawn shook his head slowly, "No."

"What is this prophecy you spoke of? Queen Gwenhwyfar has not mentioned one," Sel pressed again.

"If she has not explained, I suspect there is a reason." The god/king snapped angrily, then he sighed and said more calmly, "Sel, Melwas made his choice. I will not protect him nor will I betray him." Lord Arawn held up one finger to stop Crank from speaking. "Riona is another matter. My granddaughter did not choose to be tied to you; Blodeuwedd picked her. Why I do not know, but it was ill conceived on the goddess's part," he finished.

"I think we understand one another," Sel told Lord Arawn.

"Excellent." Then Arawn turned to an impatient Crank. "You will get your chance, Naf—but I do not think you will like the outcome."

The muscles in Crank's neck bulged, but the unseelie held his tongue. Whether that was due to the self-restraint of an ancient or the imposed will of Arawn, Sel couldn't tell.

Pleased with Crank's silence, Arawn turned his gaze to Sel once more. "Be gone as soon as the sun rises, and return by sunset. Riona will stay with me… for now."

Sel didn't like leaving her behind—not at all. "Then I will stay as well. Crank will go out alone." Sel knew he was disregarding his duty to his Queen, but he would not leave his mate to face the unknown alone. Riona was not trained in warcraft like Sinnie, nor did she have any special inherited power that could protect her from Lord Arawn, or from Melwas should the bastard return.

"Then we are at an impasse," Lord Arawn concluded.

"So it seems," Sel responded.

The god/king bid them goodnight. "I will leave you to your planning. I have duties to attend to." Lord Arawn turned to leave, a flash of a smile taking form as he disappeared along with all the ghostly specters in the hall.

"That went well, laddie," Crank said once they were alone. Pouring two drinks, he set one glass in front of Sel. "You'd leave me to hunt tomorrow without any hope of finding him… because we both know, I dinna have Gwen's vision buried in my wee skull. Lord Arawn will warn Melwas, if he hasn't already. And we are told we carry the wrong key to unlock my King's prison."

"Crank, I will not leave her behind. She cannot defend herself!" Sel snapped.

Unfazed by Sel's ill humor, Crank downed his drink and poured himself another one. "I think you are making a mistake. Riona knows her abilities better than you, laddie. I guarantee she can handle him better than the both of us."

Reaching for his drink, Sel swirled the amber colored liquid in the cup. "And if Melwas should return while we are gone. She is afraid of him, Crank, and with good cause."

"I have known Lord Arawn longer than you. He is sincere in his affection for the girl. I believe he speaks truly," Crank gently counseled.

Sel drank the contents of his cup and welcomed the burning to his throat and chest. If only he could distance himself from the uneasy feelings that plagued him. He leaned forward onto the table once more, the map of Annwn taunting him.

"Sel, you are her bloody captain. Gwen has given you orders and you have dragged me along in this bloody business. Do your duty, lad."

"I am trying, you irritating bastard." Sel pushed back from the table and began to pace back and forth. "I know my duty. I do not have to be reminded of it by someone who abandoned his own," he barked at Crank. Sel paused in his pacing to look longingly at the stairs leading up to were she slept. He was beginning to understand the dilemma Hueil had faced in his courtship of Sinnie.

"Sel, sit and have another drink with me." Crank placed a newly filled cup across the table. "Respect her choice, lad. A woman will always reward your faith in them. You'll see, I promise." Crank did not offer any more counsel, instead he refilled his own glass.

Reluctantly Sel returned to the banquet table. Looking down at the displayed map, Sel knew he would leave Riona behind by the time morning rolled around—and he hated himself for it. He would do his duty to his Queen, but for the first time in his life Sel would resent her for it.

Chapter 16

Riona remained in her assigned bedchamber long after daybreak. She told herself that she was being cautious in the game they now played. She hoped her calculated withdrawal would prompt Sel to admit his true feelings. The tried and true ploy had on many occasions worked well for her mother, but whatever comfort Riona could take from that knowledge hadn't allowed her sleep. Instead she had spent most of the evening fretting over the soundness of her rash plan to manipulate Sel. After picking a fight with him the night before, he had chosen to pass the night elsewhere.

She should have made an appearance this morning, if only briefly, Riona decided. So he would not think her angry or sullen, she should have seen him off or bid him good hunting. Suddenly, Riona felt certain she was playing the role of temptress rather badly. Groaning with frustration, she quit the safety of the bedroom and nearly tripped over one of her grandfather's white hounds in the process. It must have laid claim to the threshold some time in the night.

“Come along beastie,” she commanded. Its great head rose from its lazy repose. It then heaved itself to its feet to escort her down the stairs.

With the hound at her heels, Riona rounded the last landing and came to a complete stop. In the hall below, her father and grandfather stood together talking. Another unseelie, this one a member of the warrior caste, stood just off to the side with legs apart and arms crossed over a tattooed adorned chest in a casual display of readiness and strength. Looking up, he noticed her but did not alert her father to her arrival. A slow smile spread across the unseelie's face, a predator's leer meant to unsettle her.

Squaring her shoulders, Riona descended the last few steps on shaky legs. When the conversation ceased and all eyes turned towards her, Riona thrust her chin up slightly and issued a cheery greeting for the sake of appearances, "Good morning, grandfather." She gave her father a respectful nod, altogether ignoring the stranger in the room.

"I see you did not ride out with Sel and Naf, my dear," Lord Arawn replied.

"She is no rider," Melwas reminded the room.

"A skill easily learned," the stranger said, coming to her defense. Melwas glanced at the unseelie as if just remembering he was there.

Smiling a bit too broadly, Melwas glanced back at Riona and announced, "Daughter, I do not think you have met a most loyal unseelie. This is Aeron, a rather remarkable young warrior and one I wish you to know better."

Riona drew within arms reach of her grandfather and reluctantly acknowledged the unseelie. Aeron bowed, bending at the waist, though his eyes continued to greedily catalog her attributes.

Drawing nearer still to her grandfather, Riona kissed his mahogany cheek in greeting before dutifully addressing the unseelie, "It is fortunate for my father that such a warrior pledges his loyalty to him." She then glanced at her grandfather. He smiled at her reassuringly, but he did not seem inclined to send the unwanted visitors away.

"I am the fortunate one, Princess," Aeron said. "You are as lovely as your father professes."

Wanting to put Aeron in his place Riona asked, "Why would my appearance concern you?" For good measure, she raised one haughty eyebrow in his direction.

Her father was quick to answer for Aeron. "Daughter, I intend to tie our house with Aeron's after this disagreeable contract with the Seelie Captain is ended."

"But that could take centuries, father. Surely this can wait," Riona countered, but immediately regretted her rash reply when the all too familiar dark and malevolent cloud passed over her father's features. "Pardon, my confusion. I only wish to serve you and our house honorably," she amended.

"A noble sentiment, my dear," Lord Arawn said, patting her shoulder. "I wouldn't worry. Perhaps my son is only thinking of the future," he mused while looking rather pointedly at Melwas, his blue eyes darkening.

"Of course," Melwas readily agreed. "But one never knows. So much has become uncertain of late, father." He then turned to Riona once again, "We do not want a repeat of your disastrous contract with Calcus. Do we daughter?"

Riona swallowed the fear which had been steadily building. "No, of course not." He made it sound like she had been to blame for Calcus's bid for the unseelie throne and his subsequent death.

Melwas smiled indulgently at Riona's biddable reply. It was a practiced smile, much used to bend others to his will.

Aeron relaxed his warrior's stance and took a few measured steps toward Riona. "Princess, I think your father has business to discuss with Lord Arawn. The King and I will return shortly to Tir na n-Og. Will you walk with me and let me elaborate on your father's wishes?" He extended his arm towards her. "There is no reason to fear."

"Do not leave the Keep's walls," Lord Arawn sternly warned.

Not liking the turn of events but unable to refuse in front of her father, Riona laid her hand on Aeron's arm. "Of course not, grandfather," Riona said thankfully. She then crooked a finger at one of her grandfather's two remaining hounds, the third hound having already departed the Keep at dawn with Sel and Crank.

Firmly pinning her hand to his forearm, Aeron led her from the hall as one white hound trailed behind. Every instinct told Riona that despite Aeron's good manners, he was her father's weapon and she should be cautious.

"We are out of their range of hearing, I should think. What plotting has my father involved you in?" Riona asked as soon as they were beyond the hall. Aeron paused briefly to smile down at her. He then deftly kicked a door closed behind them, detaining her grandfather's watchful hound on the opposite side. The courtyard lay before them, and beyond that the stables and the outer wall. As they continued to stroll forward Riona tried to free her hand without giving offense but could not manage it, so she slowed their progress by slowing her pace.

Aeron ignored her question until they were in the middle of the courtyard. "Princess," he began in not an unpleasant voice, "it is a shame you have to endure that seelie's touch." He then shook his dark head and tsked more to himself than for her predicament. "An unseelie princess contracted to ride a seelie's cock and bear a child of tainted blood is truly criminal. But never fear, your father and I have plans to break this abomination of a contract." He patted her hand reassuringly. "It was never what your father had intended for you. As you undoubtedly know, as a princess, your duty is to secure alliances and bear kings for the Unseelie Court," Aeron lectured. "But instead, because of this feud between your father and the Seelie Queen you are tasked with spreading your delicate thighs for a seelie's limp cock, whose seed could not give rise to a warrior—much less a son."

Aeron's crass monologue was so shocking that Riona was momentarily rendered mute. Gone were Aeron's gracious manners, and in their place stood a crude and ruthless serpent. "Release my hand," she ordered when outrage restored her voice. But Aeron's grip tightened and he pretended not to hear, her carefully contained fear seeped out to reflect itself in her eyes.

Aeron finally drew to a halt near the outer wall of the Keep. "I first saw you when you were under the protection of Calcus, your last intended, and I have not been able to forget it. Do you know what havoc you have caused me, Riona?" Looming over her, he smiled hungrily down at her. "I have prided myself on my ability to resist temptation. I do not sway easily to a woman's charms, at least not as readily as others who have crossed your path. That is how I knew you were special, Riona. Your mother is infamous for her charms and talents as a bed-mate, but I fear she has lost the freshness that her daughter possesses."

Riona's stomach rolled violently. "I do not know what you mean," she stammered, swallowing the sudden nausea his words caused her. She desperately wanted to return to the hall, but he wouldn't relinquish her hand and she didn't possess the physically strength to fight him. For a warrior near her own age, Aeron's command of his powers was frightening. It swirled around them like a barely contained creature.

Aeron gave a mocking shake of his head. "I tell you the truth of it because one day, Riona, I will lay between your thighs. You have your mother's lust about you. Every fey can smell it on you. I can smell it on you."

Riona's free palm slapped the grinning cheek with all the force she could muster. When his cold eyes turned to her again, she began to struggle against him in earnest.

Aeron's grip tightened painfully on her hand and wrist before she could claim any real progress in her fight. He smiled, delighted by her resistance, right before ruthlessly pushing his way into her mind—an inexcusable violation.

The swiftness of his attack took Riona by surprise and before she could gather the power to throw him out, he dominated her will, bringing her struggled retreat to a temporary end.

"Don't fight my control or I will make it hurt," Aeron warned her, then one eyebrow rose as if intrigued. "Or are you like your mother in that as well?" He caressed her neck and leaned in to whisper into her hear. "When I first saw you, my cock grew as hard as stone. On that day I took a solemn vow that one day I would have you spread your legs for me. Do you know Calcus would have given you to me, after he whelped a few pups off of you?" Aeron extended her arm and placed her hand on his bulging leather pants. "I was willing to wait, Riona." He then kissed her paralyzed cheek and inhaled the scent of her skin deeply into his lungs. "But now, your father has come to my aid. He sees the advantages in giving you to me." He removed her hand from his groin but did not release her wrist. With his other hand he grazed her breasts, then lowered it further down her torso to the juncture between her thighs.

As horrified as Riona was at his free roaming hands, the battle she now waged was mental not physical. Every time she tried to push his presence and will from her mind, Aeron mentally lashed her body—the sting of a whip minus the marks to her flesh. The shock of the pain left her panting. Fleetingly, it occurred to her that Aeron would not have been able to breech her mind's defenses if only she and Sel had exchanged the vows. But out of stupidity and pride she had refused to let him, choosing manipulation over trusting the natural course of events. This was her fault. She'd left an opening for her father's poisoned weapon to strike.

"The pain can stop. I can just as easily turn it to pleasure, Riona," he murmured against her ear while slowly lifting the hem of her dress. "I have longed to have you moan for me, Princess."

If Riona thought his initial intrusion into her mind brutal, she had been mistaken. In complete control of her body, Aeron's fantasies and will now swamped her, showing her one revolting image after another. The lurid acts parading across her consciousness terrified her. Many were beyond her realm of experience and the depictions were so vivid that her body responded to his lust by contracting around his unwanted fingers when they shoved past her now wet folds. Terrified he would continue to molest her, or something worse such as abducting her from the Keep, tears leaked out the corners of her eyes.

Gratified with her body's response, Aeron withdrew his fingers.

"Stop this," she whimpered, her voice huskier than she wished. Riona watched him taste his two wet fingers.

"Riona, the sooner you rid yourself of that seelie, the sooner you can be the courtesan you were born to be." He presented the two just licked fingers to her nose. "This is who you are—a courtesan. You are a magnificent creature of lust. It is in your blood. I speak truly; it is who you are, Riona."

A small part of her heart recognized the truth of his claim. Tears were now flowing freely down her cheeks. "Sel will kill you," she promised him. Or one day she would, Riona vowed.

"Shhh," he coaxed, brushing away the tears. "No, Princess. He will gladly be rid of you." Aeron lessened his grip on her mind and eased his hold on her arm. "He will find the images I planted in your mind and know you for the disloyal unseelie that you are. He will not abide another cuckolding him. Once was enough, I think," he said with schooled gentleness.

"We... we did not," she protested. Sel had been cuckolded before? Brianna, her mind concluded. She was surely going to be sick, she thought.

"Do you think he will believe you, Riona?" Aeron snickered, smiling knowingly down at her. "You... the child of Melwas, the Butcher, and Naria, the greatest courtesan the unseelie have ever had? Believe me, she's earned the title honestly by fucking a whole army behind Melwas' back."

By this point, Aeron had completely retreated from her mind but the damage had been done. The images of her and Aeron were deeply lodged, and his physical intrusion had only cemented the false memories into place. What was she going to do? Sel would not forgive her. Would he believe her? Her heart sank, knowing he would not. Why should he?

"Princess, given time you will see I am your only option. Your father wants this, and it would be unwise to refuse him. He has already sent Naria away for betraying him with Calcus."

Riona didn't have much love for her mother, but her father was deadly when crossed. "Is she dead?" she asked.

"No, but she is regretting her nature right about now." Aeron chuckled to himself and then told her, "It would not be wise to cross Melwas, not after your mother's betrayal."

He caressed her cheek and Riona couldn't stop herself from flinching.

Impatience bloomed behind Aeron's carefully crafted civility and his voice hardened. "When the captain finds out about our dalliance, he might decide to lock you away like he did his first mate. Do not let this happen. When you leave your grandfather's lands, slip away from the captain and go to your father's hall. I will come for you. Together, your father and I will erase the contract you were tricked into by the Queen, and we will begin ours." Aeron forced her chin up so he could clearly see her face and she his. "You are an unseelie, Riona. Your place is with your own kind. I will not hold this seelie contract against you, like many of our kind might. Remember, I will be waiting. Do not disappoint me." Confidently, he leaned down and kissed her unmoving lips before telling her, "Your father comes. He will clear any lingering doubts you may be entertaining in that silly head of yours." He released his grip on her chin, and then bowed to the fast approaching Unseelie King.

Riona did not turn to greet her father, but stood like a condemned woman, waiting for the final blow to descend.

"Go ready the horses, Aeron," Melwas shouted.

"Yes, my King." Aeron winked at her then turned toward the stables, leaving her alone with her father.

Snatching her chin with one large hand, Melwas inspected her face. "Do as you are told or you will share a similar fate to that of your mother."

"What did you do to her?" Riona quietly asked, knowing her father would have been disappointed if she had not, and would have made a point of telling her anyway in order to frighten her beyond thinking.

"When she is not locked up, she is servicing who I want, when I want. She is no more to me than the enchanted she is stabled with. That, daughter, is the price for betraying me."

"Why did you not kill her?"

"I do not like to lose talent, Riona. Your mother has her talents... as do you. You live at my discretion. You were born to create advantageous alliances where I deem. And to that end, you will spread your legs and bear offspring like any well bred mare, or I will find another benefit for your long overlooked gifts."

"Yes, father." Her father lectured on but Riona didn't listen closely. He had often times told her how insignificant her life was. The sting of his hand across her cheek brought her back from the stillness she had retreated to.

"It is my business to know who is between your thighs," he was telling her. "And I know that damn Seelie Captain was the first, but be assured daughter that there are better cocks than those in the Seelie Court."

"Yes, father." She saw Aeron had returned with two saddled horses, and was smugly looking on as she was made to submit to her father's wishes.

"Good, I am pleased you understand your place. Now off with you, get that bastard to dissolve the contract and return home to me." Turning on his heel, Melwas walked away and mounted his steed.

Once the King was astride, Aeron beseeched him, "Lord, a moment more with your daughter."

Turning his horse towards the gate, Melwas called over his shoulder, "Be quick about it."

Again Aeron filled her vision, this time tethered to a nervous horse. Riona took an unconscious step backward, and gathered all her powers to keep him from entering her mind once more. From across the courtyard she could hear the padded feet of the just freed hound as it bounded towards them. Aeron did not attempt to touch her this time.

"I look forward to our reunion. You are a prize, Riona, and one I would keep close. Until then, my princess." Aeron bowed low, a courtly gesture meant only to placate her approaching grandfather.

She watched him swing up onto the prancing animal and hastily dash off to catch her father, who was already outside the outer walls of the Keep.

Her grandfather reached her side just as Aeron passed beyond the gate. "Riona, why bar me from the courtyard?" The hound followed the galloping horse for a hundred yards or more before turning back.

"I did not, grandfather. Aeron detained the hound."

"The hounds are my eyes, child. Through them I know what is afoot in my own home," her grandfather gently explained.

"Well, you missed much then," Riona replied, not caring if she gave offense. She was sick with despair and dread at her abruptly changing fate.

She didn't resist when her grandfather put his arm around her shoulders to guide her back inside. Riona also ignored the hound when it licked at her hand, its worried whimper only succeeded in encouraging a self pitying tear. She wiped it quickly away. This was her life. It had always been thus; she would never be free of it. Sel would respond as her father and Aeron intended. He admitted to not trusting her. Unable or unwilling to profess any love for her, Riona had no reason to think he wouldn't set her aside, or worse, revert to treating her as an unwanted burden fostered upon him by his Queen. She had been stupid to believe any differently.

"You do not say much."

They were back inside the hall. The banquet table had been removed, two ornate chairs were stationed at one end of the hall, and three large cauldrons now occupied the center of the room. "I have no opinions to give. I have always preferred silence to empty babble."

Lord Arawn accepted her reply, leading her to the two

chairs in silence. “My wife is absent, would you do me the honor of sitting beside me?” He indicated the chair on the right.

“If it pleases you,” Riona replied, not caring to know why he required her presence. She dutifully sat and folded her hands in her lap. Her grandfather took his seat beside her and gestured to a ghostly attendant. Riona had not noticed that the specters had returned, but now as she glanced about the hall she could see more and more spirits appearing.

Leaning over, her grandfather placed his hand on her chair’s armrest. “You are about to see something very few have the opportunity to witness. See yonder, the three cauldrons?”

“Yes.” Riona tried to turn her attention away from her bleak thoughts, but she was finding it difficult. If only she had done things differently and not tried to make Sel confess before he was ready. If only she had been able to take it on faith that he would one day shed all pretense and tell her what she already knew to be true in her heart.

“Upon each vessel there is an inscription and a design. On one you will find the fearsome boar, the symbol of power and plenty. Another displays the tree of life, a chance at a new start in the cycle of life. And on the last cauldron you will see the great salmon. Great wisdom awaits the one who chooses to fish there.”

Even in her melancholy, Riona recognized the significance of the magickal items her grandfather showed her.

“I do not extend the offer to many, child, but once I offered this choice to your father. Can you guess which vessel he chose to drink from?”

“The boar,” Riona answered quickly. Power was everything to her father.

“Yes,” her grandfather agreed, sounding somewhat disappointed. “It is the least of the three gifts.”

Riona would have chosen the salmon. Wisdom could bring power and plenty, and a wise man could live a long and productive life eliminating all need for the last cauldron. "And who do you offer this chance to today?"

"A hero who did much with his life. I hope he will choose the obvious, but you never can tell—for all three come with a cost, and some do not wish to pay."

Because her grandfather's court was silent to her ears, Riona did not notice the hush that fell over the spirits in attendance, but Lord Arawn did and he turned to the one specter who stood alone before them. Riona followed her grandfather's gaze and waited.

"Angus, behind you rest three choices. Each will have a cost unique to you, so I cannot warn you of the specific dangers of accepting their gifts. However, I offer these choices to you because of the great and marvelous deeds of your past. If you should refuse, then you will remain in Annwn for all eternity, for second chances are rarely given. If you should accept, you will immediately leave and reenter the outside world. What say you?"

The ghost known as Angus spoke briefly, but Riona was not privy to his speech.

"I guarantee nothing. She has not entered my lands and I have no knowledge of her whereabouts," Lord Arawn replied.

Satisfied with Lord Arawn's answer, Angus turned and walked toward the cauldrons.

Riona leaned over and whispered, "What did he ask?"

"He inquired after the one who killed him. Revenge clouds his judgment I fear."

Riona watched the hero, Angus, trail his hand over the relief of the boar and she knew the specter was sorely tempted. Then he moved to the salmon, she caught her breath and held it.

Again he paused, this time to ask another question of Lord Arawn.

"I do not know what age you will be when you leave my lands."

Giving a sharp nod he moved to the final cauldron. The tree of life was stamped in bright gold relief across its rounded belly. He motioned to an attendant and received a simple wooden dipping ladle. With one last look at the cauldron of power, he dipped the ladle into the waters of the tree of life and drank deeply. Applause broke out, though Riona could not hear it. Satisfaction bloomed on her grandfather's face. In a blink of an eye the ghostly hero disappeared from view.

"Well, done. Well, done," Lord Arawn pronounced.

"What will be his cost?" Riona asked.

Distracted, Lord Arawn replied, "Cost?"

"Yes, you said each had a cost."

Her grandfather grinned. "Is it not obvious, dear? He will once more have to suffer childhood and all the first pains that come with discovery."

"But is that all?"

"All? Riona, is that not cost enough? Only the most brave willingly suffer first love and loss, hunger and despair, disenchantment and hope. As you age, one forgets how painful these things are to endure."

"I have not forgotten," she mumbled.

Lord Arawn reached over and patted her folded hands. "I dare say you have not. My son has not treated you well."

Riona clamped her mouth shut. She could not begin to explain to her grandfather the many ways she had suffered at her father's hands. And now Melwas had designed a disturbing new future for her with Aeron. The prospect loomed heavy upon her heart.

"Come, child. You look like you are in need of distractions. It will do you no good to brood. We all have our fates decided for us."

"Am I not allowed happiness, grandfather?"

"Of course you are. I dare say you will have much of it with your captain."

Riona didn't comment. In one brief encounter, Aeron, acting with her father's blessing, had ended that hope for her. Sel wouldn't believe she hadn't participated willingly. After all, she was an unseelie and weren't all unseelie prone to self-indulgence and mischief-making?

Lord Arawn stood and held out his hand to her. "Come let me show you more of my Keep." Anticipating the god/king's departure, the courtiers in attendance gently parted like a curtain, leaving an opening down the middle of the hall for them to pass by.

With little enthusiasm Riona slowly rose and let her grandfather guide her though his ghostly court and beyond to an exit that had not been there before. As they left the hall and moved into the new corridor, Riona glanced back to see the archway close, the stones knitting themselves back together as if they had never been. Torches along one wall flared to life, casting an orange glow.

Riona forced a cheery smile, ignoring the trepidation she felt. "Does your home have many secret passageways? I would not want to get lost."

"Losing yourself here is no laughing matter, child," he told her sternly.

"I did not mean to offend."

Her grandfather's tone softened when he turned to look at her. "You did not, but you must always remain on your guard when in my lands. Things are not as they seem. Many have come, never to leave again because they were too curious or trusting."

They had been moving at an unhurried pace, turning left then right. The smooth stone corridor had no windows or irregularities to mark their way. Her grandfather was obviously following a path long committed to memory. The further they traveled into the depths of his Keep the more nervous Riona became. She had lost track of the number of times they had turned and which pathways he had bypassed. She was in a labyrinth. Blood relation or not, she didn't know if she could trust the god/king of Annwn to lead her back out. Hadn't he just warned her about being too trusting? This had not been the smartest thing she'd ever done. Hadn't she just committed the same mistake with Aeron? "Is it much further, grandfather?" she asked, subtlety reminding him of their family relation, should he conveniently forget.

He halted. They had reached a dead end.

"See, child. Here take my hand."

Swallowing the growing fear, Riona placed her cold hand in his warm one and gave him what she hoped was a serene smile.

As soon as her hand touched his, the wall before them disappeared. Beyond was another room, gilded, lavishly furnished, and frighteningly familiar. "It is my father's private chambers," she sputtered.

"I thought it prudent to keep an eye on him," Lord Arawn said as Aeron crossed the room in front of them followed closely by a very happy Melwas.

Fearful, Riona squeezed her grandfather's hand.

"They cannot see us," he explained, patting her hand.

Riona conscientiously relaxed her grip. There was no sound to the scene before her, but it did not slow her racing pulse to think this was only a window into Tir na n-Og. As her eyes followed Aeron's movements, her mind offered up the unwanted scenes he had planted just an hour earlier. He looked undisturbed by his actions and Riona involuntarily shuttered with disgust.

"I cannot cross into this realm or I would have intervened on your behalf, Riona. You must understand, my son has not taken my advice for a very long time. Does it comfort you to know he does not have much time remaining?"

She watched as her father slapped Aeron on the shoulder, sharing a laugh, no doubt at her expense. "Time is a relative measurement for an immortal. And no, it doesn't comfort me. I fear my near future will still be controlled by him."

"I use to love him," her grandfather murmured beside her.

Riona tilted her head to look up at her grandfather's shadowy profile. The pain in his voice, the regret and longing in his gaze startled her.

"Every parent loves their child in the beginning—before one discovers who they really are." He paused to meet her eyes. "Even the parent of a monster." He then sighed wearily and looked away. "Forgive me, Riona."

What was she supposed to say? "For what, grandfather? If he had not been born, neither would I. We would not have met. I would not have found Sel, and, and…" At a loss for words Riona clamped her mouth shut, her heart aching anew at the mention of Sel's name.

"You speak truly, child. But there was a time I thought your father the most wondrous child. I indulged him and turned a blind eye to his faults. If I had been able to see him clearly, I would have never given him the opportunity to amass the power he now wields."

Riona remained silent. Her grandfather's confession was not meant to ease her thoughts, only his own guilt. But it did help to know someone had witnessed her father's treatment of her and had objected to it, though it seemed he was powerless to stop it.

"You remind me of his mother, Riona. You and she are much alike, I think. She possessed a beautiful soul."

"Is she still among the living?" Riona hadn't given her paternal grandmother much thought. No one had ever spoken of her.

"Sadly no, child. She died in childbirth and my wife refused her admittance into my realm."

"So where is she?"

"Lost," her grandfather quietly said, still watching his son in Tir na n-Og converse with the young unseelie, Aeron. "A regret I must live with."

As Riona contemplated the possible meanings of her grandmother's fate, she watched as her father and Aeron took turns signing a document. They were laughing. The parchment was probably the new binding contract between her and Aeron, the date to be added as soon as she arrived back in Tir na n-Og. Riona fought to keep her tears from falling as she helplessly witnessed her future unfold before her.

Aeron wasn't unpleasant to look at, but his good looks belayed the depravity that resided within. No doubt, he would take great pleasure in torturing her daily. Riona had only to touch the images still swirling in her mind to know the truth of it.

"It is good you have the captain to protect you now."

Riona tore her gaze away from the scene to look up at her grandfather's concerned face. "Yes. I am lucky," she said and her heart contracted painfully.

He shook his head and tsked. "I have given you all the

counsel I can child. Have faith that he will stand by you. You must not let your past tread upon your present, or else your present will always resemble your past and taint your future."

Riona lifted an eyebrow at his circularly cryptic advice. "I thought you said we all have our fates decided for us."

"In many ways we do, and in some we do not. Your father made an unwise choice once, and now lives in fear of his own destiny. It is not a good thing to live in fear; it twists the mind and soul."

"How much of the future can you see, grandfather?" Riona asked, worried that he could somehow see into her thoughts.

"I see the ending of life, whether it be glorious or meaningless, beautifully realized or wasted. But the course which brings a soul to my lands—I can only speculate," he explained, turning back to watch Melwas.

"But then..." she began to ask how he knew of her dilemma but he forestalled her.

"I have had many years of practice, dear. Death knows the troubled heart best," he said looking down at her once again. His eyes briefly flaring an iridescent blue before changing to a cool gray.

She gave him a waning smile, sorely wanting their odd conversation to end. "Duly noted, grandfather."

Perhaps sensing her unease, Lord Arawn turned away from the viewing window. "Very well, come dear. I will escort you to your room. I have duties to attend to. You will be safe there until I have finished. I promise to come fetch you the moment I am done."

Her grandfather's statement required no reply, so she let him guide her once more through the maze until at last they reached her bedchamber door. One of her grandfather's hounds rose from its repose beside the doorway to sit on its great haunches. For all the world it looked as if it smiled in greeting, its large tail thumping happily against the tiled floor. Her grandfather stayed just long enough to make sure she entered her room before moving on. The great hound resumed its nap across the expanse of the door's threshold.

Chapter 17

Sel hadn't seen the enormous boar until after it had begun its charge. His mount having smelled the beast before seeing it shied sideways then bolted in search of safer surroundings. During those seconds, Sel had gracelessly hit the ground. And because his mind had been elsewhere, he'd been ill prepared to defend himself. Crank was now sitting on the dead beast's ugly flank and grinning like a dolt.

"That was a close call, lad. Twas a good thing I was here to save your arse," Crank said loudly, his teasing words muffled by the stuffing in Sel's ears.

"Aye, Crank," Sel replied dryly. Crank would no doubt take great delight in reminding him and others of the episode. Raising his voice Sel said, "But now that the danger has passed, we should get to the task at hand."

Crank patted the boar's shoulder regretfully and the white hound whined in agreement. "Aye. Tis a pity to waste the meat, but we must be off. We have quite a bit of ground to cover, and little time to do so." Crank stood and brushed the forest leaves from his kilt, a few remained tangled in his dark hair but Sel said nothing.

They were near the base of the mountain they intended to search. On its east side lay the trail the Queen had seen in her visions. She had placed these images in his mind, leaving it up to Sel to identify the markers along the trail that would hopefully take them to Arthur's prison.

"We will search first and then come back for the choice portions of the carcass. I don't think even Lord Arawn could transport this whole beast home."

Sel walked up and pulled two of the arrows out of the boar's flesh and then put his hand on the third arrow piercing the heart.

"Stop, lad," Crank shouted.

"Why?" Sel mouthed back.

Skirting the beast's girth, Crank moved closer so he wouldn't have to yell so loudly to be heard. "Leave the arrow in the beast's heart. Otherwise we will find our dinner has taken flight by the time we return. Things are not what they seem, lad."

Sel gave Crank a sharp nod. If what Crank was suggesting was true, then this wasn't just any boar. Sel reexamined the boar's unusually large size. He should have realized it sooner. This monster was the Great Boar of legend, a beast of mythical power. Even if they were to butcher the entire animal and consume it, the boar would be reborn the following day to be hunted again.

To cover his embarrassment, Sel went to tether their one mount to a nearby tree. They would have to trek the rest of the way on foot. With the horse secured, Sel set out in the direction they needed to go, Crank and the hound trailing behind.

Like a habit he could not break, Sel's thoughts wandered back to find comfort in Riona's image. During the boar's attack, Sel thought he had experienced a fleeting pang of fear and loathing, but in the excitement of battling the fearsome creature Sel had dismissed the misplaced emotion. Now as he and Crank climbed higher up the mountain, a worry began to gnaw at him. Could Riona have suffered some fright? They were not yet bound by the vows but their link was growing stronger by the day. He might now be able to know if she were in danger. Intense emotion between pairs could travel great distances, even beyond the boundaries of worlds.

He tapped the link between them, reaching his mind out

to her, and not surprisingly he felt nothing in return. The current distance was simply too great, he told himself while trying to disregard the alarm he felt at encountering silence. To bolster his reasoning, he reminded himself that she disliked sharing her mind with him. Knowing the sooner they could complete their search today, the sooner he could return to her, Sel brought his attention back to the path he was following.

Scanning the mountain's features, he recognized a rock cluster which matched the Queen's vision. Pointing so Crank could see, Sel headed in that direction. The hound bound forward, nose hovering near the ground as it trotted several paces ahead of them.

They climbed for another half-hour before Sel spied another marker. Then a third marker, a smooth stone etched with a rune on its surface appeared soon after. But the trail seemed to end there. Though they searched for several hours, neither he nor Crank could find anything else matching the Queen's vision. Eventually they returned to the stone with the rune.

"What now?" Sel asked. The sun was as high as it was going to appear on the horizon. They would now have to judge how much time remained to them, minus the time it would take to claim a portion of the boar. When Crank did not answer, Sel turned to look at the unseelie. He found Crank's dark head cocked, singularly interested in the hound's behavior.

Sel took his cue from Crank and studied the hound. The beast was pawing at the smooth rune stone. If a whine accompanied the hound's obsession, Sel could not hear it. "Do you think he is trying to tell us something, or just hunting a rodent?"

The hound abruptly stopped excavating beside the stone and sat on his haunches expectantly. Its red ears twitched as if it could hear something they could not.

"I think we have our path, laddie." Crank approached the Queen's marker and bent down to inspect it, running his finger over the symbol. Crank then glanced up and pinned him with a speculative look. "Perhaps..." Rising from his crouch, Crank stepped forward onto the stone twice the size of his foot and promptly disappeared.

"Bloody hell!" Sel exclaimed in surprise.

Lord Arawn's white hound barked and then bounded onto the stone's surface, disappearing just as quickly as the unseelie had. Obviously they'd found some sort of a gateway but Sel had no idea where it led, or even if Crank and the hound could return through the same gateway. Should he wait or follow?

Just as suddenly as Crank had disappeared, he reappeared. "Coming, laddie?" The unseelie grinned mischievously.

Sel gave a silent nod and Crank immediately sank downward again, disappearing from view.

Resolved to fulfilling his duty, Sel stepped onto the rune stone. In the next heartbeat he was transported into another land, a shadow realm of Annwn. The gray light of Annwn was soft and comforting compared to the depressing twilight of the barren and cold shadowland they had just discovered. There was no vegetation, only sharp rock and stone.

The hound trotted lightly off in a general southern direction. Following its progress, Sel spied the next marker, a crumbling statue of a hero long forgotten. According to the Queen, the stone sentry marked the start of a trail that would take them up the mountainside. The statue's right hand held a broken sword, fist to chest in a mournful salute. The left arm was entirely missing, as was the left side of the hero's stone face. Sel gave Crank a nod before they both set out at a jog after the hound.

Once on the pathway, it was just a matter of time before

Sel found the next marker, another rune carved into the mountain face. There would be two more after that, both easily discovered. They were now about two-thirds of the way up the mountain when Sel spotted the last sign. In a bleak land, devoid of all sun, Sel spotted what should not be possible—the dappling of green and white in the cracks of the rock face. It was the last marker. They had done it.

Overwhelmed with a mix of relief and joy, Sel paused to touch the delicate flowering plant. A lump formed in this throat as he fought back sudden tears. After losing so many good fey, men, and others in their search; after so many long years with only a vague hope as a guide, soon...very soon, they would finally find Arthur. They would take him from this awful place and restore him to his throne and to his Queen, the one who never had lost faith.

Sel glanced at Crank and knew the old commander was experiencing the same mix of emotions. "There should be a cave up ahead, where the kings-weed is thickest." Sel said despite the lump in his throat.

Spurred on by their success, they sprinted up the trail looking for the opening in the mountain face but what they found was two openings, both of them covered in greenery.

"Which one?" Crank barked in frustration. Though they stood several feet away, Sel could feel the powerful wards placed on both openings. Crank bent down and picked up two stones, tossing each into the wards. One stone burst into flames and melted before reaching the ground, the other turned to ice and shattered when it hit the ground. "Fire and Ice. Not very imaginative... but effective."

Closing his eyes to better concentrate, Sel lifted his hand and hovering mere inches away from the wards, he gingerly felt across the wards' edges. There were no weak spots, not across the open expanse of the archway or along the seam where each ward melted into the rock face. As badly as he wanted to reach Arthur, Sel knew they needed more information... and time, time to discover which doorway was the correct one, and time to find the key that would allow them to pass safely through.

Lowering his hand he said, "We should return to Arawn's Keep. We know where Arthur is. That is more than Melwas can expect. Tomorrow we will return with Riona and a way to break this barrier. We will then free the King and ride for home."

When Crank didn't reply, Sel turned and laid his hand on the old warrior's arm. "We will not leave Annwn until he is free," Sel assured him.

The pain of having to abandon Arthur to his prison for one more night brought a look of agony to Crank's blue face. Sel knew there was nothing he could say to ease his friend's disappointment, so he held his tongue.

Crank swallowed before giving Sel a resolute nod. After a moment more of silence, he then wordlessly turned and headed back down the trail, Sel and the hound trotting behind.

Because they now knew were they were going, it didn't take long to make their way back to the spot where Sel had tethered Crank's horse. The boar still lay where it had fallen. With a few deft cuts of his blade, Crank took a small portion from the Great Boar as a gift for their host, Lord Arawn. Wrapping the meat in leather, he then secured the package to his mount's saddle. Only then did he retrieve the last arrow, the one that had stabbed the beast's heart. Sel, meanwhile, located his wayward horse. Luckily, it had not wandered too far afield.

Once mounted, they then made for the safety of the Keep.

Though they galloped swiftly when terrain and vegetation allowed, the white hound never tired. It kept an easy pace and even on occasion darted out in front to take the lead, showing them the way.

Now that they had located Arthur's prison and his duty was nearly done, Sel's thoughts were only of Riona. Was she safe? Had she missed him? Wanting to reach Riona, Sel pushed his horse to run faster.

As they drew closer and the distance between them lessened Sel searched for her, reaching with his mind along their strengthening link. Only vague impressions flickered in his thoughts; worry, waiting, and fatigue.

Then when the Keep finally came into view, her image bloomed in his mind. The arching of an inquisitive eyebrow was swiftly followed by the fleeting and confused mix of apprehension and joy. The connection was then abruptly severed.

Becoming aware of his probing, she had chosen to close her mind to him. Sel ignored her reaction and soothed his ego with the knowledge that whether she'd admit it or not, his return brought her feelings of joy.

Chapter 18

Riona panicked. What was she going to do? She thrown up all her defenses, severing his connection, but only after realizing the surge of comfort and strength was in fact Sel activating their mental link. He had been able to slip into her mind without her being aware of it, and that terrified her. Just how far away were he and Crank from the Keep? Were they within its walls or still journeying toward it? And if Sel could reach her at such a distance, how would she keep him from finding the false memories Aeron had branded onto her mind?

Sick with dread and worry, Riona paced the floor of her bedchamber. Her grandfather had yet to return, and she had grown somewhat bored. But after seeing the extent to which the stones could reshape themselves, Riona thought it best not to go exploring, lest she find herself truly lost. Admittedly, she also feared the possibility of her father's return, and that of Aeron. They had ridden away from the Keep to return to Tir na n-Og, but there was no guarantee they would stay in the fey realm.

Like the stroke of a feather, Riona again felt a brush of warmth that was Sel's thoughts at the edges of her mind. She abruptly stopped her pacing. Gentle but persistent, it was so like him. He was waiting patiently for a response. Squeezing her eyes closed, she checked her mental defenses and gave no reply. She just couldn't risk it.

The idea of hurting him, even disappointing him, tore at her heart. But better to keep him at arm's length than let her father's schemes reopen old wounds for him. That would cause him real pain, and she couldn't let that happen. Somehow she would have to buy herself some time, enough time for them to leave Annwn. She would then slip away to the Unseelie Court and her father's chambers, where Sel was unlikely to follow.

He would not understand her absolving their contract, but she could at least spare him the humiliation Aeron and her father had planned. Riona flinched at the look of loathing she imagined his handsome face might wear.

Though she wished otherwise, Riona knew Aeron was right. She was her mother's daughter and her father's issue. Of course Sel would think her capable of betrayal, she thought miserably.

She almost cried when Sel's mind touched their link once more. This time questioning, but still not demanding. Riona didn't think he would force his way through her defensive walls. Though he possessed the power to break the barriers she had erected, he had given her his word he would not. What had it been, a day, two days ago when he had held her, shared his mind with her? In his arms, she had felt completely safe for the first time in her life. And only a few days before that she had run from him. And she only had to travel back a few more days to remind herself of Calcus, and her escape to Tearmann.

"Riona."

She jumped at the sound of her grandfather's voice. Turning, she found him standing in the doorway, flanked by two of his white hounds. Ignoring the quizzical crease to his brow, she forced a smile. "Yes, grandfather."

"They have reached the stables. Shall we welcome them together?"

Walking toward the god/king with her smile determinedly in place, Riona felt nothing but dread in the pit of her stomach. "I am ready," she told him cheerfully. But she knew she was anything but ready. Lifting her chin slightly she placed her small hand on his well muscled arm and let him escort her toward the great hall.

She could hear both Crank's and Sel's strong voices before she could see them. Crank was boasting loudly and heckling Sel about some exploit.

As if sensing her arrival, Sel's blond head turned, his green eyes seeking hers. Relief then washed over his features and he grinned at her.

She smiled brightly at him, surprised by the surge of joy she felt at seeing him unharmed. After her grandfather formally welcomed them back, Sel closed the distance between them.

Slipping his arm around her waist he asked in a near whisper, "Are you distressed?"

"No," she lied looking him in the eye. "What would make you think such a thing?" When she felt her bluff begin to waiver, she lowered her gaze to his chest.

"I thought..." he paused and cocked his head. "Would you tell me, Riona?" he asked, lifting her chin.

She was careful not to flinch when he touched the camouflaged bruise to her cheek from her father's slap. Riona looked him full in the face and lied again. "Of course I would tell you." The boyish grin he then gave her nearly broke her heart.

He leaned forward and kissed her hungrily, his arms wrapping around her and bringing her close. "I have missed you," he whispered when their lips parted.

She swallowed nervously, a sudden surge of heat igniting her blood as a result of his kiss. "And I you," she told him truthfully.

He kissed the tip of her nose and then stepped back, releasing her to speak with their host. She nearly whimpered with the absence of his touch. Catching herself, she checked her mental defenses and remembered her earlier plan. Falling into her old habit of withdrawing from the company that surrounded her, Riona watched the three males joke with each other. Though Sel conversed easily with her grandfather and Crank, his mind hovered at the edges of her walled thoughts, patiently waiting for her to invite him in.

He turned from his conversation with Crank and Lord Arawn and gave her a crooked grin. Reaching for her, he laced his fingers with hers and tugged her closer to his side.

Riona pretended to listen to Crank's animated storytelling, but she was heartsick inside. She knew all too well that the camaraderie she witnessed between trusted friends wasn't meant for her. Soon she would have to leave this realm and Sel behind.

She felt him squeeze her hand as if knowing the direction of her bleak thoughts. He was solely attuned to her, as if they were the only ones in the room.

She ducked her head and blinked in rapid succession to rid herself of her sudden self-pitying tears. Pushing back the darkness which could so quickly consume her, she took a deep breath and smiled once more. There would be time to mourn later, she told herself. Tonight she had to keep the charade going.

* * *

Riona was putting on a brave face, but she was politely withdrawn and it worried Sel. He knew something was not right between them. Out of desperation, he kept their mental connection open in the hopes that she would share her distress with him. But despite his patience, she remained firmly behind her defenses. And though he was sorely pressed to breach her mind's defensive walls, he did not. He'd never gain her trust if he continued to break his promises to her whenever he deemed it necessary.

Whatever the problem was, Sel hoped he could coax it out of her. But it had been a long time since he had tried to charm anyone, and honestly, he wasn't sure he had ever possessed the ability to do so. His attempts at charming Brianna had not worked out well. Quickly, he shoved that memory away and reminded himself that his Riona was not Sinnie's mother. Just because the contract with Brianna had ended disastrously, did not mean history had to repeat itself with Riona. For the most part, Riona didn't fear him to the extent that Brianna had. Riona had been willing to stand her ground and argue with him, and that alone gave him hope. Sel could still picture her cheeks flushed with anger while he sidestepped and dodged the flying projectiles from the night before. Sel had to bite the inside of his cheek to keep from smiling at the memory.

He lightly stroked the soft skin of her hand with his thumb. When she pulled her hand free of his, he didn't react, though her withdrawal touched on old wounds. He simply reminded himself again that she was not Brianna. Riona was his true mate, and would not... could not betray him with another. *But she has threatened to do just that*, his mind readily offered.

Closing his eyes, he clenched his jaw and shoved the thought away. "No!" he growled under his breath.

As light and as welcome as a warm spring rain, he felt Riona's hand touch his arm. Ashamed of his doubts, he glanced at her. She raised a concerned eyebrow and absently stroked his forearm, but did not ask him to explain his odd outburst.

This is how they passed most of the evening, with a smile, a touch, a look—both silently reassuring the other while refusing to address the problem between them. It was a tender but maddening game of cat and mouse that only continued to stir old ghosts and doubts in Sel.

Finally in the wee hours of the night, Sel abruptly announced to their host his and Riona's retirement. Sel had sensed her waning strength and as her mate it was his right to see to her physical needs. This he would do without seeking her consent.

Crank grinned, drink in hand. Sel then caught something in the look Lord Arawn gave Riona. She gave a small shake of her head, but otherwise did not utter a response.

"Til the morrow then," Sel told his host.

"Aye. Sleep well, my dear," Lord Arawn told Riona.

Riona gave her grandfather and Crank a sheepish grin and then without a whisper of protest she allowed Sel to escort her from the hall. For reasons Sel could not name, her demure conduct irritated him.

When they reached their quarters, he said, "I will pass a few hours with you, to make sure you can sleep." The hound trailing behind them like one of the Keep's ghosts stopped at the door's threshold, sitting heavily. Sel closed the door and heard the beast lean its body against the other side of the barrier.

"I do not need you to stay, Sel. What of your planning with Crank? Did you find what you sought?" Aware of Lord Arawn's far reaching presence, Riona was choosing her words carefully.

Sel was less careful with his answer. "Aye. But we have no knowledge of how to pass the wards."

Riona's brow creased with confusion or perhaps it was worry, Sel thought. Seeing no harm in telling her, he said, "He knows what we search for, Riona. Though he is not offering to aid us, he does not intend on hindering our quest."

Crossing the room, he took her hand and guided her to the bed. Fully clothed, he made himself comfortable in its cushions. "You are tired," he began.

"Do I look tired?" she asked, her mouth drawing into a tight line.

"No you do not," he cautiously replied. "But I can feel it deep within my bones. Come lie beside me and gain the rest you need. I will not bother you. This I promise," he finished, leaving her no reason to refuse his request. He then patted the space next to him.

She hesitated, but then climbed up to join him after kicking off her slippers with more force than was necessary.

Pulling her tense body close, he coaxed her into laying her head on his chest. For all his troubles as soon as the scent of her reached him, his cock grew hard. Ignoring his body's insane reaction to such a small thing, he gently stoked the arm resting across his chest. "Sleep, Riona. You are safe," he whispered hoarsely over the top of her head.

Doubting his angelic motives, she harrumphed against his chest. This caused him to chuckle.

"I cannot sleep with my head bouncing up and down," she murmured sourly against the fabric of his shirt.

"I am sorry. I will refrain from laughing. Think of me as an overstuffed pillow, nothing more."

"Pillows are silent as well," she said petulantly.

He grinned over her head, but true to his word, he did not utter another sound. He much preferred this Riona to the one who had sat like a ghost beside him in the hall.

As his body heat soaked into hers, her tense body started to relax. Eventually, he felt her breathing deepen as she slipped into a well needed sleep.

Because he could, he bent his head forward and inhaled the scent of her hair deep within his lungs. Such a small indulgence had a painfully hard consequence for his groin. Sel tried to shift his position, but then Riona snuggled closer, her leg coming up to lay across his swollen shaft.

Sel froze, and tried to think mundane thoughts, anything to ease the throbbing pressure he felt while trapped under the weight and warmth of her thigh. But his attempts to temper his body's response to her closeness was to no avail. He was therefore left to pass the next hour in equal parts agony and bliss with her soft body so temptingly wrapped around him. That is until she moved again, a thrashing motion meant to repel some unseen assailant.

Sel grunted when she inadvertently kneed him in the groin. With his free hand he captured and stilled her wayward leg before she could do any more damage to him. Riding the now unblocked link between them, he traveled into her mind to help disperse whatever nightmare plagued her, all the while telling himself she needed real rest, a rest free of haunting memories.

Sel expected to see some scene from her past life, perhaps in her father's court or among the various unseelie who had sheltered her, but the images he found her battling were disturbingly recent and hit him like a punch to the gut. He recognized the familiar setting, the worn cobblestones of the Keep's courtyard and the unseelie who pleasured her so vigorously.

Denial was the first emotion to surface. This could not be happening again, his mind cried out. What was he seeing? a fantasy, a confused jumble of dream images, a memory he asked himself.

Riona moaned in her sleep and it was all Sel could do to

keep from flinching as he saw an impassioned Riona moaning in her dream. As much as he wanted to turn away from the unfolding scenario, Sel found that he could not. Like watching an evolving disaster, he morbidly looked on as Aeron repeatedly fucked a most willing Riona.

Bile rose in Sel's throat as grief and doubt beat at him. She had been untouched before him. Sel was sure of it. Or had she preformed some spell to make him think that?

If she had indeed been a virgin, then she wouldn't have had the experience to do some of the things he now witnessed her doing with Aeron. Or did this talent come from her mother? Was this why she had recently kept him at arms length? Had she discovered the power bed-play could bring if used as a weapon? Her mother's sexual warfare had successfully raised armies for Melwas as well as against him.

Breaking into his darkening thoughts Riona stirred again, hitting him, once, twice, a third time against his chest. He grabbed her wrist to still her hand. Trembling against him, a small whimper escaped her lips. Captured as she was next to him, she then grew deathly still.

For a moment he thought she had awakened, but as he glanced down he could see she had not. It was if she were fighting the dream. Except for the one moan, she was not reacting in accord with the myriad of images parading through her mind. Needing to know the truth, Sel delved deeper. In sleep she was completely defenseless, her mind absolutely open to him. Taking the opportunity, Sel moved backward through the gut-wrenching scene, searching for the hours leading up to the tryst with the unseelie. Why had Aeron come to Annwn in the first place? Had she planned the tryst?

Sel didn't have to search much deeper to find Riona's

startled encounter with Melwas. Aeron was there as well. Riona's utter terror at discovering her father while descending the stairs permeated Sel's mind, chilling him.

Sure he had found an honest memory-triggered reaction, Sel let the memory play forward. What he witnessed made his blood boil. He knew Melwas and those he favored were evil, but he had not thought any father capable of such vile acts.

In her sleep, Riona violently thrashed out in an unconscious attempt at escaping his probing. Sel fought against her for several heartbeats, but thinking it wiser he allowed her to turn her body away from him. Finding the truth was simply too important, so Sel released his grip on her wrist, afraid that if he continued to restrain her she'd awaken. When she settled, he pressed further into her mind.

There, in the courtyard, he witnessed two overlapping scenarios. In one, Riona struggled against Aeron's attack. In the other she welcomed him, shyly at first but as the scene unfolded her shyness fell away to become the dream he had stumbled upon.

Sickened, Sel withdrew from the dark recesses of her mind. Which scenario was the truth?

Beside him, Riona had curled into a ball, her back to him.

To think of her in another's arms brought with it a rage so dark that it shook Sel to his seelie core. He would kill Aeron on sight. No warning would be given, no mercy offered—of that, Sel was certain.

Once he had determined Riona was his true mate, Sel had foolishly set out to court her. He had wanted to win her trust. But now all his foolish courtly efforts and honorable intentions seemed somehow tainted by the images which so maddeningly replayed themselves in his mind. She was in need of protection, yes, but growing up unseelie meant she had never been the innocent he had imagined, at least not the kind of blind innocence his male ego had wanted his true mate to possess.

Riona, the real Riona... his Riona, his dark princess, had dealt with impossible circumstances for much of her life, forever forced to choose between the lesser evils surrounding her.

Could this be the warning Jen had tried to give him? He hadn't been there to protect her from either Aeron or her own unseelie nature. That realization then prompted another. She didn't trust him. If she had been attacked by Aeron, then she also thought he would turn her away, believing the things he found in her mind as truth instead of any assertions of blamelessness she might make. Could he believe her guiltless of the act itself? His heart wanted her to be, but his mind warned him of who her parents were, Melwas the Usurper, Melwas the Butcher. And Naria... Naria, the Dark Enchantress, Naria the Dark Temptress.

It was in this moment that Sel's bruised heart reminded him that it had happened before. Brianna. Brianna hadn't even tried to be discrete with her lovers. Though Sel never was forced to confront the ugly gossip her unfaithfulness caused, nor did anyone offer to rebuke him for the subsequent action he took, regardless, Sel had shouldered the shame it brought to his family's house.

Sel didn't wake Riona when she slept past the expected two hours. She hadn't slept the previous night nor the night before that because of their bed-play. Had it only been two nights? It seemed like an eternity ago. He had glimpsed much while searching her mind. Things that he wished he hadn't. Not just Aeron, but acts of cruelty committed by Melwas and others.

When she suddenly thrashed herself awake, he automatically offered her comfort and she sleepily snuggled close to him. "I will protect you," he heard himself promise. The statement didn't surprise him. For all Sel's doubts, he had come to one unchangeable conclusion while laying there—he loved her. Even if their love was fated by the gods to be a tragic one, it was a fact he could not circumvent. It didn't matter what her nature might tempt her to do. He loved her and therefore his heart no longer belonged to him alone. And because he loved her, he would defend the woman beside him for as long as he drew breath. He would also bind her to himself with the vows—as soon as they reached Tir na n-Og. Even if he had to force her into saying them.

Sel sensed the time for games between them was over, so in the muted light of the dying candles, he allowed his image to shimmer. He revealed the golden glow still faintly emanating from his skin since first making love to her. Hoping her sleeping mind would hear his words, he whispered, "I love you, Riona." His warm breath stirred the fine chocolate colored hairs framing her sleeping face. "I was a fool not to tell you the first moment I realized it." He laid his cheek against the top of her head. "Find a way to trust me," he pleaded. "Take a leap of faith, as I have. I promise, I will catch you."

Pulling her tightly against him, Sel waited for dawn to approach.

Chapter 20

She was surprised to find him still beside her when she woke. Her head rested easily against his chest and the crook of his arm as if the spot had been carved just for her. For a long time Riona selfishly feigned sleep so she could lay there with his arm draped around her, breathe in the scent of him, and listen to his strong heartbeat in accord with her own. This would be the last time he'd hold her close, she thought sadly.

Sel was the first to break the peaceful spell. "We need to rise, Riona. Crank will be waiting."

She didn't apologize for her indulgence, but neither did she draw attention to it. The sweet moment had come and gone and she should not dwell on the loss.

As if it were just another morning, one of many to be repeated in the future, Riona rose and stepped away from the warmth and security that his physical presence gave her. "Give me but a moment. I will be down directly."

Sel didn't comment, nor did he rise immediately. Instead he watched as she washed her face, hands, and arms in the bowl she once broken. Then he watched as she busied herself with brushing out the tangles in her hair, before moving on to some other mundane grooming task.

Riona wrapped the room's silence around her like a wall and avoided looking directly at him, lest her resolve shatter. Today there was a perceptible glow to his unblemished skin. Perhaps it was because he could not be hers that he seemed like a treasure denied, excessively golden in the morning light.

Eventually she heard a disappointed sigh escape his lips, and then watched through the mirror's reflection as his ever increasingly blurred image strolled out of the room without a backward glance.

She swallowed back her grief, and quickly rubbed away the gathering tears. By nightfall, she would take her place in the Unseelie Court. Her time with Sel was over. He would not understand the pain she was saving him from, but given the circumstances, it was better this way.

The rhythmic thumping of a hound's tail jolted her out of her musings. She should not dally much longer. Sel had a mission to fulfill. Of late, she had not thought very kindly of the Queen but Riona had begun to understand what it might feel like to be separated from one's true mate. It was a pain like no other, and one the Seelie Queen and she would soon have in common. If she could help Sel in restoring the Absent King to his Queen and throne then for Sel's sake, as well as that of the pair's, she would. Temporarily setting aside her doubts about her own future with the larger goal, Riona squared her shoulders and headed down to her grandfather's hall.

Considering the formality of their arrival and the test at the bridge, their departure was surprisingly casual. Her grandfather walked with them into the courtyard where three beautiful horses were saddled and waiting. He kissed her cheek, and whispered his affection in her ear before saying a curt goodbye to Sel and Crank. Then Lord Arawn and his hounds returned to disappear into the fortress that was his Keep.

Riona stuffed the wool into her ears, giving herself the excuse needed to pretend she couldn't hear Sel when he offered to help her mount her horse. But her ignoring him didn't keep him from executing said aid. His strong hands easily lifted her into the air. Once she was astride, he then steadied the stirrups so she might slip her feet into them.

Else she appear rude, Riona looked at him full in the face for the first time that morning to nod her thanks. He gave a cheeky wink before moving away to mount his own steed.

Once all were astride, they headed out. Crank led the way, Riona's horse following, leaving Sel to take up position at the rear of their small procession.

They traveled over varying terrain, in a general northerly direction, towards a distant mountain. At times the obstacles in their path were considerably more challenging than Riona had prepared herself for. This was nothing like the easy path her grandfather had shown them. For the first time in her life, she had to navigate rivers, ravines, and dense woodlands.

Riona could see by the impatient looks Crank threw over his shoulder that her relative inexperience was slowing their progress. Time seemed to be against them and she was determined not to be the hindrance to their quest. Riona kicked her mare into a faster gait as soon as they came across a nearly level field. She surprised Crank, over taking him, as her over eager mare moved into what felt like a dead run—though it was more likely a lope by the others' standards. Either way, she gained Crank's approval and they crossed the expanse quickly, she clutching the mare's reddish mane until her knuckles turned white.

When they reached the far side, the horses slowed. Riona pulled back on the leather reins as best she could, but her head-strong mare moved into the trees first. A low branch nearly scraped her out of the saddle before she finally wrestled the beast to a proper stop. Sel was soon beside her to help restore order, and they resumed their earlier formation and pace, riding slowly along a narrow path into an ever denser forest.

Another hour came and went and Riona began to wonder

if her legs would work when they finally reached their destination. It was about this time that Crank stopped. He then motioned for them all to dismount. Before she could slip her foot out of the stirrup, Sel was once again there to offer his aid. She gratefully accepted the gesture with a small smile; her thighs and bottom having passed sore an hour ago. They were now moving on to numb.

"We walk from here," Sel's voice boomed next to her ear. He took the troublesome mare's reins from her.

Once the horses were secured to a nearby tree, Crank started climbing. She thought they must be at the base of the mountain, but with the stuffing in their ears it was too much trouble to ask. Instead, she rubbed her thighs to get the blood moving again before setting out after Crank. Sel followed behind.

She stumbled only once during the march upward, but Sel's strong arm was there to catch her. Riona hastily mouthed a "thank you" before scrambling away from him to move further up the slope. Was it her imagination or was he actually glowing? When she thought he might not be looking, she peeked over her shoulder.

He was.

As if sensing her eyes on him, he glanced up and gave her a boyish grin which prompted her heart to foolishly flutter. Whipping her head around, she concentrated on catching up with Crank's broad blue-tinted back.

Try as she might, she could not close the distance. By the time Crank did stop and she reached him, she was out of breath. He pulled her over to him and loudly said, "Girl, you must trust us. Step where I step." He pointed to a smooth gray stone whose surface held a carved symbol, a rune stone three times the size of her foot. "This leads to a shadow realm. It is safe. We did this yesterday."

Doubtful but resolved to follow this day through to the end, Riona nodded. Sel, never too far away, put his hand on the small of her back.

"You go first," he yelled at Crank.

Crank gave him a smirk before bounding onto the stone and disappearing.

Sel turned her shoulders so she faced him. Left with little choice, she glanced up to look into his green eyes.

"You next. Crank will be waiting on the other side. I will follow." He then gave her an abrupt peck on the lips before releasing her.

To escape having Sel so delectably close, Riona jumped onto the stone. The next moment there was a sinking sensation in the pit of her stomach, and then Crank's hands were on her arms pulling her forward.

"This way," he instructed. He set out again, striding out so that she had to jog to keep up. As he drew her along, Riona glanced over her shoulder to make sure Sel had indeed followed. True to his word, he appeared and gave her a grin. In the bleakness of this shadow realm, she could clearly make out the strange halo of light that now seemed to surround his seelie body. Because he trailed far enough behind to assure privacy, she was tempted to ask Crank if he knew why Sel seemed to be glowing. The words almost tumbled out, but with one glance at Crank's determined profile she swallowed her questions. Crank was singularly focused on getting to Arthur. And to do that, they would have to climb the rocky path that lay ahead.

They hurried by a stone statue of a forlorn and crumbling hero. As she passed under the edifice, Riona was left to wonder who had put it there and why? Who was this sad hero marking the start of the trail they must climb? Her grandfather would know; maybe her father as well.

The fleeting thought of her father brought with it a wave of despair. Riona dismissed her questions. What good would any of her questions be? She would be better served if she kept her thoughts focused solely on the next task at hand.

They climbed... and climbed.

After a while Riona wished the earlier numbness would return to her legs. Her sides ached, and her calves and thighs burned with fatigue. She was grateful when Crank paused beside a small plant embedded in the rock. "It's the final marker. Kingsweed," he exuberantly explained.

Riona said nothing. She was glad Crank and Sel had once again reached the site of Arthur's imprisonment. Soon they would ride for the border. Her time in Annwn was almost over.

With her in tow, Crank hurriedly climbed up the path until he came to two openings. Here, Crank waited for Sel to reach them.

Magick has a texture to it, unique to the practitioner who casts it. Some magick is joyous and beautiful, some whimsical or teasing, some dark. And some magick is designed to cause pain. The magick wards barring the two entrances were all too familiar to Riona. This magick was her father's doing.

Riona gave an involuntary shiver as deeply buried memories threatened to resurface. When Sel's arm slipped around her waist, she briefly leaned into the shelter of his body to draw what comfort she could.

Now that Sel had joined them, Crank began working on trying to pass through one entrance. He was pacing in front of one ward, trying to break through by using several counter spells. Some of the gestures and symbols he used Riona had never seen before.

As a child, Riona had ample opportunities to try to break past her father's wards. If only she could learn the right spell, she had naively thought. Whenever she could manage it, she'd steal away from those charged with her keeping and run to the dusty archives to study the ancient texts. In secret, she would practice what she'd learned there until someone found her. Once found, they would drag her back to stand before her father, filthy from head to toe in the dirt and grime that blanketed the forgotten tomes. She'd then have to undergo the humiliation and punishment dealt out by her father.

Riona tried to slow the memories by watching Crank. He was now drawing rune symbols along the ward's edges. In all the years of trying new spells, her efforts had never born fruit. Instead the wards, which formed the invisible box her father had used to confine her, had absorbed her spells. All her efforts to escape would only succeed in strengthening them. The repeated experience, both painful and degrading, had been his way of teaching absolute obedience. Only after she had been defeated by the painful wards and her magick spent, would he then take the time from pursuing other pleasures to lecture her on her utter foolishness. Much later, after he grew sick of hearing her pitiful moans would he allow her mother or aunt to release her.

Lesson one, no one was more powerful than him. Lesson two, it is less painful to serve him absolutely than entertain the idea of resisting. The sooner a child of his learned these lessons, the better. Thankfully, Riona had been his only child.

She closed her eyes and released a long weary breath. Despite her father's persistent efforts, she had never fully learned either lesson to his satisfaction. She had been cursed with a dreadfully rebellious nature, and her early escapes from those charged with her keeping had only bolstered her desire for freedom. Each escape taught her the skills necessary to engineer her subsequent and more lengthy flights from his court.

And yet... and yet, in the end, she was going to obey his will and return to serve him as he wished, with whom he wished. But her obedience wasn't because of any pain he could inflict on her. No, if he still only intended on humiliating her, she would have continued to resist. No, it was the humiliation and pain he intended for Sel that had ultimately gained Melwas her faithful service.

"It's not working," Sel said next to her.

"No. It is not," she replied, opening her eyes. By this time, one opening was fully engulfed in wicked looking flames. And because of the growing heat of the inferno, Crank had been forced to give up on that entrance. He was now studying the other. Sel had not been able to offer any ideas, and both fey were growing frustrated.

What her father had wanted most to instill into her was the understanding that she was powerless before him. He wanted to see her completely surrender to his will. It was what Melwas craved most from others. Absolute surrender. The power of holding a life in his hands to do with as he wished. Her mother knew this secret about him and used it to her advantage when she could. When she could not, she would hide or plot against him.

Sick to her stomach, Riona suddenly understood what she must do. Neither Crank nor Sel would be able to free Arthur unless she broke through the remaining ward. Riona knew she was the only one who had the ability to accomplish the task, the only one who had been trained from birth, the only one familiar enough with her father's magick, the only one who understood the spell-caster's awful secret.

She stepped forward to still Crank's hand as he began to weave his next spell. The first spell had already created a thick layer of ice along the entrance's rocky edges. "Stop. It only works against you," she yelled at him. "I know what to do. Step back and keep Sel from interfering."

Crank looked over her head at Sel, and then back at her. Seeing her resolve, he nodded sharply and left her side to keep Sel from stopping her.

To his credit, it didn't take long for Sel to realize what was going on. When his muffled protests reached her ears, she ignored them except to hold up her hand up to ask for silence. Closing her eyes, Riona tried to prepare herself for the coming ordeal.

Unlocking the memories of her childhood, she let them engulf her. Once more she was powerless, no longer the wayward princess who some protected, but the defenseless child who still craved the attention and approval of a parent. She pictured herself once again trapped in the center of her father's invisible box. He wanted her to bend to his will, to surrender to him.

"So be it, father. I am yours," she whispered under her breath. "My life belongs to you. I live only by your will." Now more than any other time in her life, Riona believed the words he had taught her to say.

Armed with only these thoughts, she breached the powerful ward before her.

Crossing into the magickal barrier, ice froze her flesh and numbed her limbs, making them heavy and difficult to move. Despite this and disregarding the frigid temperatures, she kept inching forward until she stood at its very center. His magick was all around her now, his power flowing through her, stabbing at her exposed flesh and stealing the air from her lungs. Unable to stop herself, she cried out in fear when pain seared her limbs.

Gasping against the terror and bone chilling burning, she opened her icy lids and watched as the sparkling mist before her came together to form an icy image of her father.

The ward's guardian confronted her, the voice of her father blooming in her mind though the phantom's crystallized lips did not move. *I recognize your blood, but you are not me. What magick do you have that I do not?*

Her lips had gone numb. Riona clenched her jaw to keep her teeth from chattering. *I am your issue and I live only by your will*, she hastily thought at the ward's guardian.

The phantom imbued with her father's spirit smiled cruelly. *My will is harsh.*

Abruptly the pain intensified, piercing her bones and leaving her light headed. *It matters not. I live only by your will,* she desperately thought. *Let me die now.* The unguarded request escaped to temptingly dance between them.

Her plea for death by his icy hands pleased the guardian of the ward and the image of the father basked in her helplessness.

The air warmed perceptibly and the burning in her lungs, throat, and limbs lessened. Though her joints protested, she took another step forward.

Whom do you serve? The spirit greedily asked as it swirled around her. Its arctic breath buffered her body while its crystallized flesh scraped against her exposed arms, taking its blood payment.

Riona closed her eyes again and took one final step forward. *You, father. I serve you.*

Chapter 21

When the warmer air of the interior cave reached her, Riona stopped inching forward and came to a halt. As suddenly as the ice had captured her, it had released her. She had done it. She had traveled through the ward. The thin layer of ice crystals still attached to her clothing and hair was melting quickly.

Forcing her eyelashes apart, she surveyed her surroundings. She now stood in what appeared to be a shallow cave. A little further ahead and off to the right, she could make out a solid metal door, misshapen and warped in its appearance, the rock having long ago magickally grown over its edges.

Glancing back the way she had come, Riona could see that the cave's opening had solidified into a sheet of ice several inches thick. From her advantage point, the distorted blue and golden bodies of Crank and Sel wavered and danced in frantic activity.

It wasn't long until she heard pounding as both warriors beat against the barrier with their sword hilts. After making very little progress for several minutes, a crack marred its smooth surface. The ward had been fatally weakened by her passing through; the ice was now only ice, no longer a magickal barrier. It would just be a matter of time before the fissure would grow larger. Each strike now added to the web of cracks. Riona backed away.

When the ice released its hold on the surrounding rock, it was spectacular, shattering into thousands of diamond shaped raindrops onto the cave's floor.

Sel was the first to charge through the gap and the only one to bark at her, his worry having turned to anger. "What where you thinking? You could have been killed!" he scolded.

Riona bristled. "Once I saw the wards, I knew what my father had done. Without me, you would still be on the other side."

Crank brushed by them, moving towards the metal door. "A blood-key," he told Sel. "She is of his blood, and like him, she can pass through his enchantments without harm. She is quite literally the bloody key to releasing Arthur."

Riona didn't correct Crank's assumption. Moving through her father's ward had been far from easy.

Noting the tightness in Sel's jaw, she knew he was upset with what he saw as reckless behavior on her part. He wanted to scold her more but they needed to free Arthur. For now he was biting his tongue, soothing his anger by healing the miniscule cuts to her arms.

After studying their next barrier, Crank returned to them and held out his hand. "Sel, I'll be needing the key around your neck."

With a gentle squeeze to her arm, Sel released her and reached under his shirt to retrieve the stag-head key.

"I do not see a keyhole," Sel said as he handed the brass key to Crank.

"Aye, nor do I see how this bloody thing is to open once we have unlocked it."

As they moved closer, Riona could only see one small opening, too big for the key and too small to pass a hand through.

Crank pounded on the door with his fist; once, twice, three times. "Arthur!" he bellowed at the metal door whose color was nearly as gray and ruff as the rock that surrounded it.

They waited. No one spoke in hopes of catching some small sound within.

Again, Crank gave the door three mighty hits. There was

no echo. The mountain seemed determined to absorb the noise.

After a few minutes of tense silence, Sel asked Crank, "What now? Can we go through the rock and bypass the door?"

The two fey now blocked her view of the cell's door, and their mutual frustration filled the confining space making it feel even smaller than it was.

Riona retreated to the mouth of the cave to let them argue about what to do next. While waiting the thought occurred to her... if she were the key to the ward guarding the cave as Crank thought, then perhaps she was the one to provide the answer to the problem before them. Returning to Sel's side, she tapped him on his back to gain his attention. When he turned to look at her, she instructed, "Let me look."

He hesitated before stepping aside. In contrast, Crank, confident she could once again help them, bounded backwards from the door to give her more room.

Riona studied the melded rock and metal. Crank had touched the door already, so she reached out to gently run her fingers over the door's surface. Upon contact, the overgrown rock withdrew from the door's surface like a living fungus, revealing hinges and a keyhole. Pleased with her contribution, Riona stepped out of the way. But before Crank could jam the key into the lock, the rock reformed over the keyhole.

"Bloody hell," Crank swore.

Sel laid his hand on her shoulder and mouthed, "Try again."

Emboldened, she held her palm out to Crank. "Give me the key."

Without hesitation he placed the brass key in her outstretched hand.

"Be careful, girl. We dinna know what foul enchantment

your father has put on this door. It may retaliate once the lock releases."

Riona gave him a quick nod, then swallowed, steadying her nerves. Once again she placed her hand on the door and the spelled rock receded. With one hand firmly on the metal, she slid the key into the lock and turned clockwise until she heard the clank of the bolt releasing. When nothing terrible happened, she glanced back at Crank and smiled triumphantly. She then caught Sel's guarded expression and her smile faulted. Thus far the rescue of Arthur had been relatively easy. What would happen now, now that the door was about to give up its secret?

Turning away from Sel's worried face and back to the barrier before them, Riona observed, "There is no handle." She had kept her hand firmly on the door's surface and the key in the lock, afraid that the rock would take back what ground they had gained.

She glanced over her shoulder to see if they had any new ideas. Crank and Sel shared look then nodded in unison. Reaching over head, they pushed on the door's surface.

At first nothing happened, but then a series of pops filled the air as the rusty hinges gave way. Slowly, the door inched inward.

Being the smallest, Riona was the first to slip through the widening gap. She was also the first to lay eyes on the Absent King.

Shock robed her of speech.

In a room not much larger than Sel's sitting room, surrounded by stacks of books in various states of decomposition, sat the oldest man Riona had ever seen. His hair was snow white and his once muscled frame gaunt. The robe he wore, once very fine but now dirty and threadbare, was gathered at his waist by a wide leather strap. He was reading, perched on a chair constructed entirely of decaying leather bound tomes. He did not react to the noise of door scraping across the stone floor or the commotion behind her, but steadfastly remained riveted to the page laid open before him. Behind her Crank's intake of breath was echoed by Sel.

No one spoke.

Perhaps realizing he was no longer alone, the ancient King carefully mark his page with a strip of folded paper and shut the brown tome. He glanced up and smiled, the wrinkles about his eyes growing deeper as his withered cheeks lifted.

Green eyes twinkling in delight, he said, "Guests. How lovely." Though muffled by the stuffing in her ears, Riona was surprised to discover that his voice was strong and pleasant. She would have expected a threadlike whisper or halting croak to come from the dusty and withered King.

While Riona remained tongue-tied, Crank pushed by and knelt before the throne of the ancient King.

"We are here to take you home, my lord," Crank's usually bold voice seemed to come out more like a reverent whisper. He then reached up and pulled the wool from his left ear to better hear his King's reply.

Riona started to remove the packing in her ears as well, but Sel caught her wrist and tugged her downward, prompting her into a low curtsy and him into a deep bow beside her. When she moved to stand again, Sel's hold tightened, keeping her in the uncomfortable low crouch. Curious, Riona peeked up and found the King wore a look of genuine surprise and then puzzlement, as if he had forgotten what to do next.

Wanting to spare him the embarrassment, she started to gently prompt him. Sel squeezed her forearm painfully, distracting her. She winced and glared at his profile, willing him to make eye contact but his green eyes would not leave the rock beneath their feet.

Finally Crank prompted, “My King, Sel, son of Selgi, his mate Riona, and I have come to free you from your imprisonment.”

Riona strained to hear Arthur's response. Her eyes darted upward to see the monarch blink in surprise.

“How is my Gwen? Do you still guard her, Naf?” he finally asked.

Without the King's leave Crank rose to stand.

Sel followed the old commander's example, releasing Riona's arm in the process. She rubbed at the spot that would surely bruise later.

“Nay, Arthur. Young Sel has taken up that honor.”

Riona nearly harrumphed at Crank's description of Sel. The captain was far from young. He was well over twice her age.

Arthur's lively eyes focused on Sel. “And what mischief has my mate been up to lately?” the King asked conversationally.

Sel shared a worried look with Crank before answering. His raised voice was overly loud even to Riona's blocked hearing. “She has spent these many years protecting as best she could your throne from Melwas's mischief.” Sel paused to choose his next words carefully. “But he has done much damage. I fear many of your court believe you lost.”

The King blanched. “Are you deaf, Sel? Is that why you speak so robustly?”

Crank interrupted. “Please, Arthur, we must be away. We have horses to take you to the border of Annwn.”

“We have time, old friend. Would you like some libations?” More agile than he appeared, the King dropped down from his perch and scuffled between the teetering stacks of tomes to disappear behind a particularly large pile of reading material. His disembodied voice called, "Wait, I seem to recall I have a smidgen of tea for our young lady. Is your party hungry as well? I can offer you some cheese. It's very nice."

"What did he say?" Riona mouthed at Sel.

"Arthur!" Crank barked, his fear and frustration rising. Working his way into the maze of literature debris, he searched for the King. "We dinna have the time. Melwas will know we have breached his wards. We must leave now."

Arthur reemerged from the maze to silently present Riona with a cracked cup half full of brown liquid and a bit of molded cheese.

She tried not to make the mistake of speaking abnormally loud as Sel had done. "Thank you," she told him taking the fragile china from his boney fingers before holding out her hand to receive the sliver of whitish cheese.

"Where the bloody hell are you?" Crank called from behind the wall of tomes.

Arthur grinned at Riona then chuckled, finding Crank's predicament funny.

"He is with us," Sel called in his booming voice.

When they heard towers of books collapsing followed by more swearing, Riona tried to stifle her giggle but failed. The King joined her in her merriment, laughing unrestrained. Sel smirked, but otherwise he was able to keep his amusement to himself.

When Crank did emerge, he was rumpled and livid. A stray scrap of parchment clung to his ebony hair and clothing. Riona bit the side of her cheek and averted her eyes from his amber glare.

Sel cleared his throat and addressed the King who was still chuckling to himself. Again he spoke too loudly. "Your highness, may I offer my aid. You will need to strengthen yourself before we journey hence."

"You are a healer as well as my Gwen's champion? Are you under the mistaken idea that I am deaf, young Sel?"

"Nay sire. It is only the stuffing in my ears. I apologize. As to my healing ability, I only have the training given to soldiers for the battlefield, but I can strengthen you."

Startled by the mention of warfare, Arthur asked Crank, "Are we at war, Naf?"

"Nay Arthur, though I dinna expect Melwas to release his hold on your throne without a proper fight," Crank told him as he picked the tissue like parchment from his kilt.

"Ahh."

Whether the King fully understood his circumstances or not, Riona could not be sure. Nevertheless, he offered his fragile hand to Sel who gently sandwiched it between his two larger ones. Sel then closed his eyes to begin the process of transferring some of his own power into that of the withered King.

Crank hastily laid his blue hand on top of Sel's, adding his magick into the mix.

Like a dried sponge drinking in water, Arthur's physical appearance visibly improved during the transference. His skin grew less translucent, his face markedly less lined, his white hair darkened to reveal traces of his once ebony locks, and his frame grew less twig-like as starved muscle greedily absorbed the magick—the very essence of their race.

As Arthur grew younger, Sel and Crank began to age. Small lines appeared at the edges of Sel's eyes, white hair appeared at his temple, and the glow left his golden skin. Riona was relieved when the King pulled his hand out of Sel's grip.

Crank immediately protested, but a revitalized Arthur silenced him with a steely look.

"You will need your strength, Naf, before this day is ended." Turning to Sel he said, "I thank you for your aid." To all he announced loudly, "We must ride for Arawn's Keep."

"But Arthur, the Queen... she awaits. Vengeance on Lord Arawn can wait," Crank carefully counseled.

As if not hearing him, Arthur turned from Crank and strolled through the cell door. Crank's face paled, then he set out after Arthur. Straining to hear their conversation, Riona and Sel hastened after him.

"Naf, do not argue with me after all this time. We ride for the Keep. I will explain after we arrive. Have pity on me my friend. After so many centuries of disuse, my voice grows tired of yelling past the stuffing in your ears."

If Crank replied, Riona couldn't hear it.

The King, it seemed, had remembered what it was to be King.

Chapter 22

The journey back to her grandfather's Keep was turning out to be considerably less difficult. She was riding with Sel at her back, one arm encircled her waist while the other controlled the mare they shared. She had very little to do except push the occasional low hanging branch out of the way as they rode past.

Once they reached open ground, their party broke into a gallop. Unlike Crank's more direct and difficult route, Arthur decided to take the long way around. Riona wondered if it was because he was revealing in his freedom as surely she would have done, or if he wanted to delay his confrontation with her grandfather.

Sel remained absolutely silent behind her though his presence continued to hover at the edges of her mind, waiting patiently for her to let him in. She would have loved to know what he was thinking; what he thought of the state of the King, why they were going back to see her grandfather instead of racing for the border, why he thought the King had chosen to remain in Annwn after being separated from his mate for so long. If such a choice had been hers to make, Riona would have chosen to reunite with Sel. But once again none of her questions really mattered except as a way of passing the time. She'd never really been given a choice. Her father ruled her life. And it was his will that she submit to serve his purposes.

It took them an hour longer to reach the Keep than their journey from it. Riona was not surprised to see her grandfather waiting for them. Unlike before, he stood in the center of the moat's bridge, which was once again missing boards except for the portion he and his hounds commanded.

Arthur brought their party to a halt at the bridge's edge. "Lord Arawn, I have come to ask a boon," the King said in greeting.

Her grandfather sighed as if knowing what the King wished to ask of him. He looked beyond Arthur to her. She bowed her head in greeting before saying, "Hello, grandfather."

Arthur turned in his saddle towards her, his brow pinched in bewilderment. Unable to bear the guilt of what her father had done to him, Riona dropped the King's questioning gaze and pushed back into Sel's protective hold.

"Welcome, Arthur. Come, let us discuss your request further." And with a wave of his hand Lord Arawn made the bridge whole.

Arthur dismounted, as did the rest of them, leaving their horses where they stood to follow the god/king into his fortress.

* * *

Sel remained close to Riona as they reentered Lord Arawn's hall. He had fulfilled his Queen's request—found Arthur and released him. Why the rightful King wasn't speeding his way towards home was anyone's guess. It had been Arthur's wish they ride to Arawn's Keep, so to Arawn's Keep they had gone. Though kings and queens might prize your skills, listen to your counsel, and reward your service... Sel's experience had taught him that royalty tended to do as they damn well pleased. Ultimately their wishes were the laws you must live by. Sel couldn't help but wonder what Crank might be thinking of Arthur's decision, but the unfailingly opinionated unseelie had yet to utter one word since leaving the cave.

Yet despite the unsettling turn of events, Sel was more

concerned with Riona's fragile state of mind. This morning he had decided to refrain from addressing the issue between them, secretly hoping she would note the faint glow to his skin and understand its meaning. But if she had, she hadn't commented or shown any signs of surprise, relief, or even comprehension of its significance. What he now wanted was to find a private moment with her, to tell her that he loved her and he had every intention of binding her to him with the vows. Though sorely tempted to breach her mind's defenses so they could converse right now in secret, he sensed such a move would be ill advised. He'd have to be patient a while longer, at least until Arthur's request had been addressed and they were given leave to travel back Tir na n-Og.

"I cannot grant your request," Lord Arawn was telling Arthur.

"But we both know it is in your power to grant my wish if I were a member of your court," Arthur countered. Freed from his prison and strengthened with a portion of Sel's and Crank's power, the ancient King was acting more and more like the king of legend.

Lord Arawn glanced over Arthur to study his granddaughter. Catching the suspicious look of their host, Arthur and Sel turned their heads as well. Raising her chin, she unflinchingly held her grandfather's gaze.

Arthur spoke first. "If you are thinking she told me of the ritual, you would be mistaken. I did not know she was your kin until our meeting at the bridge. She has not betrayed you in word or deed," he told their host.

"I did not speak of it, grandfather," Riona confirmed the King's statement.

Sel reached for her hand and laced his fingers with hers. He was starting to suspect Arthur's intentions. He hoped he was mistaken.

Crank poured himself a drink. He was becoming more agitated as the conversion between Lord Arawn and the King progressed. He downed the amber liquid like a man dying of thirst then poured himself another.

"Arthur, it must be done by another, not by your own hand. And yes, you are well informed, it is in my power to grant you what you seek," Lord Arawn said cryptically.

Finally Crank could not hold his tongue any longer, their long friendship making him bold. "I will not do the foul deed you have rattling around in that decrepit brain of yours, Arthur. I dinna abandon my exile to have it end thus."

"Will you not release me, Naf, if I ask it of you? Has your love of me withered like this ill fitting skin of mine?"

"Nay, I will not. And how dare you question my loyalty!" Crank roared back.

As strong and unyielding as the mountain which had imprisoned him, Arthur remained unaffected by Crank's rising anger. The King, having already accepted the outcome of this day, steadily led his friend towards his inevitable cooperation. "Then I am at a loss, Naf. I cannot ask this of Sel." He pointed to the captain. "To preform this service for me, he must betray my Gwen," Arthur replied.

"So you ask this of me? I, your most loyal defender. I, who have served and protected you since before the unseelie throne was yours to claim? I, who protected and loved your mate as if she were my own? I breached the realms of the gods in an effort to find and restore you. And did you know they cursed me for it?" Crank paused, sweeping a bowl of fruit off the banquet table. It clattered to the ground, its contents slowly rolling to a stop. "How can you do this?" Crank shouted at Arthur.

Riona carefully whispered under her breath, "What are they talking about?"

Sel breathed into her hair, "Arthur is asking Naf for a hero's death, so he can receive something from Lord Arawn." The King had yet to address Crank's questions, nor did it appear he intended to.

"Why can you not leave now?" Riona asked Arthur. "Grandfather, would you stop him?"

Arthur graciously turned from the enraged unseelie to address her interruption. "It is hard to believe you are his child," he observed. "I sense a good and loyal heart in you." Pausing, he smiled warmly at her. "To answer your question, no, I cannot leave Annwn."

Riona started to protest. "But surely…" Sel squeezed her hand in warning.

As if the King hadn't heard her and though none in the room had asked it of him, Arthur continued his quiet explanation. "You have only been here a few days, my dear. And I suspect you have enjoyed the protection granted to you by your grandfather and Naf's woolly stuffing. Sadly, I did not." His strong mesmerizing voice held no self-pity. "I have listened and conversed with the spirits in this realm. They have been my only company, save that of your father. The consequence is I can no longer leave Annwn. It is a rule which cannot be broken, lest the jealously guarded secrets of death become known to the living. Gwen knows this as well as I. And so, either out of grief or anger at my weakness, she has stopped speaking to me." The King's eyes grew bright as tears gathered. "I miss her voice," he quietly admitted. Taking the time to clear his throat, he then told Riona, "I miss her more than you can imagine. I am empty without her. If your grandfather will grant me the cauldron's choice, then there is a chance we maybe reunited in another life. But in this one, I am neither alive nor dead. I am lost, forever separated from my heart."

By the end of the King's speech, his eyes weren't the only ones wet with tears. Sel pulled Riona close to him and thanked the gods she stood next to him. Whatever problems they had paled in comparison to the anguish and loss he read on Arthur's pained face.

Crank, drained of his anger, had collapsed into a chair beside the banquet table and was staring at the floor, a forgotten drink still clutched tightly in his hand.

Arthur turned back to Lord Arawn who had remained surprisingly withdrawn from the discussions in his hall. "Will you, Lord Arawn, grant me the choice of the cauldrons if I am a member of your court?" Arthur formally asked.

Lord Arawn looked past Arthur to Riona and Sel. "Would you grant this king his boon, Riona, if the power lay with you?"

In the stunned silence that followed Lord Arawn's question, all eyes turned once again to Riona.

Seeing the blood drain from her face, Sel came to her defense. "She should not have to make this decision."

When Lord Arawn turned his dark face toward Sel lightning flashed across his stormy gray eyes. "No. Perhaps you are right," the god/king admitted. "Would you make it for her, Captain of the Queen's Guard? I suspect you have an inkling of what the consequences will be. Your Queen will feel death's touch as well, and I know she has no direct female heir. Who will claim the seelie throne?"

Sel's heart froze at the thought.

"If I agree," Lord Arawn continued, "and if a most persuasive Arthur can force Naf to agree, my son will have to face the threat which has plagued him for most of his life. If I deny this worthy hero who now stands before me, then I will have actively participated in my son's torture of him."

"Haven't you already aided your bloody son in this foul deed?" Crank accused.

Lord Arawn, not taking offense at Crank's question, answered sadly, "No. I am not omnipotent, Naf. I had no knowledge of where my son had imprisoned Arthur, only that he had done so to gain his throne and of the prophecy which was set in motion by Arthur's release."

Before Crank could argue with the god/king, Arthur said, "What Lord Arawn says is true, Naf. Melwas has told me as much. We have discussed many things over the centuries. If any fault lies with our host, it is between him and his son. I have no quarrel with Lord Arawn. That should be enough for you."

Sel could see that Crank had much to say on the subject, but instead of arguing further, he drank the liquid in his cup and slammed the empty goblet down onto the table.

"I need an answer, Lord Arawn."

Never taking his eyes off Arthur, Lord Arawn said, "Naf, you will need all your strength. Drink what is in your cup."

Startled by and suspicious of the god/king's instructions, Crank reached for his empty goblet and found it full to the brim once more.

Lord Arawn, having come to his decision long before today, sighed and then said, "Arthur, I will grant your request. But before we go any further, I have a condition of my own."

Disheartened further by Lord Arawn's declaration, Crank drank from the goblet clutched in his hand and sank into the chair behind him.

"I am listening," Arthur replied.

Sel held his breath. It was all happening too quickly. He had not had the time to think about what this would mean for his Queen. If he had foreseen the terrible ending to this quest, he would have refused her for the first time in his life and locked himself away as Crank had tried to do.

"Sel and Riona must leave for Tir na n-Og without delay. I am sure the captain will want to be with his Queen. And you, Arthur, must remain in my court until the next new moon."

"Upon which time, I will be allowed to choose?" Arthur asked the god/king.

Having finished the contents of the cup, Crank slowly rose from his seat.

"Aye, this I promise," Lord Arawn answered. And once his word had been given, it could not be withdrawn.

Arthur had gotten what he wanted. Sel's gut twisted.

Refusing to meet anyone's gaze, Crank stood beside the banquet table, head bent, tears running down his blue cheeks. He withdrew his sword, the foreboding sound of its metal blade pulling free from the leather scabbard filled the eerily quiet hall. He let the blade's sharp tip rest against the tiled floor.

"Then I am ready," Arthur told the god/king. Turning to Sel he asked of him, "Tell my Gwen that I love her, and that I do this for us."

As if in a dream, Sel felt himself agree to Arthur's request. It can't end this way. Not now, not after all they had been through to find him, Sel's mind screamed.

Wanting to comfort him, Riona encircled his waist and laid her head against his chest. Her small hand covered his heart as if she could prevent the pain from reaching it.

"Now if you would do me the honor, Sel. I am in need of a sword."

Sel stood as if frozen. He could not do it. Even with Arthur patiently waiting, emerald eyes boring deeply into him, willing him to help. His hand just wouldn't obey the gentle order of this King and reach for his weapon. He couldn't give aid to one who would cause the death of his Queen.

After a several excruciating minutes where Sel grappled with his loyalties and the right and wrong of it all, the weight on his hip lightened as Riona withdrew his sword from its scabbard. Understanding his dilemma, she had taken it upon herself to relieve him of the impossible choice between the tortured King standing resolutely before him and his loyalty to a most beloved Queen.

"Thank you, child," Arthur responded when Riona presented him with the heavy sword. "I am sure Naf will return it."

The sword, once gifted to him by Gwenhwyfar had been one of Sel's most prized possessions. With it he had defended her reign, protected those in need, and served the interests of the Seelie Court. But most importantly, because he had taken the life of Calcus with its blade it had brought Riona to him. "I do not want it back," Sel told Arthur. "It is a cursed blade now."

Still holding the once cherished weapon between them, the King nodded kindly. "I understand. Perhaps you are right. But now I think it is time for you two to make your way back to court."

Sel, desperate to stop the unfolding events, tried once more to gain Crank's attention. Surely he would continue to fight this. "Crank!" Riona gently pulled on his arm but he ignored her. "Crank. Look at me," Sel barked.

When Crank slowly lifted his head and turned to lock eyes with him, Sel wished he hadn't insisted. True madness swam just below the surface of Crank's grief-stricken amber gaze. Despite this, Sel knew he had to try. “Crank. Stop him. He has to listen to you.”

But the unseelie Sel pleaded with was no longer the fey he had called commander and friend. Clothed in living flesh, Death replied, “Tell Melwas I hunt for him. The god's curse has come to pass.”

Riona was tugging on his arm in earnest now, and her fear flowed into him. Unable to do anything to stop the coming tragedy, Sel let her pull him from the hall.

Chapter 23

"I should have said more," Sel told her as she pulled him out of the Keep. "I should have done more."

"Listen to me, Sel. I have seen the look the King wears. He has made up his mind and no one will change it, not Crank, not you, not even my grandfather."

They were crossing the courtyard now. "I have killed my Queen," he said aloud.

Coming to a halt, she spun him around. "Listen to me, Sel. You have not killed her. I will not have you bearing this guilt," she snapped. "He's the one who is choosing to end their lives, hero's death or not the result is still the same. It is selfish of him." She paused to lay her palm against his cheek. More gently she told him, "But you have it in your power to help ensure that they will be granted another life. I have witnessed the ritual Arthur is seeking. Sel, he will live again, and so will Gwenhwyfar. But they will not be given this second chance if we delay. We must leave as my grandfather has instructed or else it is all for naught."

With his world crumbling around him, Sel found himself anchored by his mate's words. Oh, how he loved this woman, he thought. Out of the evil events of this day, she had found and offered a hope for him to cling to. He kissed her palm and laced his fingers with hers. "You are right. We must ride for the border."

Finding their horses still at the bridge, Sel moved into action. Picking the swiftest of the three, he mounted and then reached down and swept Riona up into his lap. He knew he could get them to the gateway faster sharing a horse than if she rode beside him.

With little urging, the big gray leapt forward. Sel galloped recklessly across the field, up the slope then plunged down the other side. He could hear the whispered voices Arthur had befriended and Crank had warned against. Promises sweet and low tickled his ear. In their haste, they had not thought to replace the wooly stuffing to block the enticing voices.

Riona didn't complain about the speed at which he traveled, though her fingers gripped the horse's mane in front of her, knuckles white. To be honest, Sel was afraid to slow down. To distract her from the reckless ride and the even more dangerous pleas of the dead, he began singing to her. They were bawdy ballads he had learned while serving in the ranks of the Guard as a tracker. Why such songs sprang to his mind now, Sel had no idea. But he sang them anyway, loudly and enthusiastically.

When they finally reached the rowan grove Sel was forced to slow their pace to a walk. He stopped singing as he navigated them through the tree's tightly overlapping branches.

When Riona began singing to him, he was stunned. But he was not surprised to discover that she had a beautiful voice, low and sultry. Unlike his raucous songs, her melody was more of a lullaby and it didn't take much of a leap for him to picture her one day singing to their child. The thought warmed his heart and at that moment Sel realized he had very little to fear from the promises floating by them on the breeze. Everything he ever wanted in life, he now held in his arms.

* * *

Riona began singing because she feared the earlier despair she had seen in Sel's eyes. It was obvious he had started singing those outrageous songs to keep from listening to the promises of the dead swirling all around them. Feeling the need to protect him, she had taken up the task when his voice had finally faltered.

She had witnessed the moment Sel realized he was about to lose his precious Queen, the driving force of his life. Sel was many things but first and foremost he was the Gwenhwyfar's champion, her captain. His entire life had been dedicated to the Seelie Queen and Court. And now all that had defined him was coming to an end.

His newly lined face and graying hair was a testament to just how much of himself he had been willing give in an effort to restore the Absent King to the Seelie Queen. Riona didn't mind the new lines, but she did fear he wasn't as strong as he would need to be in the coming darkness which now faced the Seelie Court.

Because Riona worried for him, she sang. She sang because he was just now beginning to grieve for Gwenhwyfar, the Queen he cherished. She sang because the despair she had seen in his pained eyes scared her and because the whispers swirling around them seemed desperate to be acknowledged. Her songs were a feeble show of support, but considering what she'd have to do once they reach Tir na n-Og, it was all she could do for him. She needed to make sure he got to Gwenhwyfar's side to say his good-byes. It would be her final task for the day, and a last gift to him.

From their current advantage point, she could see the white beach below. Choking on the thought of leaving him, Riona's song fell silent mid-phrase.

"We are almost there," he said close to her ear. He then carefully picked their way down the hillside the three of them had climbed two days before.

A wave of jealousy stabbed Riona. Gwenhwyfar had not asked for their love, but nevertheless three men had loved her completely and had been willing to profess it for any who cared to hear. Arthur, her mate, who was bound to her by the vows, loved her. Crank who had protected and come to love Arthur's mate as if she were his own, loved the Queen as well. And then there was Sel—the golden captain of her court and her truest servant. Gwenhwyfar's death would be hardest on him.

His mind brushed lightly against hers and Riona's heart ached in her chest. Sel should belong to her, not Gwenhwyfar. But even now, his actions were solely aimed at reaching his monarch's side. Had he not already openly admitted to being in love with Gwenhwyfar?

Riona stifled the despair she felt. Because he refused to say what she knew to exist in his heart Riona could only conclude that Sel didn't trust her. It could be because she was unseelie and her mother's daughter, reason enough for most; or it could be because she was her father's issue. But these circumstances of birth paled in comparison to Riona's true fear—that there was only room for Gwenhwyfar in his heart.

At least after she returned to the Unseelie Court, the captain would be able to soothe himself with the knowledge that he had never professed loving an unseelie, even for a moment. No one would be able to claim he had been a fool or mock Sel for being cuckold as they had with Brianna.

Actually it occurred to her that in the coming days, Sel would undoubtedly have much more important matters to occupy his thoughts. The turmoil in the Seelie Court would distract the court's attention away from her father's high-handedness in supplanting Sel's contract with Aeron's newer one. No one would be concerned with Sel's private affairs, her abandonment, or the shortness of their contract. And the members of the Seelie Court weren't likely to hear the ugly gossip her father and Aeron were bound to spread. For Sel's sake, Riona hoped Aeron had plans to lock her away. Whatever he planned for her, she would submit if it kept him from parading her in open court.

They had reached the dunes, and Sel brought the sweaty horse to a stop. Dismounting first, he then helped her down before securing the reins to the saddle. Giving the animal his freedom, Sel slapped the horse's rump and set him on his way home.

Avoiding his gaze, she walked across the white sands until she reached the water's edge. When she sensed him near, her hand unerringly reached for his. "We must hurry," she said unnecessarily.

Unable to persuade them to stay, the whispers of the dead grew still.

With his hand still holding hers, Sel was the first to step into the brackish water. The fog parted for them as it had done during their first crossing. In less time than she would have liked they were walking through the archway furthest to the left and emerging onto the solid ground of their own realm.

There was a seelie guard waiting for them.

"Liam," Sel greeted the guard, returning the customary salute.

"The Queen has fallen ill. She is asking for you, sir."

The news, naught but a terrible thought at this early stage was most probably being kept secret from most of the court, Riona thought.

Sel had flinched at the news, before he had calmly nodded. Both he and Riona knew it wasn't an illness Gwenhwyfar would recover from. Soon Liam would know it as well.

"Go now," Riona urged him. Choosing her words carefully so as not to lie, she said, "I will return to your rooms in the Seelie Court to wait." She could see the relief of not having to worry about her reflected in his eyes.

"Our rooms," Sel corrected, letting go of her hand.

"Of course." Now was not the time to argue with him she told herself.

Turning to Liam, he instructed the guardsman, "Escort my mate to our quarters and remain there. I go to the Queen."

Surprised, but not in a position to question his superior, the guardsman, gave his captain a crisp nod and salute. Without a final word to her, Sel disappeared, leaving the startled guardsman alone with her.

She should not have been hurt by his abrupt departure but she was. Burying her feelings, Riona took a deep breath and gave her best performance yet. Lifting her chin in a royal manner, she said, "Well, Liam. Let us go then." Without needing his guidance she folded space and pictured the place where she most wanted to be. A heartbeat later she stood surrounded by the dark greens of Sel's study. Liam arrived two heartbeats later.

Turning to him she used her sweetest voice, "Unlike Sel, I understand all the guardsmen would like to be near the Queen at this desperate time. I see no need for you to stay. I am content to wait for Sel until the danger to the Queen has abated."

Doubt crossed Liam's face. "I was ordered to stay."

"Yes, I know, but I am sure it was an oversight. Sel adores the Queen. Did you not notice him flinch when you told him of her falling ill?" Riona felt bad for Liam, caught as he was between her and his captain. But she needed him to disobey Sel and leave her, and yet still feel confident he wasn't disregarding a direct order.

"At least go and report to him that I am safely in our quarters." Riona had to make her self say "our" instead of "his" when in truth these rooms would never belong to her.

Liam brightened with her last suggestion. "Aye. Tis a wise idea," he said because it gave him the excuse he needed to glean the latest news on the Queen's health.

Riona smiled sweetly at him. "You do that. I need to change should he call for me," she said indicating the state of her muddy clothes.

That was all the encouragement Liam needed. He vanished, leaving her blessedly alone.

Not trusting Liam would stay away, Riona didn't waste any time with self-pity. First, she shimmered to rid herself of the muck clinging to her. She then clothed herself as she thought her father might wish for such an occasion; an eggplant colored silk gown with little embellishments, cut lower than she would have liked to accent her breasts, a tightly fitting bodice to emphasize her waist, and a full enough skirt so as not to constrict her movements. Her shoulder length hair she left unbound. Her father preferred her hair long like her mother's, but Riona could not bring herself to change this one act of open rebellion just to suit his liking. It should be enough that she was returning to him as instructed.

When Riona was sure she had struck the right note of feminine softness for her father and austere stylishness to remind Aeron of her rank, Riona dashed into Sel's bedroom to retrieve the only trinket her father had ever given her.

Digging through her trunk she found the ugly silver medallion at the bottom, wrapped in a scrap of discarded fabric. On one side it was completely smooth, the other bore the stamp of a great black boar. She had never understood its significance until witnessing the cauldron ceremony with her grandfather. The boar was the symbol of power gifted to him by the cauldron's waters. Wearing this adopted emblem predominately in front of Aeron would please her father, and it would declare her loyalty to him despite the signing of the contract. Stringing a black ribbon through a hole at its top, she tied it so that the medallion settled just below the hollow of her neck.

Riona ignored the other belongings in her small chest. She wouldn't need them, nor did she want to be burdened with the happy memories they could ignite.

Steeling herself for what was to come, Riona shifted to her father's private rooms.

Chapter 24

Riona materialized at the center of the lavishly furnished audience chamber she remembered so well. Not much had changed, the room's theme was still black and gold intimidation. The marbled walls, floor, and ceiling were all black. Most of the heavy furniture had copious amounts of gold inlay, the tapestries and embroidered accents either prominently displayed her father's boar emblem or deceptions of him as the warrior king of the Unseelie Court.

There was only one unseelie waiting to greet her—Aeron. As promised, he was there to collect her from her father.

He stood near her father's ornate chair, one hand resting along the garishly carved backrest. Like most in the warrior caste, he went shirtless in order to draw attention to his blue-tinted muscled chest and whatever battle tattoos he had earned. He was minus his sword. Her father trusted no one and wouldn't have allowed an armed fey into his inner-sanctum. She gave a small nod of her head but otherwise she held her tongue.

Since her arrival his smile had grown wide, taking his time to appreciate her form. Finally he bowed gallantly to her and then said, "Welcome back, Princess. May I say, you look absolutely ravishing today." He took several steps down from the raised platform on which her father's chair sat. "I should warn you, your father is in an ill mood this afternoon." His handsome face grew mischievous, a cruel delight dancing in his amber eyes.

"Thank you for the warning. I have come as he bid," she replied politely. Refusing to let Aeron gain the upper hand, she held his gaze, daring him to be the first to drop eye contact. Once he crossed the distance between them, his gaze did drop, but just low enough to take in the swell of her breasts. His lips twitched, giving the impression he might be fighting the urge to lick them, like a dog anticipating its dinner.

Riona ignored his leering. Raising her chin slightly she began to ask him if she could see the new contract when her father marched into the room. As soon as he spotted her, she dropped into a low curtsy and heard Aeron casually move away. She held the curtsy for longer than was necessary, but she wanted to portray a submissive nature to her father. By the time she stood again, it was too late to prepare herself for the strike to her cheek. The force of it sent her tumbling down onto the black marble floor, where she knew from experience she should remain.

"You betrayed me!" he screamed at her. "I know they freed him!" Melwas pulled his arm back to strike her again, but refrained when he saw the medallion about her neck.

Holding a hand to her stinging cheek she quickly lied. "Father, I have not betrayed you. Each day they rode away from the Keep and left me with grandfather." She knew from experience a half truth was easier to tell.

He cock his head, waiting for the rest of her explanation.

"I swear it. Grandfather can attest to my ignorance of any wrong done to you."

Her father lowered his hand, but she knew there was more to come. It was a test. He hadn't yet given her leave to rise from the floor so she stayed where she had fallen. If she stood without permission, he would strike her again. She let her eyes grow wide and clear and said nothing about his unprovoked attack. Riona couldn't help but note that Aeron hadn't attempted to intervene during her reunion with her father.

Still towering over her, Melwas asked, "What do you know of it? Surely they let something slip while in your company."

Riona swallowed then told him, "Nothing. Neither trusted me enough to explain why we had gone to Annwn in the first place. I returned with the captain. I came as soon as I could get away, just as you bid me. Cr… Naf," she quickly amended, "remained behind. I do not know why."

Beyond the shadow of her father, Aeron asked, "Did the captain find my gift swirling around in your mind or were you successful in hiding our bit of fun from him, Princess?"

Seemingly satisfied with her explanation, her father stalked away, leaving Riona with a clear view of Aeron. His form would have tempted most females, but his looks left Riona cold.

"The Queen's illness took precedent," she told the gloating warrior.

"Really? Does she have a runny nose? Did he need to rush back to wipe it?" Aeron asked, taking a delighted pleasure in knowing the Seelie Queen suffered.

Her father's pacing abruptly stopped.

Riona dropped her eyes to the floor when he looked at her.

"Rise, girl," he ordered impatiently. Then he barked, "What illness?"

While gracefully rising to stand, Riona told her father about being met at the gateway by the guardsman, Liam, and the captain's hasty departure shortly thereafter. She watched as her father's complexion paled. To see a glimmer of fear in him was satisfying.

"Nothing was explained to me," she lied again. It was becoming easier now. Riona was starting to remember how to play the game; a half truth shared in confidence, a bold-faced lie given with a demure smile, absolute truth offered as proof so all seemed plausible to the listener.

Intent on seeing to his own interests, Aeron addressed her father, while managing to slither within reach of her. "My Lord, I know you have much on your mind. May I suggest we move forward with the signing of the contract."

Riona had noticed her father grow dangerously still, but Aeron either wasn't paying attention or he was beyond stupid.

The young warrior held his blue hand out to her, one dark eyebrow lifting.

The thought of touching him was absolutely repulsive to Riona, but her father was watching her like a hawk for signs of rebellion. Riona managed to place her hand into Aeron's without flinching. She even gave him a shy smile.

"Show her where to sign, Aeron. But then I have a task for you," her father instructed. When Aeron's mouth opened to offer protest, Melwas cut him off. "I am giving you what you want most, boy. Now is not the time to get greedy. After seeing how well behaved my daughter is being, I have a mind to take back my gift before you have had time to unwrap it. Perhaps there is someone in my court who is more worthy than you."

For once Riona was happy her father liked torturing his men.

Seeing the disquieting effect of his threat on Aeron's face, her father taunted Aeron further. "Have you taken the time to truly look at her, Aeron? Is she not worth all that I might put you through? Now that I think on it, you have the good fortune of being only the second fey to bed her. I doubt the captain has much skill. She will undoubtedly be a virgin in most things. I think her price has just gone up."

Masking his panic as best he could, Aeron gave the Unseelie King a partial bow and said, "You're daughter is a most marvelous prize. And you are most gracious to entrust me with her care, my King. How may I continue to earn your favors?"

Melwas smirked. "Get the bloody paper signed and stow her away. Her charms can wait, I have an unseelie for you to hunt."

With a tight rein on his natural arrogance, Aeron managed to sound honest when he told the King, "As always, I live to serve."

Her father's smirk never faltered, but the brief distraction that Aeron's lust provided had worn thin. King Melwas waved them away. Riona was sure he was fretting over the release of Arthur and what it meant for him. Discovering the Seelie Queen was ill had only troubled him more.

As Aeron pulled her away from her father and towards a side table, her Aunt Morgain entered the room dressed in an exceptionally sheer gown. Her ebony hair was haphazardly piled atop her head, as if she had just risen from the King's bed. Riona knew her aunt had entertained her father in the past. Perhaps she had finally been successful in supplanting Riona's mother as the King's favorite mistress.

Noticing Riona's attendance, her Aunt said, "It is nice to see you have finally taken your rightful place in your father's court, niece. Better late than never."

Riona ignored her aunt's barb. "Hello, Aunt Morgain." Because Riona's father had encouraged and rewarded submission in the female sex, most unseelie males enjoyed total power over their female counterparts. Morgain was exceptionally adept at playing the subservient role.

Aeron stopped to give Morgain a polite nod and greeting. "As always, Morgain, it is a pleasure to be graced with your lovely presence." As the King's favorite, she wielded the power of influence. He respected that, but nothing more.

She smiled at him, but otherwise ignored him. The King was exceedingly jealous when it came to his bed partners. Unlike Riona's mother, Morgian's sexual nature had never once wavered from the King.

Riona briefly wondered if her grandfather were watching this family reunion. Riona watched her aunt approach her father. She spoke a few words and then retreated the way she had come.

Aeron regained Riona's attention when he handed her a gold quill and tersely ordered, "Sign there. Your father has already signed, but I do not want it said that you were forced." He gave her lower back a light shove.

Sick to her stomach, Riona leaned over the parchment. Aeron moved his hand from the middle of her back to her buttocks. He then squeezed, startling her. Biting her tongue, Riona ignored his exploration as best she could and tried to steady her hand. Despite her efforts, it continued to shake. To gain time so she could settle herself, she asked conversationally, "What are the terms of the contract?" Her heart was racing now. The fear of being alone with this fey had started to grow difficult for her to hide. and She had also began to doubt the soundness of her reasoning for coming back to her father's court.

Her mild question annoyed him, and he leaned close to hiss, "The terms, Princess, are that you belong to me."

Stepping back, quill still in hand, she persisted, "Yes, I understand I am bound to you by the contract, but is it like the contract with Calcus? At what point does my father regain his rights?"

She was now wishing she had never come. At this moment anywhere else would have been preferable.

Aeron didn't answer her right away. By the way he cocked his head and narrowed his eyes, Riona knew she had somehow pushed him too far.

"You are very much like your mother, I think. So I will be honest with you."

He pulled her close, and spoke into her ear so as not to be overheard by her father.

"Riona, my very own princess... because it gave me pleasure to do it, I have done unimaginable things to fey and halfling alike," he told her as easily as if they were talking about the weather. "I sup nightly on the terror of others, gorging myself on their pain. Do you really want to test my patience with silly questions?" He paused to stroke the skin along her neck. "For the moment, you are a prize to me, something to be cherished and enjoyed fully. But all new things tarnish over time."

His hand dropped lower to cover her breast, he then pinched her nipple until she winced.

"This is not the time to become dull to me. Sign the contract without a fuss in front of your father." He let go of her nipple and carefully smoothed the wrinkle in the fabric. "Please me for as long as you can, Princess, and I will try very hard to remain interested in keeping you in good health." He loosened his grip to read the fear on her face.

She saw a hint of disappointment at the corners of his mouth when he found none. The only thing keeping the abject terror from overflowing onto her serene face was the years of practice spent avoiding her father's fury. With her voice quivering slightly, Riona gave him the words she sensed he craved most. "My father spent many years teaching me to live by his will alone. I now see that all his hard work was so that I might serve and please you as you deserve. Forgive me, Aeron, for not understanding sooner."

She was rewarded by his self-satisfied smile. His blue

fingers briefly stroked the pale skin along her cheek. Without being prompted again, she bent over the table and signed her name to the foul contract.

Chapter 25

Sel arrived in the Queen's outer hall and was met by Fain, Digon's twin and Sel's second lieutenant. The two brothers were nearly identical in their looks, expect for a prominent scar that ran from the corner of Fain's eye to his jawbone.

Without saluting, Fain told him, "She collapsed about an hour ago."

"Does she still live?"

"Aye, but she cannot speak. Only a few are able to communicate with her by mind link; Tristian, myself, Airem, and of course you will be able."

Fain fell into step as they crossed the white hall. The news of the Queen's condition was spreading quickly. Many of his guardsmen and some members of court had already gathered; their mood was somber, reverent, and not surprisingly... nervous. This was just the beginning, more would arrive within the hour as rumors flew.

"Fain, we will need to inform all the noble clan chiefs. Send out men to gather representatives from the most powerful seelie houses."

"Tristian has already dispatched them."

The massive bronze doors leading to the Queen's audience chamber opened when they drew near and he and Fain swept through. Sel paused only long enough to issue an order to the guards on the other side. "Let only the family heads pass into this room, but no further, until I speak with her."

"Aye, Captain," one of the four guardsmen replied. All four saluted. He returned their salute, fist to chest, before moving on.

It had surprised Sel when Fain had informed him that his Queen still hung on to life. He had expected to arrive to news of her passing. For a fleeting moment, the unrealistic hope she might recover seized him.

They traveled quickly through the formal audience room into a smaller waiting area which served as a buffer between the public and private rooms of the Queen. The intimate space was filled with more guardsmen who parted for them as they strode through, many quick with a salute, but none tried to delay him. The heavy bronze doors he and Riona had moved through only days before stood ajar, and the once powerful ward Arthur had created to enhance the protection of the doors was no more. It had ceased to exist upon Arthur's death. For Sel, it was the tangible proof a great era ended. Gwenhwyfar was indeed dying.

Fain brought him to Tristian who stood guard in front of Gwenhwyfar's closed bedchamber door, his face drawn with worry. They clasped forearms in a warrior's handshake.

"She is waiting."

Sel nodded. "I am glad you were with her when I could not be."

Tristian's eyes were red with his own grief. Releasing Sel's arm, he cleared his throat. "There is a handmaiden of Arianrhod with her now. Her mother, the goddess Danu, has come and gone as well. Our Queen bargains for more time."

Sel had always been able to count on Tristian to keep a clear head during times of crisis. This was no different.

"Will Arianrhod grant it?" Fain asked.

"As of yet it is undecided," Tristian told them, then turning he unlocked the door and stepped aside for Sel to pass. None followed and the door was gently closed behind him.

The usually bright room was now cloaked in shadows.

The heavy sky blue drapes were drawn closed and sweet smelling candles had been lit. The handmaiden, robed in white, stood near the Queen's low bed. Hearing him enter, the handmaiden turned, her face still obscured by the cowl of her hood. Silently she moved away to give him some privacy with the Queen.

As Sel drew closer to Gwenhwyfar's side, the reality of what had occurred in Annwn finally descended upon him.

His most beloved Queen was propped up with pillows into a sitting position. Her once glowing skin was now gray, her face showing lines that had never existed before. She looked empty, as if her very essence had been drained from her. Seeing her so diminished, tears gathered in his eyes.

Dropping down onto one knee, he said in a choked voice, "My Queen, I have failed you."

When her sweet voice bloomed inside his head, Sel wanted to weep. Despite his efforts to remain strong, his shoulders shook under the weight of his grief as his tears fell unhindered.

Sel, the failure is mine. I have tried to win a game that has no winners. Arthur tried to tell me as much, but I refused to listen to his counsel. I am the one who has failed. Do not blame yourself for my arrogance.

Woven into her words was a sense of contentment which helped to lighten some of Sel's sorrow. Knowing she needed to say more, Sel reached for her limp hand and wiped at his eyes with the other. He knew contact would make conversing easier for her. There were decisions to make and his Queen could only communicate with a select few; her three most trusted guardsmen, and Airem—her enforcer who was dragon-kind and unlikely to be of any service to her now. "What are your instructions?" he asked aloud, his voice thick with emotion.

His unwavering ability to anticipate her needs put a smile on her face.

Listen closely, Sel. I have been granted a little time by Arianrhod, but I have much to accomplish. Bring Sinnie to me. Though she is not the daughter of my womb, she is the daughter of my heart. I have already told Tristian she is to inherit my crown. I have watched her closely. She is of a noble house, she will have the love of her guardsmen, and I fear the Seelie Court will need the strength of a warrior queen in the coming days.

Silence.

Sel took a deep breath and began to nod, but stopped when Gwenhwyfar voice continued. *This is only half of your task. Now I come to the difficult part.*

Sel remained silent.

Hueil, Sinnie's bound mate, must claim the unseelie throne. If the prophecy is fulfilled, then Naf will make this task much easier for him. But it is imperative Hueil becomes King.

"I cannot imagine a crown on that one's head," Sel told her honestly. In response he heard her laughter tumble through his mind, and it gave him much joy.

I believe he is the only unseelie with the ability to heal the damage done to Arthur's court by Melwas's rule. I have believed this for a long time. He does not know it, but I have protected him over the centuries, providing him with helpers while he languished in exile.

That was news to Sel. He wondered how Hueil would react if told of Gwenhwyfar's efforts.

It is in the past. Hueil is better off not knowing.

Sel smiled at her quick response. "As you wish," he replied. He rose and kissed her ring, as he had done countless times. "I will go now to fetch my daughter and her mate." When he started to pull back her cold fingers tightened around his hand.

Realizing she had more to tell him, Sel leaned over the bed which seemed to swallow up her petite form.

Delay the announcement of my dying until Sinnie has been brought to me. Once she arrives, I wish to be alone with her. Bar the door. Not even Hueil may be present when I pass my powers to her. It has been done this way, Seelie Queen to Seelie Queen, from the beginning.

"It will be done just as you wish, my Queen," Sel promised her. His mind was still reeling from the idea of his daughter as the next Seelie Queen. He had no doubt she'd be a good and fair ruler, but she was still very young. And Hueil... Sel's mind simply couldn't picture Hueil as the King of the Unseelie Court. Sure, he had lived long enough to amass quite a bit of power, his being of the warrior caste gave him even more strength than a noble of the same age. But King?

To ease his doubts, he asked Gwenhwyfar, "What have you seen of the coming days, of Sinnie and Hueil's rule?"

Still holding her fragile hand, the Queen's eyes closed. Sel waited, knowing she was looking inward to find the answer. Eventually she opened her eyes and pursed her lips, her brow creased making the new lines in her face deeper.

I fear, I see only darkness. My gift of foresight has left me, just as the strength has left my limbs. They will have to rely on their own skills and the talents of those loyal to them. Now go, do this final task for me." Giving into her weakness, she released his hand and closed her eyes again.

Sel turned to white robed figure in the room. "How much time does she have?"

Before answering his question, the handmaiden removed her hood.

Sel's initial reaction was that she was shockingly young to be in the service of a god. Her honey blonde hair was piled atop her head, wisps framing a heart shaped face. She would have been considered extraordinarily beautiful, even among the race of the fey. But try as Sel might, he could not tell what race she was; not fey, not dragon, not shifter. The clear blue eye color indicated divinity, but he could not sense any god powers surrounding the handmaiden. Still, there was something strangely familiar about her features.

"Mother has given your Queen until the next new moon. I am here to witness the exchange of power, and give the goddess's blessing to the new Seelie Queen and that of her reign," she told him.

"The Queen has said none are to be present save that of my daughter," he replied.

"An oversight, nothing more. A handmaiden of Arainhrod has been present at every coordination of the Seelie Court. Your Queen will verify this—when the time draws near."

Until the next new moon, Sel thought. Gwenhwyfar had less than two weeks to guide and train Sinnie in her new duties. Turning from the maiden, Sel let himself out of the Queen's bedchamber.

"Tristian, I go to escort the new Queen home. I think it best if I step aside and let her pick a new captain for her guard. I will recommend you as my choice."

"But Sel…" Tristian began.

Sel cut him off. "I am her father. I cannot also be her captain, Tristian. You are more than qualified than any other, but we all know Sinnie to be head-strong. She might chose another, simply because you are also her uncle by blood."

"Almost all the fey in the Guard think of her as theirs," Tristian replied.

Sel couldn't help but smile. He hadn't raised his daughter

alone. Sinnie had long ago become the living heart of the Guard, cherished by all.

Turning to Fain, Sel said, "I need someone I can trust to guard my other daughter until the new Seelie Queen releases me from my responsibilities. Will you do this for me?" With every member of the Guard wanting to be with the Queen in her time of need, Sel had the ongoing problem of providing security for Jen and Steven after Sinnie and Hueil had returned to Tir na n-Og. And then there was the problem of Gwenhwyfar's refugees housed at castle Tearmann. He would need to get a message to Digon. Arthur's choice to seek a hero's death was having long reaching consequences.

"The handmaiden said Gwenhwyfar only has until the next new moon. Make no announcements to the nobles until I return with Sinnie," he told Tristian.

He didn't need to see Tristian's nod to know his order would be carried out, nor did Sel need to tell Fain to follow him before shifting.

"Sinnie?" Sel called as soon as he had materialized in the hallway of Jen's and Steven's house. Fain appeared a moment later.

Poking her head out of one of the front rooms, she shushed him, her index finger to her lips. "Jen is sleeping. She had another nightmare last night."

As sick as Sel was about Gwenhwyfar's pending death, to see his daughter worry over her half-sister's health warmed his heart. "Daughter, where is Hueil? Has he returned? I need to speak with both of you."

She motioned him and Fain into the room and closed the door behind them. "Yes. He returned a day ago. He is feeding the horse this morning with Steven. What has happened? You look...

tired, father," she said, unable to hide her concern.

"I look old."

One of her red eyebrows lifted. "You have looked better. Where is your uniform?"

Sel glanced down and realized he was still dressed in the clothes he'd worn leaving Annwn. The murky waters at the border had stained them from the waist down and his boots were covered in mud. "I will explain as soon as Hueil arrives. Other than her trouble sleeping, how is Jen's health?"

"Good. The child she carries is healthy as well. Tomorrow is their wedding. I have been creating a bouquet for her to carry. She says it is traditional to have one. What do you think?" Sinnie reached for the bundle of flowers laying on the coffee table. "I used a little spell to keep the flowers fresh."

"They are beautiful. I am sure she will love what you have done," Sel told her, realizing Sinnie would now have to miss witnessing her half-sister's human ceremony. Before he could say anymore, Hueil materialized inside the room.

"Bloody hell, Captain, you look damn awful," Hueil exclaimed in greeting. Then turning to Fain, who had remained silent thus far, he said, "Is Fain to join us?"

"No, Hueil. We have come to fetch you and Sinnie," Fain replied.

Sel held is hand up to forestall Fain from saying any more. Addressing Hueil he asked, "What of Gloric? What was the outcome?"

While taking several steps towards Sinnie, Hueil delivered a concise report. "He is living with a woman who is dragon-kind. She more or less owns him, according to their laws. There is no danger of him upsetting the treaty with the dragons, or of him traveling beyond their lands. We left him as we found him."

"And of your brother, Neb. Where is he?"

Hueil frowned and looking slightly shame-faced at Sinnie he said, "He went to see Bran, my other brother."

"The one who maintains a pleasure den?" Sinnie snapped. "Did you go?"

Hueil cringed and then he asked her, "Do you really want Neb here—with no entertainment?"

Before his daughter could gather anymore steam in picking a fight with his son-in-law, Sel interrupted the couple. "Sinnie, forget Neb. There is much more at stake right now."

Catching the seriousness of her father's tone, Sinnie asked, "What has happened, father?"

Sel paused to take a deep breath. "Sinnie, there is no easy way to say this." Sel hesitated again.

"Spit it out, Captain," Hueil prodded.

"I am not here as your father," Sel began, "but as the Captain of the Queen's Guard. Queen Gwenhwyfar is dying. You are to inherit her crown." Sel watched as the blood drained from his daughter's face, the impact of his words dawning. "She is asking for you," he said more gently. We do not have much time. I failed. The Absent King..." Sel looked from his daughter's stricken face to Hueil, "he is dead."

Several long minutes passed where no one breathed, much less spoke. Shattering the stunned silence, Hueil spewed a string of curses not usually heard outside of battle. Sel watched his daughter closely. She had not moved. She was still cradling Jen's flowers in her hands.

Fain went down on one knee and bowed his head to the new Seelie Queen. Sel glanced at Hueil's panicked face and then he too bent his knee and bowed to their new Queen.

Finally Hueil told Sinnie, "I think you bloody well have to tell them to rise or they will remain thus until hell freezes over.

In a wooden voice Sinnie said, "Rise, Father. Fain."

When Sel stood once more, Sinnie demanded, "What is she thinking? What of Melwas? What of Jen and the other halflings she protects?"

From behind him, Fain said, "Gwenhwyfar has faith in you, as do we all."

Sel answered another one of her questions. "Fain will remain to guard Jen and Steven until you can choose a new captain, and I can take up my responsibilities here." Knowing time was against them, Sel gently reminded her, "Take a moment to gather your things, we should not delay."

As in a trance, Sinnie carefully laid Jen's bouquet onto the sofa behind her.

When his daughter turned to leave the room, Sel said. "May I suggest you arm yourself. By the time the court hears of your ascension, they will expect to see a warrior queen."

Tucking a loose strain of red hair behind her ear, she nodded before slipping silently from the room to retrieve her weapons."

When Hueil started to follow, Sel grabbed his arm and spoke quickly. "Gwenhwyfar has said that you must claim the Unseelie throne. She believes Crank will clear the way by removing Melwas. I believe her. Hueil, I hope you still have friends you can call on because you will need to amass powerful supporters among the unseelie."

When one corner of Hueil's mouth lifted, Sel knew Hueil had already begun to plan. Hueil was many things, but unresourceful he was not.

Sel said in a rush, "Sinnie can hold the seelie throne; the

Guard will support and protect her as will most of the noble houses. Despite what Melwas claims, he only ruled because Gwenhwyfar allowed it. The Seelie Queen has always chosen her King, never the other way around."

Hueil's amber eyes showed no fear. If anything, he seemed eager. "I will see Sin safely delivered to the Queen before I leave to make my claim."

Sel let his hand drop away and Hueil shifted from the room. It didn't surprise Sel that Hueil hadn't argued with him or tried to deny he had once entertained the idea of being King. Hueil's confidence added to the hope Riona had been able to give him. Twice now, an unseelie had given him hope to hold onto when the world around him seemed to be flying apart.

When they were once again assembled Sinnie was dressed in her usual black leather and knives, her flame red hair was braided and pinned at the nape of her neck. Hueil had dressed in the unseelie warrior way and nearly matched her for weaponry, the black sword he had wielded against Melwas was predominately displayed strapped to his hip. Sel thought they made a striking pair, both were warriors, natural leaders, and capable of inspiring loyalty in others.

Hueil gave Sinnie a kiss then told his mate, "You are going to make one hellacious queen, Sin. I hope Gwenhwyfar knows what she's doing."

Sinnie playfully glared up at him before holding out her hand for him to grasp. "Shut up, Hueil."

In unison, the three of them shifted to the Queen's audience hall and found Bradwen waiting for them. Taking point, Bradwen parted the gathering nobles so Sinnie could pass. Sel and Hueil followed a step behind.

Guessing at the significance of Sinnie's arrival, a few

nobles bowed or curtsied as they swept through. By now, news of Gwenhwyfar's wishes had filtered into the smaller waiting room, and the guardsmen in attendance bowed to Sinnie as she moved past them. Sel couldn't help but be proud of the way his daughter handled the unfamiliar treatment from those she had called friend, teacher, and on occasion uncle. Each time they entered a new room, more guardsmen bowed, some verbally declaring their support by greeting her as "my Queen".

Finally their procession reached Gwenhwyfar's bedchamber door. Here, Sel would say good-byes to his daughter. As Seelie Captain, he had other duties to see to; Tearmann and the refugees, the nobles and their concerns, and he had to make the formal announcement of Queen Gwenhwyfar's dying while paving the way for Sinnie's rule.

"Tristian, is Arianhrod's handmaiden still with the Queen?"

"Aye. The Queen confirmed she must be present."

Sel didn't like it, but it seemed he had no choice in the matter. Before letting his daughter take the final steps into the room that would soon become her own, he kissed her forehead like he had done so many times. "Sinnie, she has asked to speak to you alone. Tristian will lock the door behind you and none will be allowed to enter until you give the command. When you reemerge, you will be the new Seelie Queen."

Taking a fortifying breath, Sinnie stole a quick glance at her mate. Sel was encouraged when his unseelie son-in-law winked back.

Never one to back down from a challenge, Sinnie confidently told her father, "I am ready. Open the door."

Sel watched as she bravely walked into Gwenhwyfar's room. Once inside, he ordered Tristian to close the doors and lock it. Sel then called Bradwen to him. The usually jolly guardsman's eyes glistened with unshed tears, much like the rest of the assembly. "None enter, until our new Queen has emerged. Keep Hueil on this side of the door," he said, glancing sideways at Hueil.

Hueil gave him a shrug, as if saying, "Who me?"

"Aye, Captain." Bradwen gave Sel a crisp salute. "I always knew our Sinnie was special."

Sel's heart began racing. He ignored it, thinking it was just fatigue. He clapped Bradwen on the shoulder. "Yes, my friend. I am so..." Sel paused when the fear swept through him, leaving him lightheaded.

"Captain?"

Panicked, Sel searched the link to Riona and found it harder than expected to reach her. When he registered the wave of terror on her end, Sel shifted.

Chapter 26

Pain exploded inside him as Sel collided against the ward. Before it could completely tear him apart and absorb all his energy, Sel reversed course and materialized once again outside the Queen's bedchamber. Severely weakened, he stumbled back.

If it hadn't been for Hueil's arm catching him, Sel would have slumped onto the floor.

"Captain?" Tristian and Bradwen spoke at once.

All Sel could be sure of was that Riona was in mortal danger and for some reason he could not reach her. "Riona..." he croaked.

Seeing their captain weakened to the point of collapsing rendered Tristian and Bradwen temporarily mute. Hueil was the first to press for more information. "Where is she? Concentrate, Sel," he ordered.

Sel tried to follow the link to her again, but he kept running into a barrier. Tristian laid his hand on Sel's shoulder and began to transfer much needed strength into him. Bradwen followed suit. Having noticed their captain's need, and without asking permission, two other guardsmen joined in. With each passing second as the gifted power flowed into him, Sel's body regenerated. His senses became sharper, his reflexes swifter. He could sense her much better and he was able to push through the wall separating them.

Seeing through her eyes, he tried to determine where she was. "She is in the Unseelie Court. Melwas's private rooms, I think," he heard his voice say. The thought of her there made Sel sick and his gut twisted. Why the hell had she left their rooms? He suspected the reason, but hoped he was wrong.

"Those rooms are warded. No doubt that is what robed you of your strength. We will have to find another way in," Hueil told him.

Sel waved the hands on his body away. "Thank you," he blindly told the mass of green and gold uniforms crowding around him. Just as Aeron came into his mind's viewing, Riona's terror exploded in his mind.

Because he had to release the link in order to think clearly, Sel broke the connection with her and barked at Hueil, "The room just beyond his private audience chamber." Sel then shifted without waiting for a reply.

* * *

Sel arrived first, then Hueil and Bradwen. They were in a black marbled room devoid of any furniture. Similar in design to the Queen's Court, this room was a buffer between the formal audience hall and the royal private rooms. A handful of unseelie were present. Each waiting to see the Unseelie King; two warriors, two craftsmen, and a noble. A visit from the Seelie Queen's Captain was not uncommon so no alarms were sounded at Sel's abrupt arrival.

Hueil approached the one warrior who was not guarding the King's chamber door. Stationed near the entryway they needed to get through sat a table on which any and all weapons were expected to be deposited. Sel noted the sword and three knives lying there.

"Bran? Why are you at court?" Hueil hailed his brother. "I thought you hated court. Where is our little brother, Neb?"

Bran wasn't overjoyed at seeing his brother. Hueil had recently changed his allegiance from the Dark Court to the White, which no doubt still rankled the Unseelie King. And consorting with the source of Melwas's displeasure was dangerous.

"Hueil," he said, drawing out Hueil's name so it sounded more like a question than a greeting.

"I've come to claim the throne," Hueil told him boldly.

Bran laughed, as did the two craftsmen who overheard the boast. The noble's expression of cautious curiosity remained the same. While Sel and Bradwen moved to approach the only guard, the noble went to speak with Hueil and Bran.

Once Sel was within a sword's length of the guard, he said, "I am here on behalf of the Seelie Queen. I carry a message for Melwas." He had delivered messages many times before. Sel knew the guard wouldn't have cause to deny him. They just needed to get him to deactivate the ward by unlocking the door. Bradwen started to unstrap his sword from his hip.

The warrior regarded Sel, then made a point of looking down at the empty scabbard still strapped to his hip.

"I know the King's rules. I dinna bother bringing my sword," Sel told him.

Finding Sel's lack of self-preservation funny, the blue-skinned warrior chuckled to himself. "I will announce you. Wait here." He then turned his back to them to unlock the door.

The moment they heard the faint click of the lock release, Bradwen put the tip of his sword under the warrior's exposed throat. "Thank you for your assistance. My captain will announce himself." Leading the guard by the sharp point of his sword, Bradwen maneuvered him out of their way.

Sel picked up the discarded sword and scabbard from the table and called, "Hueil, is this one friend or foe?" Turning, he noticed the noble and one craftsman had disappeared from the room. The other was talking intently with Bran, who seemed to be making an impression on the other unseelie.

Turning, Hueil smirked and then said, "We should ask."

There was a heating of the air as Hueil unleashed his power into the room. The craftsman's eyes grew wide right before abandoning the room. Bran shifted as well. The superior strength of Hueil's uncloaked power rendered the unseelie guard that Bradwen still detained relatively docile. Most in the warrior caste heeled to the rule of the wolf pack when faced with a more powerful alpha male. And Hueil was about as alpha as it got.

"What are you called?" Hueil asked.

Sel had to give the poor fool credit for not stammering when faced with the ancient unseelie who was soon to be his King. Sel had even seen Bradwen blanch at the unexpected strength Hueil so casually contained.

"Olwen."

"I am Hueil, son of Caw, and I am here to claim my throne. Which side will you take?" Hueil's approach was simple and direct, much like his fighting style. Declare against him, or step aside.

With typical unseelie bravado the warrior leaned into Bradwen's blade. "I serve the Unseelie King, and the last time I checked, you were not him."

Hueil shrugged and glanced at Bradwen. "Kill him."

Bradwen cut his eyes to Sel, seeking conformation. "It is his court, not mine. Do as the rightful King orders," Sel told him.

Surprise flickered across Olwen's face. "What do you mean, rightful King?" he blurted.

As if expecting the question, Hueil patiently explained to the young warrior. "There is a new Seelie Queen this day. I am her mate, which by right makes me the Unseelie King."

"But?"

Hueil's dark eyebrow lifted. Leaning forward until he was nose to nose with the sorely outmatched Olwen, he asked, "Do you wish to change sides, Olwen? Unlike my predecessor, I can assure you I possess a tolerant and understanding nature."

Tolerant my ass, Sel thought. Sel bit his tongue, as did Bradwen.

The warrior swallowed nervously. "Aye."

Bradwen lowered his sword; Hueil had yet to unsheathe his.

"Good, then be of use to me. Show me to my private rooms. I hear it is infested with rats."

As impatient as Sel was to reach Riona, he couldn't help but be impressed with the way Hueil was handling his take over. He had yet to kill anyone. Given the unseelie way of doing things, Sel had expected nothing short of a blood bath.

Following Hueil's newest convert to the doors, Sel unsheathed the borrowed sword and reached for Riona through their link.

Chapter 27

Sel's desperation bloomed vividly in her mind when she put ink to paper. Careful to guard her thoughts from him, she did a fast check of her mental defenses and found them still in place. He had somehow slipped in without force, as if they now shared one mind.

She straightened, turned to Aeron and gave him a practiced smile. Was she imagining Sel's presence, her own desperation mocking her?

Taking her wrist, Aeron removed the gold quill from her hand with a self-satisfied smirk. "Give your father one last curtsy to impress, and then I will take to your new home."

Riona knew she had made a terrible mistake coming to her father's court. What had seemed like no choice at all, was most definitely the wrong one, but Riona had no idea how to extract herself from the situation.

With her panic mounting, she softly whispered, "Yes, Aeron," before turning away. The fear of her knees giving way made the first step the hardest. She moved woodenly, no longer able to achieve a graceful gait. The closer she came to her father, the harder it was not to run. She stumbled when Sel's mind connected once again with hers. When his voice filled her mind, she stopped transfixed before her father.

Riona, I am just outside. Delay.

Her racing heart began to beat erratically. The terror Aeron had fanned in her was nothing in comparison to the fear of Sel's impending appearance.

When she did not immediately speak, her father's eyes narrowed. "A final farewell?" he prompted.

Sel's strength flooded her mind, helping her to focus. Lifting her chin a fraction she looked up at her father. "I wanted to thank you," she paused to search for the right compliment.

One of her father's eyebrows lifted, and yet he still gave the impression of boredom with his surroundings and with her.

"To thank you for helping me understand how to best serve you." Riona then dropped into a low curtsy at his feet.

"Ho ho!" her father exclaimed, delighted by her flattery. "Has my daughter finally accepted her fate?"

Gracefully she rose to stand before him. "Yes, father. As must we all." As if on cue, the doors behind her opened. His eyes left hers to identify who had dared to enter unannounced.

Hueil, Sel and Bradwen marched in.

"You!" Melwas roared at Hueil.

Riona hastily moved away from her father and toward Sel, but Aeron reached her first, grabbing her wrist and yanking hard.

"I come with a touch of bad news, Melwas," Hueil called out tauntingly.

Sel, sword drawn, bore down on Aeron.

Riona tried to distract Aeron by asking, "Where is your sword?" Then she directed the desperate thought at Sel, H*e will not let go*.

Aeron, never taking his eyes off of Sel, snapped, "Be quiet, dear. I will handle the captain. He is woefully ill informed. I am sure once he knows you have been sharing your charms with others, regardless of your contract with him, he will be happy to be rid of you."

Her father was yelling now. Hueil's voice gave a reply which set her father into a violent rage. But none of it mattered. Aeron's grip on her arm was tightening, and Sel was all Riona could see.

"She is my mate. Release her or lose that hand," Sel declared coldly, pointing the sword he was carrying at Aeron.

Aeron ignored the warning. "Captain, do you really think the daughter of Naria is capable of being faithful?" Speaking to Riona he barked, "Open your mind to him. Let him see for himself how you begged for my attentions. Let him see how lusty you truly are." Aeron's vise like grip tightened again and Riona cried out, collapsing into a kneeling position beside him. "Just like her mother. Always on her knees."

But instead of feeling Sel's probing, she heard him whisper in her mind. *Can you get him to release you?*

She thought back, *I didn't do it. Please. I didn't do it.*

Riona, trust me. Placate him. Get him to release you.

She looked up to see Sel lower his sword, the pain of betrayal etching lines into his handsome face. When Riona dared to look into his eyes, she saw the disgust she had most feared reflected back. "Keep her," Sel told Aeron harshly.

The grip to her bruised wrist eased.

"Just like that?" Aeron asked the captain, suspicious but wanting to believe he had taken the prize from him.

Riona couldn't breath. Aeron and her father had been right; Sel didn't want her.

Before more Sel could answer Aeron the marble walls seemed to shake with the calling of her father's name. "MELWAS."

Riona barely recognized the deafening roar as Crank's voice.

Abruptly Aeron dropped Riona's wrist, snatched her by the back of the neck and moved closer to the King.

Shadowing Aeron, Sel moved as well.

"Sounds a lot like destiny to me, Melwas. Perhaps you

would like a running start," Hueil taunted, his black blade now drawn.

Seeing Aeron dragging Riona towards him, Melwas snapped, "Aeron, let go of the bloody girl and defend me!"

Torn between King and satisfying his own agenda, reluctantly Aeron obeyed.

Having seen the deep revulsion in Sel's eyes, Riona simply stopped moving when Aeron's hand released her. Her golden captain hadn't even tried to argue with Aeron. Whatever love Sel had secretly felt for her had been utterly extinguished. She had seen it, and now nothing mattered to her.

Hueil and Bradwen took several steps away from Melwas when Crank appeared in the doorway.

As if in a daze, Riona watched as he charged toward Melwas like a rabid animal, swords drawn. She hardly recognized the old commander; he was what nightmares were made of, a red eyed blue demon covered with blood—Arthur's blood.

Seeing what hunted the King, Aeron changed his mind about defending him. Turning away he moved to reclaim Riona.

Sel struck without warning, sword blade swinging and then descending, separating Aeron's head from his body. Riona numbly looked on as the spinning orb hit with a dull thud and then rolled across the black marble floor, spraying bright droplets of red until it came to a rest, the grisly severed neck exposed like some strange fruit.

Hands were on her, patting her hair, her shoulders, feeling further down but she could only see Aeron's head and the awful disgust she had seen in Sel's eyes. She was wrapped in a cloak and then pulled into a tight embrace. She didn't fight it. All the fight had drained from her. They could take her wherever they liked.

Riona closed her eyes to block the sight of Aeron's head from her vision, but she was unable to remove the image of Sel's revulsion from her mind. She let herself cry as grief and loss engulfed her.

Time and space was folded around her and the one who held her shifted.

* * *

Riona didn't know how much time had passed, but the warmth of his embrace ended. He stepped back and held her at arm's length to study her. She kept her eyes down, knowing what she would see.

"I am not like your father, Riona. I am not going to punish you for leaving me," he said gently.

Still looking at his chest, she whispered, "I did not..." but she choked on the rest of her denial. If only she hadn't played games with him. If only she hadn't taken those fateful steps outside her grandfather's Keep with Aeron. Surely part of the fault lay with her.

He stroked her cheek. "Will you not look at me?"

She shook her head no and heard him sigh.

"I have tried to earn your trust, Riona, but you have not even tried to meet me half way."

She glanced up and read the sadness in the small lines etched at the corners of his mouth.

"If you had for one moment looked into my mind, you would have known my heart." He carefully brushed a hair away from her cheek. "I love you, Riona."

Confused by his confession, Riona whispered, "But he said... and the way you looked at me."

Cocking his head, Sel said, "I just told you that I love you. Why persist in believing your father's lies, and the lies of that dog, Aeron? Riona, what are you afraid of? Look inside my mind. It has always been open to you."

Afraid to hope but unable to refuse him, Riona tapped the link between them and cautiously slipped into his mind. His warmth, strength, and security surrounded and supported her, as did his love.

She had been a fool.

Sel, I'm so sorry. I shouldn't have followed him into the courtyard. I should have known better. She thought miserably.

He pulled her closer, putting his arms protectively around her. *Shh. I was wrong to hide the glow of my skin from you, but it took me by surprise.*

"What does it mean?" she murmured against his shirt. She felt raw and bruised, fragile enough to break.

He chuckled, his amusement running through her mind as well as vibrating in his chest. "When a seelie finds their true mate, we glow."

She giggled through her tears, then sniffed and wiped at her wet cheek. "Now what?"

"Well, I hoped you would agree to say the vows with me." He stepped back and gently raised her chin so he could read her face when she answered. Smiling up at him, Riona enthusiastically nodded yes.

Joy bloomed inside Riona's heart as the music of his relieved laughter danced around them. With all they had been through, he had still worried she would turn from him. Never again, she thought. Never again.

To her delight he hugged her close. Perfectly happy to remain in his arms, she rested her head against his shoulder.

"With the Queen dying, Sinnie becoming the new Seelie Queen, Hueil claiming the unseelie throne, and Crank hunting your father, I fear we must wait awhile longer. Will you promise me, Riona, not to sign anymore contracts with any other fey until I can carve out some time for us. I grow weary of executing your prospective mates."

She didn't answer right away. Riona found herself thinking at him, *Sinnie is to be the Queen?*

Pleased she had initiated the private communication between them, Riona felt the echo of his smile in her mind. "Yes. And because the Seelie Queen chooses her King, Hueil, is the rightful Unseelie King. I think he will do a good job of it."

"It seems I am no longer a princess," she told him.

Sel released her long enough to soundly kiss her. *No, but you are my queen.*

Her blood warmed and she sighed, delighted with her new title.

"No more contracts?" he asked again.

"I promise," she whispered against his lips.

"I will hold you to this promise," he said, his green eyes searching hers.

She could feel the relief and contentment her answer gave him, but Riona could also taste the weighty sorrow he carried for the dying Gwenhwyfar.

"I will miss her too," she told him. And she would, no matter what ill feelings she had harbored over the past few days toward the dying Queen. Gwenhwyfar had been a stabilizing force in Riona's turbulent life, a mother figure in many ways.

"She is content with Arthur's choice, and so must we all be."

Chapter 28

For the rest of the day, Riona accompanied her mate as he set about fulfilling the list of difficult duties which lay before him. Though her physical presence seemed to satisfy him, Riona wanted to do more so she kept her mind open to him. In this way Riona was able to share in his burdens.

First, they went to check in with Tristian and found him still guarding the Queen's locked bedchamber door. Sinnie had yet to emerge, which worried Sel.

"Arianhrod's handmaiden had recently departed," Tristian told Sel. "I am sure she will appear momentarily."

Catching Riona's eye, Bradwen smiled warmly.

"All is restored to rights?" Tristian asked, his eyes darting back and forth between her and Sel.

Denying Tristian the private details, Sel confirmed what Bradwen had no doubt already reported back, "Aye. Melwas is on the run. Hueil is doing what he must to secure the unseelie throne. Tell our new Queen I will return, but first I must see to the affairs of her court."

Tristian and Bradwen knew their captain well so they refrained from asking any more questions. Instead they crisply saluted their friend in unison, fists to hearts. The gesture was mirrored by the few guardsmen closest to them.

"Aye, Captain," Tristian replied, a grin tugging at his lips.

Without further comment, Sel slipped his arm around her waist and shifted.

Sel's next duty was his announcement to the heads of the noble houses in the Queen's formal audience chamber. Sel left her side to climb the few steps leading to Gwenhwyfar's throne.

Standing beside the empty chair he informed those assembled of the final fate of the Absent King, and its consequences for their beloved Queen. Almost embarrassed, Sel then formally announced the Gwenhwyfar's successor. As Sel had predicted, they supported the Seer Queen's choice. When one nobleman suggested a bias on the Queen's part, he was soundly shouted down by his peers. Though some might have questioned in private the captain's influence over the dying Queen's decision, no other accusations of foul play were entertained in the open.

Riona breathed a sigh of relief when the nobles dispersed to relay the news to their families.

Catching hold of her hand as he passed, Sel then strode from the hall into the antechamber still filled with guardsmen. He selected a handful of them to take messages to the craftsmen guild leaders who had pledged their loyalty to the Seelie Court. Liam was not among the guardsmen he picked.

Do not blame him, Sel. I can be very persuasive when I want to be. She thought at him.

Sel turned his green eyes to her and then his voice floated through her mind. *He did not follow my orders. That must be dealt with, but I will let Tristian handle it. I do not trust myself to be fair where your safety is concerned.*

Riona didn't press him any further on the subject. If Liam had refused to leave as Sel had ordered him, then perhaps she would not have been able to travel to her father's hall.

While Sel was giving each guardsman their assignment, a mourning Urias arrived to hover just off the captain's shoulder. Sel held out his palm and Urias landed, his wings drooping low. Moving off to the side, Sel took the time away from his duties to share with Urias the whole sad tale. The gentleness Sel displayed in dealing with the smallest of the Queen's supporters tugged at

Riona's heart.

Once informed of Gwenhwyfar's choice of heirs, Urias's slumped shoulders straightened and his wings began to flutter excitedly. Able to hope for the future once more, he then volunteered to take the news to the various clans of the lesser fey. Sel gave his blessing and the sprite vanished, a streak of blue iridescent light speeding away over a sea of fair-haired fey.

Once the messengers to the craftsmen were all dispatched, Sel's thoughts turned to Tearmann and the refugees of the Queen. Sel held his hand out to her once more. With his fingers laced with hers, they shifted leaving the Seelie Court behind.

When they materialized beside the heartstone of the castle, they found Digon waiting for them.

"What news? The castle did not move at sunset,"

Without preamble Sel said, "The Queen is dying. Tearmann is no longer protected. Call all into the hall and I will explain."

Digon's face paled.

"All is not lost, Digon. Tell them Melwas's reign is at an end as well."

Nodding more to himself than to the captain, Digon took a deep breath and then set out to gather the castle's residents.

As they walked toward the hall, Riona asked, "What will they do if Crank fails to?" She couldn't finish her question. The idea of her father's influence and reign coming to an end was too foreign for her mind to fully accept. She had escaped her father's reach because of Sel, but could the rest of the refugees be as lucky?

"Crank will succeed. I do not know how long it will take, but these souls must be protected until Hueil can effect real control over his court."

"Do you have a plan?"

"Those who want Sinnie's protection will need to relocate to her court. From there, Tristian or I can provide the protection of the Queen's Guard. But it must be their choice."

When they reached the hall, a handful familiar faces were there to greet them. More arrived as the seconds ticked by. Once Digon assured Sel that all had been summoned, the Queen's Captain explained the circumstances surrounding the past few days and it consequences. Once again Riona was struck with how patiently Sel answered the questions directed at him. Finally, he told them, "You know my daughter to be just and fair. She will offer the protection of the Seelie Court to each of you without prejudice; seelie, unseelie, other, halfling, human or god."

"Do we have to go with you?" Tara asked.

"No, Tara, I will not force anyone to take the Queen's protection."

"Good. I do know your daughter, Captain, and despite Queen Gwenhwyfar's confidence in her, I do not think Sinnie has the power to protect any of us. I for one decline your offer."

A few grumbled their agreement, but most took the safer course and chose to depart Tearmann with Sel and Riona.

"For any who are not coming with us, you must leave this place. Melwas may be on the run, but this castle is too well known. An unseelie seeking Melwas's favor will hunt for it in an effort to collect the bounty set upon your heads."

Knowing their lives were once again in danger, the hall cleared quickly. Belongings were hastily gathered, and those leaving for the Seelie Court returned to the hall. Sel took Riona's hand and told the anxious refugees, "Follow me."

Sel led them to his private hall. The residents of

Tearmann appeared in small groups, seventeen souls in all. Digon was the last to appear.

"There are no more coming," he told Sel.

Night had fallen in Tir na n-Og, but Sel didn't seem to notice. Several more hours passed as each refugee was assigned a set of guardsmen. Riona noted that once again Sel overlooked Liam when parsing out the duties. She felt bad for the young fey, but she didn't question Sel on the matter.

While the captain had worked to address the interests and concerns of the Seelie Court, Riona had spent part of her time floating among his thoughts. He was putting off facing Digon. His reasons seemed clouded by guilt. Careful not to dig into matters he'd yet to share with her, Riona left the problem of Digon to him. But eventually, Digon was the only soul remaining in the colorfully decorated white hall.

Sensing Sel's need for privacy, Riona stepped into the green study. She didn't eavesdrop, but whatever was said between the two troubled Sel greatly. After several long minutes, Sel came to find her. A flushed and brooding Digon followed.

Catching Sel's eye, Riona's eyebrow arched.

"Digon has agreed to remain here until I can send Fain back from Jen's."

Riona started to ask why, but the strain lining Sel's brow made her bite her tongue. Instead of questions, she sent him what support she could through their mental link and received a surge of gratitude back.

Drawing her near, Sel put his arm around her waist. "We should check on our new Queen before traveling to inform Jen of the changes at court. It has been a long day and you have not eaten. Are you all right?"

She smiled up at him, all the day's events falling away

until it was only the two of them. “I am stronger than I look.”

He gently laid his forehead on hers and breathed, “Aye. You are. Your presence at my side has been a balm.”

With his forehead still touching hers, his power wrapped around her like a warm cloak and they shifted.

Chapter 29

Once again they were met by Tristian and a locked door, but this time the news was more encouraging.

"Our new Queen is waiting for you inside… both of you," Tristian told Sel. Then he turned and unlocked the door, stepping aside for them to pass.

Taking her hand firmly in his larger one, Sel led her into the Seelie Queen's darkened bedchamber. Though Gwenhwyfar should have captured her attention first, she did not. Glowing in the dim light like one of the candles that surrounded Gwenhwyfar's bed sat Sinnie. She was dressed not in a gown, but in leather, much like an unseelie might, knives sheathed along her black leather bodice and on her leather clad thighs. But her's wasn't the only skin casting off light. Sel's skin also gave off a faint glow. It would not have been noticeable except for the lack of light.

Looking at the two of them, Sinnie smiled knowingly. She then glanced back at the frail form of Gwenhwyfar and whispered, "She sleeps."

Though it felt odd to show deference to Sel's daughter, Riona remembered her courtly manners and curtsied to the new Queen. Prompted by her actions, Sel bowed beside her.

Sinnie stood and crossed the room towards them.

"Father, Riona. I am so happy for you both," she quietly gushed. Reaching out, she gave her father a fierce hug. When she released him, she asked, "When?"

He reached over and took Riona's hand, before he whispered back, "We have not exchanged the vows, as of yet." Sinnie frowned at hearing this news. Explaining, Sel said, "There was much to do this day, my Queen."

The "my queen" had sounded forced to Riona's ears, but it had been expected of him.

Sinnie, not yet used to her role pursed her lips with distaste. "Father, I understand you must address me as queen in public, but not in private. I am still your daughter."

"And you will always be, but as Seelie Queen, I must ask you for my release as your captain. Another would serve you better. Tristian perhaps. He is level headed and skilled."

Riona could see Sinnie didn't like her father's choice by the wrinkling of her nose. "I love Tristian. He is my one true uncle, but he is too prone to lecturing. Do you have a second recommendation, Captain?" she asked teasingly.

It was Sel's turn to purse his lips. Riona was touched to see such closeness between the two.

"Digon has returned from Tearmann. He is as able as Tristian, but he has just been told that his twin lives. And Fain, who has yet to be told, is led too easily by his anger. There is Bradwen. But to overlook Tristian's worthiness is a mistake. His niece he lectures because he loves her. To his Queen he will offer sound counsel."

Sinnie gave him an understanding nod. "I will have to think on it." Turning to glance over her shoulder at the still form on the bed, Sinnie then said, "Gwenhwyfar wants me to remain by her side for the time yet remaining to her. She has already gifted her powers to me, but has much to teach me. How is Hueil? Tristian told me he went with you to the Unseelie Court." She cut her emerald eyes to Riona and then back again to her father. "He blocks his thoughts from me," she confessed.

"Hueil is doing what he must to secure the throne," Riona told her. Unlacing her hand from Sel's, Riona untied the knotted ribbon from around her neck. She then removed her father's medallion and presented it to the new Seelie Queen. "The symbol of my father's house," she explained. "Like my true mate, I pledge my loyalty to you, Queen Sinnie."

Caught off guard by Riona's unexpected gesture, the new Seelie Queen silently accepted the medallion.

A surge of pride from Sel swept through Riona's soul and mind. Slipping his arm around her waist, Sel gave her a gentle squeeze.

"Thank you, Riona. The new Unseelie King will be pleased as well to hear that the daughter of Melwas openly supports the new rule." Turning from Riona to her father, Sinnie asked, "What of Jen?"

"Once you give me leave, I will go and take up my responsibilities there. I will watch over her, but I cannot guard her and be your captain," Sel persisted.

Knowing her father had made up his mind on the matter, Sinnie sighed. "I expect regular reports on the health of my sister," she finally told him. "You and Airem will guard her until I find a better solution."

"Airem?" Sel snapped. Then remembering to whisper, he asked. "You now control Airem?"

"Yes, I do."

"Who's Airem?" Riona asked, Sel's concern blowing through her mind.

Sinnie looked directly at her, emerald eyes flashing. "My enforcer. He served Gwenhwyfar, but now she has passed him to me."

"He is dragon-kind and unpredictable," Sel supplied. "He will not like being transferred from one queen to another."

"He will guard Jen with his life, and unlike the fey, he

isn't a direct threat to the humans," she snapped at her father. "And I don't care if he doesn't like serving me. He was pledged by his court to serve the Seelie, so serve he will."

Riona realized the edge in Sinnie's retort was a direct result of the raw power flowing through her. Sel stiffened, recognizing the sudden change in his daughter. Riona tilted her head to glance up at Sel's profile and saw that he was clenching his teeth. It wasn't anger, but worry that made him do it.

"Does Hueil know you are bonded to another male's mind and he to yours?"

"It is a part of being Seelie Queen," she hissed at her father.

"Have you already sent him?" Sel asked.

"No," Sinnie said, sounding more like herself. "And no, Hueil doesn't seem to know of the bond yet."

Riona suspected Sinnie was fretting over how Hueil would react to the news. If Sinnie could talk to this Airem in her mind as well as her true-mate, then could Hueil also hear Airem's thoughts?

"So as not to alarm Jen, let me prepare her for the idea of a dragon." When Sinnie glared at him, he went on to add, "Please, for Jen's sake."

Not wanting to cause upset to her sister, Sinnie agreed, nodding her head. "I will send him in two days time."

Relief made Sel smile. "Thank you."

Through all this, the ancient Queen appeared to have slept, her tiny form lost in the vast bed.

"She knows you are here, Riona." Sinnie said. "My mind and hers are linked... for now. She tells me I must send you both away." For a moment Sinnie looked pained by the thought, but it passed to be replaced by a small smile tugging at the corner of her mouth.

"As your Queen, I accept your resignation as my captain," she said in a rush. "As a member of my guard, I order you to keep the halflings, Jennifer Mackell and Steven Dunne, safe for the length of their natural lives. During the execution of this duty, I hope you will find time to bind this most beautiful unseelie to you." The new Queen's half contained smile broke into a grin. "It would give me great pleasure to know you are happy, father," she finished.

Grinning back, Sel said, "I live to serve my Queen's wishes." He then bowed to his daughter with a flourish.

Sinnie giggled then waved them away, moving back to Gwenhwyfar's bedside.

Sel's eyes settled on Gwenhwyfar's still form, and Riona shared in the tide of grief he felt. "Does she need me?" he asked his daughter.

"No, father. She is at peace with all you have done for us. Her last wish for you is to be happy. She will call for you before the end comes. You and she will have a chance to speak once more, I promise." Tears came to Sinnie's eyes. "Now go. You have been commanded by not one Queen but two."

Riona put her hand on his arm. "It is time," she prompted.

"Weekly reports," Sinnie called when Riona turned him towards the door.

"Aye, my Queen." Sel replied as they were exiting the room.

Tristian locked the door behind them.

"I am no longer your captain. She will choose another, Tristian. I am sorry, I do not know if she will take my recommendation."

Riona couldn't tell if the news upset the blond lieutenant.

Tristian gave Sel a nod and said, “I serve the Queen's wishes, as do we all.”

Sel didn't argue with the fey. “I have been given another mission. If you have need of me I will be in the human realm.”

The two clasped forearms. Nothing more needed to be said.

Chapter 30

Riona was surprised when Sel brought her back to his bedchamber in the Seelie Court. "I thought we were going to your daughter's home?"

"It can wait until morning. We have a few hours until the sun rises. You need rest," he told her.

"And you need to regain your strength," she countered when he pulled her close.

"Do the few lines on my face repel you?"

He didn't mention the gray she had noticed in his otherwise blond locks. "Never," she assured him. "But you gave much of yourself to Arthur," she said, reaching up to caress the new lines at the edges of his eyes. She thought the newly weathered appearance of his face only enhanced his handsome features.

"Aye. I did. Some food then," he suggested, a glint of mischief shining in his green eyes.

"Yes. I would like that, but what about Digon?"

Sel's face fell and Riona giggled. He had forgotten about the seelie fey.

"In the study, you think?" he asked her.

"Probably."

"Bloody hell!" His plans having been frustrated, he released her and stalked out of the room.

"Digon!" Sel's voice bellowed.

Poor Digon, Riona thought. She sank down onto the bed's soft mattress to wait. She was still wearing the dramatic gown meant to appeal to her father's sensibilities and the hunter green cloak Sel had wrapped around her in her father's hall. Had Crank caught up to him yet? She shivered despite the warmth of her attire.

The day could have ended so differently. She could have been locked away somewhere in the Unseelie Court and at the mercy of Aeron. She shuttered again and pushed the disturbing thought away.

Not wanting to think about such things, she kicked off her slippers and touched Sel's mind. He was making arrangements for Digon to spend the remainder of the evening elsewhere. She smiled to herself. Shimmering, she exchanged the eggplant silk gown and cloak for the simple russet dress Sel loved to see her wearing.

He believed all the trouble between them had stemmed from her unwillingness to trust him. It was a symptom, yes, but not the cause. From childhood, she had nurtured the belief that a happy life was meant for others, not for her. What a fool she had been.

Sel's voice floated in her mind. *I'm coming. How hungry are you?*

Ignoring the unexpected growl from her stomach, she thought back. *I'm not hungry. Just hurry.*

Silence.

Lying. How very unseelie of you. He teased her.

She giggled and amended the thought. *A little hungry.*

He materialized at the foot of the bed, holding a tray of meats and cheese, a crooked grin on his handsome face. "Do you love me?"

"I think you know the answer to that."

He deliberately sat the tray down on the bed and moved to stand before her. "You have not said it aloud."

"Have I not?"

He cocked his head and said nothing.

"Surely I have," she protested. When he slowly shook his head no, a blush rose to her cheeks. Then searching her memory she realized he was right. She had withheld the words, for fear of being rejected. Standing, she cupped his face. "I love you with all my heart." She then kissed him.

When the kiss grew heated, he ended it.

"Riona," he paused to clear his throat. "I give you my heart, for it will beat for no other. I give you my body, for it will desire no other." Touching his lips to hers, he gently kissed her and then withdrew. "I bind my fate to yours, for I will follow no other. I give my love to you—through time and eternity, for I will have no other." Having said the vows that would bind them together, his finger lightly traced the edge of her jaw until it reached her chin.

Wanting to prolong the wonderful moment, Riona remained silent and watched as his confidence gave way to concern. When his jaw tightened, she bit the inside of her cheek. Teasing him, she asked, "Do you do this because your new Queen requests it?"

Indignation flared along their link, and lightning flashed across his eyes. "Riona, repeat the vows," he growled.

She giggled. "Is that an order, Captain?"

"If that is what it takes, then it bloody well is!" he nearly shouted at her.

When he tilted her chin up so he could study her hooded eyes more closely she purred, "Duty then."

"Riona, do not tease me."

With a single thought he sent a deluge of pleasure through her body, swamping her mind and senses. Her knees buckled. Without his support, she would have collapsed onto the floor.

Then as abruptly as the sensation had begun it ended, leaving her breathless and her heart hammering in her chest.

While she tried to form a coherent thought, he whispered next to her ear, "I warned you when we first came together. I have the power to bring you to your knees, my love. I will abuse that power if I must." His lips then slowly trailed kisses along her cheek and jaw. "Please, Riona, bind yourself to me. Your teasing is killing me."

"Such pleasurable punishment," she sighed. She let his lips roam their way down her neck before finally giving into him. Gently, regrettably, she pushed him away. Reaching up, she encircled his neck with her arms and started to repeat the vows. "Sel, son of Selgi, I give my heart to you, for it will beat for no other." He gave her a boyish grin. "I give my body to you, for it will desire no other... because you have trained it thus," she playfully added. When his smile faltered, she stood on her tiptoes to kiss him. "I bind my fate with yours, for I will follow no other." Knowing he was anxious for her to finish the ritual, Riona took her time saying the last line, relishing every word. "I give my love to you—through time and eternity, for I will have no other."

In one breath the god-storm of uniting descended upon them. The once faint glow emanating from Sel's golden skin erupted, cocooning them from the outside world. This was a uniting of souls, blessed by the gods. Clothes fell away and Riona welcomed the searing heat of him against her ivory skin now made soft by his hard hot flesh. The compulsion to become one physical being overwhelmed her senses.

When he pushed into her wet embrace, she clung to him, legs wrapped around hips, arms around his neck. Instinctively, Riona held fast, trusting in her love for him and the frenzied forces driving them. Firmly anchored in each other's minds, the winding and weaving of binding-threads tightened drawing their souls ever closer together.

Beyond all thought, save that of claiming her completely, Sel hammered into her. Each powerful stroke was a primal answer to her siren call, and she joyously vibrated with the need for him.

Riona was lost to all but the sensation of him blending his essence with hers. His power flowed through her mind and body, his soul consumed hers like a wolf devours a lamb, like fire burns a leaf to ash. She burned from the inside out, until finally… the god bolt struck.

What was once two separate beings became one newly born entity. One heart beat. One set of lungs inhaled for the first time. One mind erupted in utter bliss, floating freely between worlds—beyond all limits, as one soul sighed in wonder.

Time stopped.

The being of light and magick, which had been forged by the creation fires of the gods, eventually had to cool or else cease to exist.

As the light dimmed, time resumed its measured pace and the soul that was something more divided and settled into flesh. Two hearts now beat in unison. Warm breath mingled as two sets of lungs exhaled together. Two minds held one smiling thought, while two bodies tenderly cradled one another.

Never again would she face the future alone. Sel was a part of her now and she a part of him.

"Riona," he whispered into her ear.

"hmm…"

"There is a life-spark in your womb that was not there before."

Her eyes flew open to find him smiling down at her. "You

are certain of this?"

"Aye, my love." He kissed the tip of her nose, his pride and joy filling her mind.

She thought of Arthur and the ritual of the cauldrons. "Do you think?"

"Does it matter?"

She smiled, her heart bursting with love for the golden seelie who held her so tenderly. "No, nary a bit."

Epilogue

On a clear fall evening, Neb stood on the brick walkway outside Jen's and Steven's eatery. What did his brother Hueil call it? Ah, yes... a cafe. The cafe was closed to outsiders today. He peered through the windowpane anyway.

The couple sat at the head banquet table, surrounded by friends and family. They had just performed a completely useless ceremony. He searched his memory for the term. Yes, a wedding. Fools, Neb thought. The couple's souls were already bound to one another through the fey vows. A wedding had been a complete waste of time in Neb's opinion.

He shook his head. Humans were difficult to understand. In the face of real danger, often times they would stand and fight, but when the Seelie Court offered aid to the fledgling race, they habitually shunned the gesture... preferring their science to true magick. Except for the pleasure a well-trained human could provide, Neb had very little interest in the species.

The thought of enchanted humans brought Bran to mind, having recently come from his brother's home. Ever since their brother Hueil's defection to the Seelie Court at Mabon, Bran's business had suffered. The challenge to the King's power had resulted in the loss of the King's favor for the Caw's pleasure den. After having endured an earful from Bran about Aeron and the den's subsequent revenue loss, Neb had returned here, to Madison, in hopes of speaking with Hueil. What help Hueil might lend Bran was questionable. Bran, on the other hand, had traveled to court to take up the matter with the King. "Good luck with that," Neb muttered under his breath.

Traveling first to the home of the halflings Hueil and Sinnie guarded, Neb was disappointed to find the spacious house empty. Next, he had tried the halflings' eatery. Fain, a seelie guardsman, hovered nearby but Neb could not detect Hueil's presence at all.

For Hueil's sake, Neb had taken great pains to look human. His image was relatively satisfying, he thought as he critically studied the reflection in the large window. Having worked harder than the rest of his brothers to become a true member of the warrior caste, Neb disliked hiding his blue tinted skin and warrior tattoos. His black hair was shorter than usual, bound at the nape of his neck with a simple cord, but otherwise he looked much like himself.

Catching the movement of swinging blonde hair and hips crossing the street behind him, Neb turned away from the preoccupied humans. Leaving the wedding party behind, he followed the enticing feminine sway, like a cat stalking a mouse. The female was young, and well rounded in all the right places. In the back of his mind Neb thought about Bran's recent losses and wondered if the little beauty would be missed if he were to take her.

She was now crossing another street, moving with purpose. Neb got a quick glimpse of her profile when she turned to look for on coming traffic. He'd have to hurry to catch her.

Pausing on the opposite side of the street, Neb waited to see which direction she'd head next. When she cut across the grass of the town's square, Neb searched for the best place to head her off. A large pine tree stood on the opposite corner, its lower branches grazing the ground. A prefect location to pounce on his prey, he thought. Timing his reappearance so he'd take her by surprise, Neb shifted and materialized between her and the tree.

She stopped dead in her tracks and glared up at him.

Neb had expected fear, but her perfectly formed features and shocking blue eyes seared him with a look of scorn. For a heartbeat, Neb could only stare at the beauty before him. She was absolutely breathtaking. He hastily rethought his earlier plan. There was no way he was going to share this human's charms with anyone, let alone Bran.

"You're in my way."

The sound of her voice touched on an old memory, but try as Neb might he could not recall it. "Do I know you? I feel as if we have met before."

She arched an eyebrow.

Wanting to hear her speak again, he said, "My name is Neb."

She took a step to the side and then another, keeping her distance from him.

He matched her move for move. No bloody way was he letting her escape. He may not know her, but by the gods he damn well wanted to.

"I know Jen and Steven," she told him.

He gave her a charming smile. Ignoring the sound of tumbling dice bouncing around inside his head, he replied, "As do I."

She took another step closer to the tree's branches.

Neb 's smile widened. The closer to the cover of the tree they danced the better. He took another step. "What do they call you, sweetheart?"

"Hostess," she quipped.

Though Neb could not detect any fear in her pretty face he did notice the rise and fall of her luscious looking chest had picked up its pace. "An odd name," he counted while taking another step towards her, forcing her to take another towards the tree's cover.

The blue eyes never left his face. "Cora," she said, daring him.

Something in the way she acted bothered him. Yes, she was glorious to look at, as beautiful as any fey he had ever seen. Yet, Cora was definitely human, no trace of his race's blood flowed in her veins. At least she had no magick he could detect. But she acted as if he could do her no harm. And those eyes...

why did he know they weren't truly blue? The distracting noise of rolling dice grew louder in his head, making it hard for him to think clearly. Holding his hand out to her, Neb coaxed, "I promise, Cora, I will not hurt you."

Her scornful glare and haughty indifference faltered as hurt furrowed her brow. The clear blue of her eyes darkened, until they flashed with iridescent green fire. "You said that once before, Neb. You lied."

Before he could react to the change or frame a response, she dove for the tree and disappeared into its trunk.

With his heart pounding in his chest and the dice ricocheting off the inside of his skull, Neb knelt down to place his hand on solid bark. Who was she? What the bloody hell was she?

You said that once before, Neb. You lied. For reasons he could not understand the wild accusation angered him, but not nearly as much as the lost opportunity to capture her. Just the thought of touching her made his mouth water. Standing, he cursed long and loud in a language not often heard in the human realm. With her escape, the sound of tumbling dice faded from his mind until it too disappeared.

"Hey, buddy...you okay?" a man called from beside his parked automobile.

Finding the onlooker's casual familiarity offensive, Neb shimmered, reclaiming his true warrior form.

Fear robed the man's face of blood and any further speech. With a shaking hand the human hastily unlocked his car to slide inside.

Smiling to himself, Neb shifted away from the town's square; the glow of his amber eyes were the last to fade from view. If Madison was where this tempting creature was living, Neb thought, then Madison was where he would stay until he found her again. And next time he wouldn't waste time bantering with her.

Reoccurring Terms and Themes:

The Mabinogion (MAW-ben-oh-geee-yen) An incomplete collection of stories taken from Celtic oral tradition and written down in approximately the 11th century.
Tuatha De' Danann (TOO 'ha dA Dah n'n) The Children of the Goddess Danu, the race of the fairies or fey (fae) who once called Ireland home.
Tir na n-Og (TEER- na- nog) The Land of Youth also known as the fairy realm where the fey retreated to after leaving the human realm.
Sidhe (SHE) An entrance or gateway which can take you into Tir na n-Og. Usually found in a hillside, or mound.
Seelie (SEA-lee) Blessed or holy. Derived from Scottish mythology, the Seelie Court of the fey or Court of Light maintains a benevolent attitude towards the human race. Though prone to their own form of mischief, the seelie fey are typically fair haired with light or golden skin. They love order and tradition.
Unseelie (Un-SEA-lee) Unblessed or unholy. The unseelie fey are very often malicious and evilly inclined. The Unseelie Court or Dark Court is the mirror opposite of the seelie and delight in causing trouble to those they run across. Typically dark haired, the unseelie are pale in complexion, except for the warrior caste who have blue-tinted skin.
Halfling – Any human who possesses a fey ancestor. Many halflings mistake their fey gifts as supernatural, and therefore call themselves witches.
Magick – A derivation of the word magic. The added "k" is used by the witch and Neo-pagan community to draw a distinction

between illusion and slight of hand used by stage magicians from the practice of influencing events and physical phenomena by supernatural, mystical, or paranormal means.

Shifting – A mode of travel or teleportation used by the fey to move them quickly through time and/or space.

Shimmering – A term often used interchangeably with shapeshifting. This is the fey magickal ability to change one's appearance or glamour. It can be a small change as in clothing choice, or a large change like ones entire form such as transforming his or her form to resemble an animal. A large change requires more magick to accomplish.

Life-Debt – The fey law that requires a life be given for the taking or saving of another's life. It is a debt no fey wishes to incur.

Fey Binding Vows- The Binding Vows are different from a Binding Ritual or Binding Contract which is a written formal agreement between two fey houses that typically only binds a couple together for a specified number of centuries. The exchange of binding vows is a magickal act that binds two souls together for all eternity. A couple bound by the vows will share the same fate. Reciting the binding vows is usually not attempted unless a fey finds his or her true-mate.

"I give you my heart, for it will beat for no other.
I give you my body, for it will desire no other.
I bind my fate to yours, for I will follow no other.
I give my love to you—through time and eternity, for I will have no other."

Fey Society – Fey society is made up of four distinct castes; Nobility, Warriors (unseelie warriors and seelie guardsmen), Craftsmen, and the Lesser Fey or Elementals (Sprites, Pixies,

Doxies, Boggarts, Brownies, etc.)
Tearmann (TEAR-men) A Gaelic word meaning sanctuary. Tearmann is a magickal castle kept by the Seelie Queen for sheltering individuals she wishes to protect from King Melwas. Castle Tearmann constantly shifts through both space and time until finally resting at nightfall. If traveling there, it is best to go with an ancient who has the power to reach Tearmann's heartstone.
Guardsman's Hall motto: The guardsman's motto is written in Ogam as a reminder to the seelie guardsmen of their vow of serve to the Seelie Queen and Court. North Wall; *Seek Wisdom* East Wall; *Defend Truth* South Wall; *Challenge Death* West Wall; *Love Beauty*
Ogam - An ancient language derived from tree lore and once taught by the fey to the Celtic bards and shamans of Ireland. Shown as a series of slashes along a straight line, the ogam consists of 25 letters, each letter has additional meanings or phrases, revealing a spiritual quality to each tree letter.
Arach Mountain – Arach means dragon in Gaelic. The Arach Mountains lies on the western edge of Tir na n-Og. It is where members of the unseelie warrior caste took refuge during the Unseelie King's purge. This portion of Tir na n-Og belongs to the Dragons.

Celtic Gods

Lord Arawn (AHR-aun) Celtic god/king of the underworld known as Annwn. Lord Arawn is also know as the Lord of the Hunt.
Arianrhod (ah-ree-AHN-rud) Goddess of the Silver Wheel, the Celtic Weaver of Fate. (Welsh) Beautiful and pale of

complexion, she was the most powerful of the mythic children of the Mother Goddess Don. The willow is her tree.
Blodeuwedd (bluh-DIE-weth) A Celtic spring goddess, The Ninefold Goddess, Flowerface. Most Beautiful and treacherous (Welsh). Cursed by Arianrhod, Blodeuwedd transforms into an owl every night.
Danu (DAN-u) Celtic goddess and ancient goddess of Ireland who is thought to be the mother/creator of the entire **Tuatha De' Danann** race. She is also known by the names Anu, Ana, Cat Ana, Aine. She is Queen Gwenhwyfar's mother.

Seelie Fey

Gwenhwyfar (Gwen-nah-far) the Welsh version of Guinevere. The fey Seelie Queen has lived for approximately six thousand years. She was forced into accepting Melwas's reign in order to protect the life of her true-mate, Arthur. Her name can be found in the Mabinogion as the wife of King Arthur.
Sel, son of Selgi (Cell) A seelie and Captain of the Queen's Guard. His name appears in the Mabinogion as a kinsman to King Arthur on his father's side. He is Sinnie's father and is approximately four thousand years old, give or take a century. History records his name as Sir Gawain, the green knight.
Sinnie (sin-NIE) The daughter of Sel, raised within the ranks of the Queen's Guard, she is more warrior than maid. Her name means sun gift and she is the true-mate to Hueil.
Krist (Kres-t) Pronounced with a hard K. A young seelie fey and a tracker within the Queen's Guard. He and Sinnie are childhood friends. His father is Fain.
Fain, son of Alar (Fain) A seelie guardsman who bears a moon shaped scar on the left side of his face. He is Sel's second

lieutenant and Krist's father.
Digon, son of Alar (DIE-gone) A disgraced seelie fey, Keeper of the Castle Tearmann and Fain's twin. His name can be found in the Mabinogion.
Bradwen, son of Iaen (BRAD-win) A jolly seelie guardsman whose name can be found in the Mabinogion as a kinsman to King Arthur on his father's side.
Tristian (Tris-tan) A seelie guardsman and Sel's first lieutenant and next in command within the Queen's Guard. He is Sinnie's blood uncle, his sister Brianna is Sinnie's mother. His name can be found in the Mabinogion.
Brianna (Bree -anna) a seelie noblewoman who was once forced into a binding agreement with Sel by her brother, Tristian. She is Sinnie's mother.

Unseelie Fey

King Arthur (Ar-thur) The true Unseelie King, also known as the Absent King. Arthur's reign as Unseelie King predates Melwas's. He is approximately six thousand years old and is Queen Gwenhwyfar's true-mate.
Melwas (MEL-was) The current Unseelie King. He is the bastard son of Lord Arawn. Born within the warrior caste, Melwas rose to the throne due to King Arthur's absence. History records his name as Mordred. He has one child, Riona.
Riona (Ree-on-ah) An unseelie and bastard daughter of the Unseelie King and Naria, his mistress. Contracted mate to Calcus.
Hueil, son of Caw (HUGHel) Second youngest of thirteen siblings, he is an unseelie warrior who is approximately three thousand years old. His title is "The warrior who never submitted to a Lord's protection" (hand). His name can be found within the

Mabinogion among a long list of warriors belonging to King Arthur. Sinnie is his true-mate.

Neb, son of Caw (Neb) An unseelie warrior, he is Hueil's younger brother. Neb's name also appears in the Mabinogion.

Calcus, son of Caw (CAL- cus) A recently deceased older brother of Hueil and Neb, Calcus made an unsuccessful bid for the unseelie throne. His name can be found in the Mabinogion.

Bran, son of Caw (Br-ann) An unseelie warrior and brother to Hueil, Neb and Calcus. Bran is possibly the last brother to survive the Unseelie King's purge. He has no desire to live at court. Bran runs the House of Caw's pleasure den with his only daughter Ena.

Naria (NAR-ree-a) An unseelie seductress, noblewoman and the favorite mistress of the Unseelie King. She is Riona's mother and an old lover of Hueil's. History records her name as Morgaine le fey, confusing her with her lesser known sister, Morgain.

Morgain (More-gain) An unseelie and Naria's lesser known sister. She is Riona's aunt. Morgain has long wanted to supplant her more famous sister's position as Melwas's mistress.

Naf (Naf) An unseelie warrior more recently known by the alias "Crank". He is the original owner of castle Tearmann and was King Arthur's first defender and most loyal friend. He is an ancient who was cursed by the gods during his search for his beloved King. History records his name as Lancelot.

Brodie (Bro-dee) Unseelie warrior. One of Calcus's generals.

Durstian (DUR-Sten) Unseelie warrior. One of Calcus's generals who fell under Melwas blade after Mabon.

Aeron (Air-ron) An unseelie warrior, who was one of Calcus's young generals. Aeron has a disturbing liking for torture.

Brom (Brr-om) Unseelie warrior.

Gloric (Glor-ick) Unseelie warrior who during the King's purge escaped by becoming a dragon in the Arach Mountains on the

western edge of Tir na n-Og. He is thought to be Steven's grandfather.
Olwen (Owen) Unseelie warrior.

Other

Urias (Your-az) A male sprite and a member of the lesser fey, who serves Sel and the Seelie Queen. Why he has pledged his life to these particular seelie, no one knows.
Airem (Air-m) The Seelie Queen's enforcer. Airem primarily lives in the human realm hunting down fey who intend on harming humans. Airem is dragon-kind and shares a mind link with the Seelie Queen.

Halfling

Jennifer Mackell- Daughter of Sel, and true-mate to Steven. A halfling whose empathic fey gift is developing into that of a seer. She and Steven are under the protection of the Seelie Court.
Steven Dunne- Grandson of Gloric, and true-mate to Jen. He possesses the fey talent of persuasion.

About the Author

Tarrant Smith graduated from Queens College in North Carolina with a degree in English literature. She currently lives near the beautiful town of Madison, Georgia, with her husband, son, horses, dogs, and the odd assortment of stray cats. As a self-described kitchen witch, she has always sought out and nurtured the magick that she finds in the mundane trappings of everyday life. For more information about the author and the Darkly Series please go to www.tarrantsmith.webs.com

Made in the USA
Charleston, SC
10 May 2011